FISH TALES

FISH TALES

EDITED BY
RAMONA DEFELICE LONG

INTRODUCTION BY CHRIS ROERDEN

WILDSIDE PRESS

FISH TALES

Published by Wildside Press LLC.
www.wildsidebooks.com

CONTENTS

INTRODUCTION

BY CHRIS ROERDEN

guppy, a small topminnow, one of the most popular freshwater aquarium fish species in the world. The ability of guppies to tolerate fluctuations in water conditions puts them among the hardiest of all aquarium fishes. They are prolific live-bearers.

Guppy, a member of the online Guppies Chapter of one of the most popular organizations of crime writers in the world, Sisters in Crime. The ability of Guppies to tolerate fluctuations in publishing conditions puts us among the hardiest of all writers. We are prolific mystery creators.

Our Guppies Chapter, like its parent organization, is made up of women and men of all ages whose mission it is to promote the professional development and advancement of women crime writers to achieve equality in the industry. In addition, Guppies enjoy the unique role of providing a safe harbor for aspiring crime writers, who may feel their professional development is adrift, their advancement is caught in a riptide, or they are drowning in a sink-or-swim effort to get published.

Our name, Guppies, reflects the circumstances of our group's origin as the "Great Unpublished." However, since 1995 when the concept of unpublished writers teaching other unpublished writers was initially floated, a steady stream of Guppies have gotten contracts in the mystery field and bubbled up to the big pond.

With a membership currently tipping our scales at 400, one in twenty Guppies continues to keep a mystery-credentialed fin dipped in the buoyant waters of our little pond. That's where our long-time friendships—and new friendships, too—help keep a Guppy's head above water. It's where grateful authors can pay forward by supporting others. Besides, there's nothing like publication to convince a writer of the need to keep learning.

Though the majority of Guppies may be working on their first mystery novel, not all are as wet behind the ears as you might think. Many have been published in other genres and possess expertise in a broad range of fields and professions, including legal, medical, forensic, and law enforcement. Guppies live and work throughout the United States and Canada—even in Europe—and travel the globe. Our varied experience contributes to a pool of knowledge that enriches the entire school of Guppies.

Chapter activities include forming separate groups for brainstorming book ideas, exchanging manuscript critiques within the different subgenres, analyzing and deconstructing selected mystery novels, and pursuing the quest for an agent. Periodically we challenge ourselves to pour forth daily word counts. The digests that deluge our e-mailboxes keep us hooked, and our bi-monthly newsletter lets us soak up in-depth information while encouraging us to flood its editor with practical articles of our own. And whenever a Guppies-only online class is held, member discounts help conserve our liquid assets.

At conferences from the Atlantic shores to the Pacific coast, badges proclaiming "I'm a Guppy" facilitate our matching new faces to familiar names and gathering in large shoals at restaurants and watering holes. When not attending conferences, Guppies survive on chocolate.

One activity that spawned an annual celebration is cyber-crowning a Queen of Rejection. Based on the largest number of "thanks but no thanks" responses received by a Guppy in the first three months of the year, this honor signifies not failure but success in taking the greatest plunge required of a writer: submitting regularly all year long.

Our intrepid group is now surfacing with its first anthology, a volunteer effort in which every Guppy who entered a story also read three other entries and gave each of them feedback—no names disclosed. Stories were then edited by a non-member, so that no Guppy would judge the writing of another.

A key feature of this project from its start was to provide an educational experience for those who participated. Of the 22 stories ultimately selected, most were written by Guppies with no prior publishing credits, as you'll see from the author bios.

Now I invite you to help the Guppies make a splash by diving into our fishpond and submerging yourself in this collection of mysteries. If you haven't guessed from the clues so far, one element runs through these pages: water.

Chris Roerden's *latest books are* Don't Murder Your Mystery, *recipient of the Agatha Award for Best Nonfiction Book, finalist for the Macavity and Anthony awards, and a selection of the Writer's Digest Book Club, and its all-genre version,* Don't Sabotage Your Submission, *recipient of the 2009 Benjamin Franklin Award for Literary Criticism, the Florida Writers Association Book of the Year Award, and ForeWord Magazine's bronze medal for Writing Book of the Year. Authors she's edited are published by St. Martin's Press, Berkley Prime Crime, Midnight Ink, Perseverance Press, Viking, Rodale, Walker & Co., and others. She is proud to be a Guppy.*

THICKER THAN BLOOD

BY LESLIE BUDEWITZ

From the shore, the setting sun looked as if it had been pierced by two burnt lodgepole pines still standing on a distant ridge. Not even last summer, when the fires raged for months, had she ever seen the sun so red.

And her hands. Nothing more red than fresh blood.

* * * *

"You're the third person in twenty minutes to ask me where dildo head is and I don't know." Annette slammed the pitcher of my Montana Snow Cap Ale on the bar and a good two or three swallows splashed out. She grabbed the customer's twenty and stalked to the till, not seeing the look on his face. But I own this joint, and I knew that look—aggravation at not getting his full money's worth mixed with irritation at the sticky pitcher, made worse by rudeness. So I topped it off, wiped it off, and handed it back, all before she slapped his change on the counter with the same force.

"Thanks," I told the customer. "Enjoy."

He nodded, looking more congenial, and took his pitcher to a table. I turned to my bar manager and whispered, "Where is Zach? What do you mean, the third person? And don't call anybody dildo head in my brew pub. You might as well say your dog pissed in the keg."

Her face suggested she might do just that. "First, Kathryn. Then those two." She jerked her head toward two men sitting by the front door, not nursing beers. I should have noticed them sooner. They weren't in uniform, but they didn't need to be.

"If I count them separately, you're number four. I don't know where he is. With him, you never know. He said he'd be here, and I have to pick up Jade in ten minutes." She had her apron half-untied even though she hadn't asked if she could leave without a replacement, but she didn't need to ask. She was going to leave no matter what, and she knew I'd say yes. When it came to daughters—hers or mine—I always did.

I grabbed the apron before she could toss it onto the wet spot the dripping pitcher had left. "Go. And watch your speed—those aren't the only two cops out tonight."

They weren't after her, though; they hadn't moved since I'd first seen them, but their body language said they were waiting for me. Annette grabbed her bag and dashed out the back before I had the strings tied, a tidy bow in front. Not the usual thin white stuff. We had a lakeside theme going on, and I'd sewn the aprons myself from sturdy cotton with a fish design. I made the beer, I made the aprons, I cleaned up the messes I hadn't made.

I wiped down the bar and called out. "Get you fellows anything?"

The lanky one slid off the stool and approached the bar, wallet badge open. "Cheryl Christman?" I nodded. "Detective Anderson, Sheriff's Office. This is Detective Lee. Can we talk somewhere?"

I opened my hands, gesturing at our surroundings. A bar and stools, a few tables, and a wall of thick glass windows that revealed the brew room's vats and pipes. We had a deck with a lake view for summers, but by mid September, evenings were cool and the deck was an afternoon thing. Other than a storage room, a small office upstairs, and the john, this was it.

"My bartender's running late tonight, guys. I'm on my own here. What can I do for you?"

"Your bartender, ma'am. Zachary Delorme?" Lee had some beef to him and a slightly flushed face, like he'd drunk a few beers in his life. "His body was found this afternoon out near the end of the point. Washed up on a private beach. Some kids found him."

Body. Oh, God. That meant dead, didn't it? Oh, God. I groped for a stool. "Zach's dead?"

"Yes, ma'am. Sorry to break the news so abruptly. We're trying to trace his whereabouts the last twenty-four hours, talk with everyone who's seen him. We wanted to talk with you, of course, as his employer, and your daughter."

"Why Kathryn?" She'd just been here looking for him.

Anderson spoke. "We understand they have a history."

"Well, yes." If they'd talked to someone who said Zach worked here—Friday and Saturday nights, the last three or four months—then they'd probably heard about Kathryn, too. In a community this small, half a dozen people would spill what they knew about

Kathryn, or thought they knew. "They know each other. Everyone knows each other around here."

"Nonetheless, Ms. Christman, we would like to talk with her," Anderson said.

I let out a long sigh, weighted with all my dreams for Kathryn, that she would grow out of the faulty personality traits and biological defects her father and I had given her, find some way to tame her compulsiveness, and live a regular, dependable sort of life. Like the one I'd made, with effort and time and help. But dreams aren't visible to other people, so the detectives just kept watching me.

"Annette said she came in maybe twenty minutes before I got here, asking for Zach. His shift starts at six"—about an hour from now—"but he promised Annette he'd come in early today. So you just missed her."

"Why didn't she wait?"

"A reasonable expectation of anyone but my daughter, Detective. She's a little ADD. Okay, a lot ADD." I tried to laugh. "Always got a million things racing through her head. She probably had five other people to see or things to do."

"Unless she had an idea where else he might be."

"I wouldn't know."

Detective Lee responded as if we were just a couple of buddies in a bar on a Saturday evening. "Ms. Christman—Cheryl. You know how people talk. We've been hearing a lot of things about your daughter and her, well, *interest* in Delorme. Why don't you give us your perspective?"

Be careful, I told myself. He's friendly and he acts concerned, but he is not on your side. I got up and poured myself a glass of water, drank half, dumped out the rest, and poured a glass of stout. Took a long draw, sat down, and forced myself to match their self-control. "Sure I can't get you anything? The only alcohol I can serve is the beer we make, but we do have soft drinks."

They shook their heads. I took a sip and told them about Kathryn, short version. When I finished, I said, "So you see, she is impulsive, but also very focused—obsessive at times. The doctors would never say for sure—I think they wanted to protect me from my own worst thoughts, but I know." I tapped my chest. "It's the drugs we did while I was pregnant, and before. I've been clean a long time—clean enough to do this for a living," I said with a wave toward the brew room. "But I still live with it every day, because of what it did to her. She's just wired differently. The flip side is that she is also passionate and loving and extremely generous. She comes on too strong sometimes, but she is not violent."

They watched me, seeming to consider what I'd said.

Finally, Anderson spoke. "We understand she threatened to kill him more than once."

"And I've threatened to move to Canada every time we elect a Republican president, but I'm still here."

Both detectives smiled. "Where would Kathryn go if she were in trouble?"

I shook my head slowly. "Look, guys, I understand when someone turns up dead, you look hard at everyone around him. You can't just take a mother's word that her child isn't capable of hurting anyone. I've been honest with you about Kathryn's faults, but really, truly, she wouldn't hurt a flea. She can't even stand the sight of blood." A big problem when she hit puberty. Monthly histrionics for the first few years. But they didn't need to know that. "And she had no reason to hurt Zach."

"Who did?"

"I don't know. He's only worked here a few months, but he does a decent job and he's been reliable." In truth, I'd sensed something more to him, something mean and a little sneaky. But I've learned, when you can't be specific, it's best to be silent.

"Why did he keep working here after your daughter threatened him?"

"He didn't take her seriously. And she wasn't the only young woman who noticed him. A good-looking guy who's new in town is always popular." I shrugged. "Easy work, free beer. Close to home. He's caretaker of a place up the hill. Really, you should have asked Annette."

"Why?"

They didn't know? "He's her brother."

* * * *

The sun, the hot red sun, the blood red sun. Kathryn held two fingers parallel to the horizon, at arms' length. Fifteen minutes a finger, her father had said, that time when he was out of prison and came to the lake to see her. But it was true. Thirty minutes or so, then, dark.

Would the people leave then, the people scrambling around the gravel beach and yard next door, some in brown uniforms, others in black with yellow stripes? They looked like bugs. Kathryn hated bugs, hid from them. The first time she saw someone squash a bug, she'd screamed for hours. Whenever one got inside, her mother would pick it up on a tissue or with her fingers and carry it out.

If she screamed now, the bugs would see her and come crawling over. She scrunched down against the house and pulled her jacket tight. Soon it would be dark and there would be more bugs. Her mother said sometimes that she needed to get hold of herself because she wouldn't always have a mother there to protect her.

That's what Zach had said, too, and Annette.

Now Zach was dead, and Kathryn had blood on her hands.

So did someone else. She thought she knew who, but who would believe her? Not the bugs.

Not with blood on her hands.

* * * *

Annette ran her fingers through her hair, jerking loose a tangle.

She should not have lied to Cheryl, not now or before. Cheryl's own troubles had made her generous and understanding, not harsh and judgmental like it did some people. She should not have let Zach move up here or take the job at the brewery, and she should not have let him behave so badly toward Kathryn. The girl couldn't help herself. Zach could, but he liked messing with people's minds.

And now he was dead and things were tangled beyond belief.

Annette paced the living room of her cabin, as if answers would emerge from between the chinked logs or descend from the dusty rafters. As if, somehow, the problem of Zach's death could be solved by revisiting his life.

As if she, his older sister, who loved him more than anyone else loved him—who should have protected him—had not killed him.

How had it happened? She stepped into the kitchen with its still-damp floor. Right here, not twenty-four hours ago. He'd been standing with his back to the window, the window that overlooked the lake. He'd been laughing. He liked to laugh, always had, since he'd been a little bitty guy.

No. Go back to the beginning.

"Heather's getting married," she'd told him. "Her fiancé has a job in Alaska and she's taking Jade."

"So?" he'd said.

His indifference infuriated her. "What do you mean, 'so?'"

"So what's that got to do with you or me? Heather's her mother. You fought for custody and lost. Get over it."

"Get over it? I raised that child for five years, when neither of you gave a shit about her. You still don't. Then Heather decides a kid's a great accessory, everybody else has one, and she wants one, too." Her voice shook, and she crossed her arms to steady herself.

"That's not exactly how it happened," Zach replied, cool, calm. As if they were talking about a stray cat instead of his biological child, his and Heather's, the child they'd abandoned to her. To her. She'd been mother, not aunt. Legal guardian when Jade had had no one else. Until Heather had come back, pretending to have her life in order.

"Jade belongs with me."

"She belongs with her mother. You always knew that could happen. Besides, Heather said you could visit, like a regular aunt."

"How can you trust her? For five years, she called twice a year. Sent birthday presents that looked like they came from the Salvation Army, or the dump. Never sent a penny. You both wanted Jade to live with me. You wanted me to raise her, to let her call me Mommy." Annette had collapsed against the kitchen counter. Jade had been the child she'd never had, never could have, her life, her heart, her future. Wasn't that thicker than blood?

Zach was right about one thing: she had always feared Heather's return. And when it happened, she'd been too terrified to tell anyone about the legal battle. Not even Cheryl.

Heather had been a stranger to Jade. Annette had been the only constant in the child's life. But the court said Heather met all the legal requirements, had never given up her legal rights, had the legal right to full custody. All Annette's arguments about what was best for Jade meant nothing in the face of Heather's rights.

It wasn't right. It was all wrong.

And what made it worse was that Zach hadn't lifted a finger to help his own sister keep his daughter in the only home she'd ever known.

"Why did you move up here," she'd asked him, "if it wasn't to help me keep Jade?" He stood there, in her kitchen, drinking Cheryl's beer straight from the growler. "If you'd asserted your rights as her father—"

"You still couldn't have kept the kid. Nothing could have kept Heather from terminating your guardianship and preventing you from adopting her." He wiped his mouth with the back of his hand and laughed. When had he turned into this cruel man? "Face it, you dumb cunt. You did it to yourself. You gave up years of your life for somebody else's kid, and you've got nothing to show for it but a sad story and a pile of legal bills."

She grabbed a knife from the wooden block on the counter. Though he was younger and stronger, he hadn't fought her off, too slow to recognize danger from such an unlikely source. That had given her the advantage, and she'd stabbed him, first in the neck, cutting the carotid artery, then in the heart. The only sign that he even had a heart was the blood spewing out of his chest.

Spewing onto her kitchen floor. Then it stopped and she saw what she'd done. Her baby brother's blood soaking the rag rug.

If she were discovered, she'd never see Jade again.

She looked around, but the cabin gave her no answers. The lake. She backed her Subaru wagon up to the front door and spread a tarp near the body. It must have been adrenaline that kept her going, that gave her the strength to wrap Zach in the rug, tie it with an old rope, haul it on to the tarp, and drag the load to the car. Getting him in was a bitch. Finally, she crawled in herself and pulled, using the tarp as a sort of sled.

Back inside, she scrubbed her hands with soap and rage. They shook. The growler Zach had taken from the brewery sat on the counter. Well, that didn't matter. Why wouldn't her brother bring beer to her house and drink it before he left town? But it reminded her that she'd have to do something with his truck and his things.

Later. Later.

Oh, God, Zachary. What had she done? He had deserved it, hadn't he?

Blood had dampened the wooden floor. She couldn't stop to think about that. She had to get the body to the lake. The lake was huge, and cold, and the currents would wash him away.

He had loved the water, to the extent that Zach had loved anything except himself and messing with other people's minds.

Just past eight, getting dark. She had to get going, though she would wait until full dark to dump the body. Where? Even in mid September, the campground at the state park was still busy. That left the fishing access, a well-kept local secret. Only one road led out there, but no one would notice a car driving by, unless she gave them reason.

The fishing access had been deserted, as she'd prayed. No stragglers packing up their fishing gear or loading boats on trailers. No teenagers drinking by a bonfire or making out in parked cars. The setting sun glowed—from forest fires in Washington or B.C., no doubt.

She'd backed down the boat launch as far as she dared, then slid the tarp out of the car and on to the ground. How had Zach suddenly gotten so much heavier? The plastic might trap air and keep the body from sinking, so she unwrapped the tarp, rolled up her pant legs, dragged the load into the lake. Pushed it away from her, into the water, away, away, away.

She stood, looking, watching. *I'm sorry, Zachary,* she whispered. *But you betrayed me, and Jade.* She'd looked down at her hands then, and seen that once again, they were covered in blood.

This morning, she'd cleaned Zach's things out of the caretaker's apartment and driven his truck far into the woods, up one of the overgrown logging roads where it wouldn't be found for months, or years. Then she'd gone to work and acted like normal.

Until Kathryn came in, looking for Zach. There'd been a wild look in her eyes. She knew, Annette had realized. She must have gone to his apartment, seen that he was gone, come to the bar hoping to be wrong.

But there was no way she could know what really happened.

What if she did? Hadn't Kathryn threatened to kill Zach just two weeks ago, in front of the entire Friday night crowd? Hadn't she repeated the threat the next morning at the Grill?

He'd laughed. He'd dismissed her as a drama queen, spoiled and undisciplined. Annette would have to find her, scare her into silence, and make sure the investigators saw her for a crazy, violent lunatic. Then she could focus on getting Jade back.

"I'm sorry, Cheryl," she said. "I'm only doing this for my daughter. You understand, don't you?"

* * * *

As soon as the detectives left, Cheryl called a friend and asked him to handle the bar for the night.

Where would Kathryn go? Home seemed unlikely, but Cheryl checked first, looking in all the closets and under the bed, in the woodshed and the pump house. No sign.

The detectives had said Zach's body washed up on private property not far from the fishing access. The access itself would be blocked off and crawling with cops, even as dark fell, but there was a private road that led to the nearby homes. She'd been to some of these places, knew her way around a bit. So did Kathryn.

As Cheryl drove, she weighed her certainty that Kathryn was not involved. That she could not have hurt Zach. Obviously, if she'd killed him, she would not have asked Annette where he was. She might be unstable, but she wasn't stupid.

Holy shit. Cheryl had misunderstood. She'd told the deputies that Kathryn probably left rather than wait because she had other things on her mind, but what if Kathryn had come in already knowing Zach was gone? Maybe she'd been to his place, or seen or heard something. And she'd left in anger, thinking Annette knew and wouldn't tell her.

Or was it even worse? Had Kathryn known Zachary was dead and suspected Annette?

Annette had been acting strangely the last few weeks. She'd asked Cheryl to sign an affidavit attesting to her steady employment and good character—something about her ex and Jade's child support, she'd said. Cheryl hadn't asked questions, assuming that was the cause of Annette's occasional lateness and frequent sharp temper.

But what if there was some other explanation, something to do with Zachary?

Cheryl slowed as she drove past the trophy houses along the lake, wondering which yard, which beach was the one. Surely there would be a patrol car, a crime scene team, that garish yellow tape.

She stopped suddenly. No yellow tape, but wasn't that Kathryn's car? She backed up and crept down the steep driveway. Kathryn's beat-up blue Honda sat haphazardly behind an RV, beside a darkened house. Cheryl blocked the driveway with her Jeep, parked, and got out cautiously.

"Kathryn? Kathryn?" No answer. She looked around, then walked down the driveway and alongside the house, toward the lake. A deck jutted off the back of the house, and she glanced beneath, where sloping ground created the perfect place to hide. A flash of color caught her eye, and her throat. "Kathryn?" Cheryl crouched and called to her daughter. The girl turned, her eyes fevered and wide. Cheryl started toward her, and then saw her point toward the lake and the beach next door. Half a dozen men and women in uniform, taking measurements, photographs, notes. That was the place, then, where Zach had come to rest.

Cheryl crept toward her daughter. Wordless, she wrapped her arms around the thin shoulders. And then she saw the girl's hands, covered in blood.

* * * *

Annette held the phone to her ear, steering the curves on the road to the lake with one hand. She could hear adult voices yelling in the background as she waited for her daughter.

"Jade honey, it's Mommy." The two-word response stabbed her. "Yes, Mommy Annette. Listen, honey. Can you keep a secret, like a big girl? I'm coming to see you, soon. Don't tell anyone. It will be our surprise."

Zachary was wrong. Jade *was* her daughter. The love she felt, and the pain of separation, proved it. She would take Jade away from here, to safety.

But first, other matters. The mother would lead her to the girl. And sure enough, Cheryl turned down a driveway and left her car, never glancing back.

There they were, underneath the deck. Caught up in each other, unaware of anyone else, the perfect mother and daughter. If she moved quietly, they would never know. She had intended only to frighten the girl, but if she moved quickly, and cut their throats—arteries and trachea—they would die silently, as Zach had, and never be a threat to her and Jade. She tightened her grip on the knife in her pocket.

* * * *

The bugs. The bugs.

Kathryn's screams pierced the air. Down the slope, next door, the men and women in the bug suits turned toward the sound. They started running, some toward the deck, others toward trees that gave them cover as they approached the women under the deck.

Annette froze. Dare she move now, with all those eyes on her? She had to, had to make the break. Get Jade, and get away.

Hands grabbed her ankle and held her tight. "How could you?" Cheryl said, gasping. "You killed your own brother, and you meant to kill Kathryn and me. How could a mother kill anyone?"

Then they were surrounded. A deputy pried the knife from Annette's fingers and dragged her into the open. Another deputy helped Cheryl ease Kathryn out from under the deck. Cheryl brushed the spiders off her daughter, and the screaming quieted.

"Your hands. Are you hurt? Were you stabbed?" a deputy asked, shining a flashlight over a shaking Kathryn. She put her hand to her head, to a shiny patch on her skull.

Cheryl stopped herself from answering. It was time for Kathryn to speak for herself.

"I—I think I hit my head on a board." Kathryn's voice was thready. "Under there." She pointed under the deck, and in the beam of light, they all saw the blood on a deck joist.

Over her daughter's shoulder, toward the lake, Cheryl watched the sun drop below the horizon.

Leslie Budewitz *lives in northwest Montana. Her book,* Books, Crooks & Counselors: How to Write Accurately About Criminal Law and Courtroom Procedure, *will be published by Quill Driver Books in fall 2011; her website is www.LawandFiction.com. Leslie's short mysteries have appeared in* Alfred Hitchcock's Mystery Magazine, Ellery Queen's Mystery Magazine, *and* ThugLit.

THE SECRET OF THE RED MULLET

BY NANCY ADAMS

Rome, A.D. 380

"Marcellina! Look what that cat of yours has done now!"

Sagitta leaped out of the impluvium with a small fish in her jaws and shook herself off, scattering even more water over the atrium floor. A big gulp, and the fish was gone.

"Your brother is very fond of those fish!" Priscilla continued her scold.

I ignored my old nurse's words. The maidservants who were scrubbing the floor kept their heads down. Sagitta retched, her sides heaved, and a stream of brown liquid spewed out of her mouth. All over the floor. An intricate mosaic of tiny little tiles with tiny little spaces between. The maidservants looked at one another in resignation.

"Another hairball!" Priscilla grumbled. Her eyes narrowed to slits in her broad, fleshy face. "That animal is no better behaved than you."

I knelt down by Sagitta, stroking her fur in sympathy. Sunlight poured in, illuminating every dust mote, every drop of liquid on the floor. And something caught my eye. Something glinted gold in the unsavory wad of cat hair and fish bones. A disk of gold with a loop for a chain, Greek and Latin characters engraved around the rim. A defiant rooster stood in the center, crowing to drive away the dark. It was an amulet. A charm to ward off evil.

I plucked the amulet out of the muck and held it up to the light. The inscription read: "Hygia Valerius." For the health of Valerius. The maidservants crept closer, their irritation momentarily giving way to curiosity.

"Sagitta must have swallowed it," I said. "But the fish must have swallowed it first. Where do you think it came from?"

Even Priscilla was intrigued. She met my eyes with no trace of her usual grumpy expression. "Your father buys them from that fish market by Trajan's Forum," she said. "He got some new ones just a few days ago. I overheard him telling your brother about it. Red and gold fish with whiskers like the one your cat just ate."

"Hmmm." I stared at the amulet thoughtfully. I was beginning to form a plan.

* * * *

Seeing Trajan's Market for the first time was overwhelming. All the twelve years of my life, I'd been confined to the streets around our house; it was only on holidays in the country that I was allowed to roam very far. I had no idea that this amazing labyrinth lay just on the other side of Broad Street, only a few blocks from home.

I followed Priscilla through the crowded forum's square, gawking at the huge open space filled with more people than I'd ever imagined together in one place. Then through an archway in the surrounding wall, and there it was before me.

A half-circle of brickwork stretched out to embrace us, three tall stories high. Above it rose three stories more. I craned my neck to see the top. Colorful displays of fruit and flowers lined the half-circle before us. People milled around each booth, talking rapidly and gesticulating as they bargained with the merchants. Business was brisk.

"Built right into the Quirinal Hill," Priscilla said. Speechless, I followed her round the corner into a great entrance hall. I looked up at a vaulted ceiling higher than any I'd ever seen. Galleries on either side overlooked the space, and I longed to fly up to their lofty heights and gaze down at the hall from above. Enormous amphorae lined the walls on either side. Merchants stood behind stone counters filled with cups and pitchers, pouring out fragrant samples of olive oil and wine.

Priscilla led me through the hall to a flight of stairs at the back. We emerged on the corner of a busy street where vendors of every kind were hawking their wares. Exotic spices wafted through the air and delicately woven silks caught my eye. Even better was the view of Trajan's Forum three stories below. I stopped and gazed down at the scurrying crowds. We were at the top of the half-circle layer.

Priscilla tugged on my hand. "The fish ponds are on the top floor," she said. "You can see even more from there."

Priscilla was right. The windows on the top floor were so wide it was almost like walking beneath a covered portico. I stared out in open-mouthed amazement: you could see the entire city. Priscilla had to tear me away.

"We came here to find out about the fish, remember?"

I followed her reluctantly.

But the fish ponds were almost as fascinating as the view. There were six in all, each holding a different kind of fish, and I stared down at the colorful, shimmering shapes flitting through the water, entranced. The bearded mullets, the kind that Sagitta had swallowed, were especially handsome, with their iridescent shadings of red and gold.

A man strode up to us, and Priscilla pointed to the tank with the mullets.

"Do you raise them here, or do they come from somewhere else?"

"The red ones?" he said. "We get them from old man Gabinus outside Neapolis, down Campania way."

"Gabinus!" I said to Priscilla. "Our neighbor in Campania?"

"Must be," she replied. "I know he raises a lot of fish and sells some of them. And we'll be traveling there in a week or two, just as usual. I heard the master and mistress discussing the arrangements only yesterday."

We looked at each other in a rare moment of accord.

* * * *

My brother Gaius and I had always been a little afraid of Gabinus, who owned the neighboring villa just west of our family's summer retreat. Once he had caught us trespassing on his land and threatened to throw us into his lamprey pond. He'd laughed a big booming laugh. "Then I'll watch the little butchers tear you to pieces." Gaius and I had fled.

I took out the amulet from the little pouch tucked in the girdle at my waist and looked at it with fresh eyes. Its owner doubtless lay at the bottom of Gabinus's fish pond.

I couldn't wait to find my brother and tell him the exciting news.

But Gaius was unimpressed. He had turned fifteen only a few months ago and now considered himself too grown-up for my company.

"He just said that to frighten away a couple of little kids." Gaius dismissed my news with an irritatingly superior look. "He read the story about the man who supposedly fed his slaves to the lampreys and thought he'd get a good laugh out of us." He shook his head disdainfully, dark curls bobbing.

"I've read the story, too," I said impatiently. "That doesn't mean somebody couldn't really do it."

"You'd do better to worry about pirates," my brother said. "I overheard Father talking last night. There have been raids all along the coast in Campania."

"Oh no! That's not going to keep us from staying there, is it?"

"He said we'd take some extra men for protection, so I think they're still planning to go."

"I hope so, I've been looking forward to it so much! We always have such a good time there."

"You won't if the pirates kidnap you!" my brother taunted.

"And you won't if Gabinus feeds you to his fish!" I stuck out my tongue.

Gaius turned over the amulet in his hands, looking thoughtful despite his scornful words. He walked away without deigning to answer, still holding my prize.

I snatched the amulet back. "You think you're Apollo on Mount Olympus, just because you've turned fifteen!"

* * * *

Once we settled in our summer home, with no boys of his own age for company, Gaius dropped his snotty air, and we slipped back into our old roles as fellow explorers and conspirators. The excitement of being back in the country overshadowed the affair of the mysterious amulet. I had almost forgotten its existence when Priscilla brought it up again.

"Marcellina." My nurse stepped into the courtyard where Gaius and I were lounging after a morning spent along the shore picking up shells and stones and threatening to push each other into the sea. She dangled a thin strip of leather in front of me. "For that charm. I thought you could wear it around your neck. Be safer that way."

"Thank you." I took out the amulet and threaded the leather through the loop at its top. Priscilla waited expectantly, but I said nothing else and took up the scroll I'd been reading. My nurse scowled and stomped back inside.

As soon as she left the courtyard, I turned to Gaius. "The moon's almost full; it'd be a perfect evening to do some exploring on our own. We know the amulet came from Gabinus's fish ponds." My brother, so stodgy in Rome, could never resist an adventure in Campania, and we arranged to meet outside as soon as the household retired for bed.

The moon was rising behind us when we slipped out of the courtyard. The sky was a deep, dark blue, mirroring the water in the bay below. Above us rose the wooded ridge connecting the two villas, a dark mounded mass punctuated by the crowns of ancient umbrella pines poking above the rest of the foliage like the heads of beneficent, shaggy-haired giants. A small dark shadow flitted into the trees before us. A bat.

Entering the woods was strangely peaceful. At first. Moonlight illuminated the well-known, well-beloved forms of the venerable holly oaks beneath whose branches Gaius and I had played since I could remember. The trees were dappled with lacework of light and shadow, dressed up in evening finery rather than the everyday wear of sunlight. My brother and I stared in silence, awed by the magic of the night. The only sounds the low cicada hum, the occasional hoot of a small owl. Beneath these, a deep hush that seemed to come from the floor of the forest, the depths of the trees, the darkening sky, the glowing moon. I forgot the purpose of our journey and gave myself up to the wonder of it all. The moon rode our backs in friendly silence as we threaded the familiar path through the wood. By the time we saw the row of cypress that marked the clearing where Gabinus's villa stood, she had risen clear above the treetops. We were nearing the end of our journey.

Angry voices shattered the silence, like a slap in the face. Beneath the sheltering limbs of a great holly oak, Gaius and I stopped as if we'd been turned to stone. We held our breath, listening.

"The master's going to be angry, Hermes. You agreed to go along."

"I didn't know anyone was going to get hurt!" Hermes' voice was high-pitched and shrill with fear.

"Who said anything about getting hurt?"

"It's for the pirates! Of course he's going to get hurt!"

A sharp slap rang through the trees. Someone started to sob.

"Shut your mouth, Hermes! No loose talk! Master's going to be angry when he hears about this."

"Please, don't tell him," Hermes sobbed.

"You were all ready for your share of the gold," the first man sneered. "Where'd you think it'd come from?"

"I thought we were just goin' to steal something," Hermes mumbled.

"Leave the thinking to someone else. It's not—"

A gust of wind blew dust in our faces and Gaius sneezed. Loudly.

Hermes shrieked. Footsteps pounded close, closer. A ghostly figure appeared in the swatch of moonlight next to our tree. White face, haloed in reddish wisps, mouth open in a silent scream. We could hear his gasping breaths as he raced past, and his hand brushed against my hair. I swallowed a shriek myself and Gaius grabbed me by the shoulders, pulling me further beneath the tree. I clutched my brother round the waist and buried my head against his chest. My mouth was dry and my heart thudded into my throat. Gaius's heart was thudding, too.

The remaining man cursed. I opened my eyes and peered through the leaves. A long, silver blade flashed in the moonlight. Twigs crunched underfoot, grew softer, gradually died away.

I released my strangle-hold on Gaius and drew a deep shuddering breath as we left the shelter of the holly oak. My brother's face shone ghostly pale in the moonlight. We turned back for home without a word.

* * * *

The next day our family paid the obligatory social call on our other neighbor, who owned the villa to the east. A funny old man named Censorinus, who loved nothing as much as the bearded mullet fish he kept as pets.

Sure enough, we found him by his fish pond, feeding the mullets out of his hands. One of them even had a miniature jeweled tiara tied on top of its head. Gaius and I exchanged a grin. Visiting Censorinus was always fun.

Plump, good-humored, he creaked to his feet and greeted us affectionately. We joined him at the pond's edge, feeding the fish and dabbling our hands in the water to stroke their scales. Censorinus claimed they knew their own names and would come when he called—except they didn't feel like it at the moment. Too excited by our company, he explained.

When we tired of the fish, the grownups sat around the pond exchanging neighborhood gossip while Gaius and I wandered into the gardens, basking in the sunlight and breathing deep breaths of the clean, salty air. Last night's scary adventure seemed worlds away.

"Hermes!" A man's voice. The same voice we'd heard last night. Coming from the other side of the boxwood hedge. Gaius and I sank to the ground and peered through the foliage.

The man speaking was big and muscled like a gladiator. His companion, Hermes, pale, red-haired, and thin, cowered under the other's glare.

"We're goin' back tonight," the big man said.

"But he's got guards!" Hermes protested. "We almost got caught last night! Why can't we wait till the moon's dark?"

"There's no time. They gotta leave tomorrow. Come on." The two men crept away.

"They must be planning to do something to Censorinus," I whispered. "You know what Gabinus is like. I bet that amulet belonged to someone like Hermes, some slave who wouldn't go along with one of his wicked schemes, someone who got thrown in a fish pond and drowned."

Gaius frowned. "But why would they be over here in broad daylight?"

Thoughtfully we made our way out of the garden, back toward the fish pond where the others sat chatting.

The talk was putting me to sleep when a maidservant appeared at my elbow to ask if I'd like a honey cake. Behind her stood a man holding a platter of food. I almost fell off my couch. It was Hermes!

"I didn't mean to wake you, Lady," the maidservant apologized, fortunately taking my open mouth and clumsy moves for remnants of sleep.

"Of course I'd like a cake. Thank you," I said, recovering my poise and tearing my stare away from the red-headed slave. I threw a glance at Gaius, who was masking his own amazement with a tremendous yawn. Talk would have to wait.

* * * *

"What does it mean?" I burst out once we were home. "I thought Hermes belonged to Gabinus."

"Maybe Gabinus sent his man around to bribe the servants of Censorinus," Gaius said. "That would explain why Hermes didn't want to hurt him."

"Or maybe Censorinus is up to something," Priscilla's voice came from the door.

Gaius and I started. My old nurse smiled, smug at having caught us out.

"I've got some interesting news," she said. "But you go first."

I cut in quickly, before Gaius could open his mouth. "We were walking over towards Gabinus's villa yesterday and heard two men talking. It sounded as if they were planning something bad. And one of them was that red-headed slave we saw today at Censorinus's place."

Priscilla didn't have to know we'd seen them at night.

"Hmm." She knit her brows thoughtfully. "Well, the gossip at Censorinus's place isn't as free as it used to be. Things are different this year. They all act as if they're afraid of something, but nobody will talk."

"What about the servants of Gabinus?" I asked.

"Gabinus? They're all devoted to him. It's a good place to work. He's like your father, treats everyone fair. But there's not much interesting news from Gabinus's household. Except that his young grandson's visiting. A boy much younger than either of you."

"But I thought Gabinus was mean!" I said. "I've been frightened of him every since he threatened to feed us to his fish all those years ago!"

Priscilla laughed until the tears streamed down her plump cheeks. "He likes his fun, from what I hear. He must've enjoyed giving you two a scare."

Gaius and I exchanged a look. Something strange was going on. The big slave had said they had to do it tonight—whatever "it" was.

Priscilla's next words echoed my thoughts. "There's something going on with Censorinus. Some fishy business, if you ask me."

* * * *

The full moon followed us through the trees as Gaius and I retraced our steps of the previous evening, heading through the woods to the villa of Gabinus, where something wicked was afoot.

We crept to the edge of the clearing where the villa stood. White-marbled columns stretched into the distance, a long line of porticos overlooking the sea. The pillars glowed in the moonlight against a dark backdrop of trees and night sky. The wind moaned like a creature in pain. At the seaward side of Gabinus's land, a thicket of oleander masked the abrupt drop off a jagged cliff, whose steep, rocky slope ended at the water's edge. The surf below growled in the darkness, a dragon in its lair, lying in wait.

Two figures slipped out of the villa, carrying a long bundle wrapped in cloth. What was it? Hermes had been reluctant because he didn't want to hurt someone. The bundle must be a person. Suddenly everything became clear.

I screamed as loud as I could. Several times. Gaius stared at me in shock.

One of the men screamed too and dropped his end of the bundle, fleeing into the woods. Hermes.

The remaining man shook his fist, then picked up the bundle once more. He headed straight for us. A thin line of silver gleamed in the moonlight. His dagger. I screamed again.

He was so close I could see every hair on his chin. Then he stumbled and fell to the ground, tripped by my brother's long leg. The bundle he'd been carrying rolled into the trunk of an oak. A small child's head popped out of the cloth, his mouth opened wide in a bewildered wail.

"Grab the dagger!" Gaius said. "I'll take the boy."

I obeyed without thinking, hurtling over the kidnapper's prostrate body to seize the thin gleam of silver that had fallen from his clasp. Gaius clutched the bundle of cloth to his chest. A thin whimper came from its folds. We ran to the villa as fast as the wind. Already Gabinus's men were pouring out.

"He's over there." Gaius pointed. "In the trees."

* * * *

"I can't thank you enough." Gabinus held his little grandson in his arms, tears raining down on the boy's dark brown hair. We were sitting in one of the reception rooms that looked out over the sea. "What were you two doing here, anyway? I can't imagine your parents let you roam around in the middle of the night. Not that I'm unhappy about the result." He grinned.

So I told him the tale from the beginning, when Sagitta had eaten the fish.

"May I see the amulet?" he asked.

I pulled the leather strap off my neck and handed it to him. Gabinus threw back his head and roared with laughter. "The Goddess of Fortune has a strange sense of humor. Val!" he said to the boy, who had fallen asleep. "Look!"

The little boy opened his eyes and yawned sleepily. But when he saw the amulet, he sat up, wide awake.

"My charm!" he said. "My charm! I thought it was lost."

Gaius and I stared in amazement. Gabinus grinned again. "Valerius lost this on his last visit, a few months ago. It fell into one of the mullet ponds. The servants dived in and dug up the entire bottom, but it never turned up. A fish must have swallowed it." And he repeated the story for his grandson's benefit. The little boy smiled and slipped the leather thong over his head. He pressed his face against Gabinus's chest and fell asleep again, the amulet clutched fast in a chubby little fist.

"Did your servants catch the kidnapper?" Gaius asked.

"Ah, he met with rather an unpleasant fate." Gabinus barked out a grim laugh.

"Did you feed him to your fish?" I was horrified.

"No, little mistress, I did not feed him to my fish. Whatever made you think that?"

I explained. Gabinus roared with laughter again, and then sobered enough to relate the kidnapper's end.

"He was running from my men and he ran right off the cliff into the sea. May he rot there forever, the venomous snake! Kidnapping a little child to sell to the pirates! Can't think of a crime worse than that. And if I find out that Censorinus had anything to do with this—well, little mistress, maybe I'll feed him to my fish after all." He hugged his grandson tight.

* * * *

We left Gabinus's villa escorted by an army of servants, for who knew whether any of the kidnapper's pirate friends were lurking nearby. The moon was high above our heads; the waves below gleamed with phosphorescence and moonlight. The scene was magical, yet full of foreboding. The dragon of the sea on the rocky shore below growled with subdued menace, appeased for the night at least, by the libation of the kidnapper's blood.

Nancy Adams *is a theological librarian with a Ph.D. in music history from the University of Pennsylvania. She lives in the Philadelphia area with her husband, Patrick, and is working on a series of historical novels that feature older versions of Marcellina and Gaius. Research help was provided by Michael Markowitz, Carolyn Snively, Catherine Collins, and Matej Zupancic via the Late-Antique listserve. Many thanks.*

ACCIDENTS HAPPEN

BY JAMES MONTGOMERY JACKSON

On my drive through the woods I passed two gutted deer hanging in hunters' camps and one more posed rack forward strapped to the top of a car. November 15th—first day of deer season in Michigan's Upper Peninsula—was proving successful for the hunters, less so for the deer. Every camp I passed had a smear of smoke drifting from its chimney and a half dozen trucks parked in the yard. Opening day is almost a national holiday hereabouts and many businesses shut down for the first week of deer season. Only the mine was open; it ran 24/7. Since I don't hunt, it seemed like a good day for the fool's errand I was on.

I was on my way to meet Glen at the mine's security gate. Glen and I owned neighboring camps deep in the woods, fifteen miles from the nearest place you can buy anything. Toward the end of his annual Halloween party, his wife, Margie, cornered me and Jon Nyland, Glen's boss. She convinced Jon to bring me onsite to look into the mine's mysterious deaths. "A serial killer is on the loose," she said. "Glen could be next."

I asked myself again what a forensic accountant, city born and raised, was doing investigating mine accidents. Sure, Margie knew that, working for Criminal Investigations Group, I had solved a couple of murders. Fortunately, my financial sleuthing uncovered the killers before they claimed me as their next victim. Once Margie laid her hand on my arm and asked, "Seamus McCree, are you going to help me?" my desire to be useful trumped my common sense.

At the guard's booth, Glen handed me a visitor's pass and I followed him to Jon's office, a closet so small we both had to stand.

Jon cleared his throat. "I looked at the accident files again," he said. "The three electricians worked here a combined eighty-seven years. Before their fatal accidents, the worst thing that happened to any of them was one guy slammed a car door on his pinkie."

"You know this is a waste of everyone's time," Glen said. "Margie's just paranoid."

"Look, Seamus," Jon said. "I know Margie caught us after we'd had a few. I got no budget to pay you and I don't even know what you can do, but I do have a bad feeling about these accidents."

"I'm not a licensed investigator," I said. "But if you want, I can look around, ask some questions. Best hope is to kick up something to get the cops interested again."

"Can't ask for more," Jon said, "but I can't pay you."

I dismissed his concern with a wave. "After the party I talked to Margie again. She wouldn't take no for an answer. She's so worried she promised to take me to Glen's secret spot for brook trout next spring."

"She did what?" Glen shouted.

"Fair enough." Jon removed a file from a dented cabinet that might have been beige a century ago. "Here's a list of the guys in the Electrical Department. I don't think anyone else could rig these deaths. If there is a killer, he's here. Shift change is in fifteen minutes. I'll get both groups together and let them know what you're doing . . . or is that a bad idea?"

"Might as well address it head on," I said. "I don't know enough about electricity to fake being an inspector."

He circled three names. "It's an old seniority list. These are the fatalities. The top six guys are on vacation. These twelve," he placed a circled "1" in front of their names, "are on the shift that's about to end. Glen and the others are on second shift. We got some replacements who aren't on this list, but since they weren't here you don't need to worry about them. I'll have Glen take you around. If you need to talk to the first shift guys, stick around for shift change again or come back in the morning. They ain't gonna stay here any longer than my speech."

"Do you know who was working when each of the supposed accidents happened?" I asked.

"Not off hand. I'll get the information from personnel. Might not be until tomorrow though."

"They got *us* working twelve-hour shifts," Glen said. "But *they're* long gone."

Jon checked his watch. "Showtime."

* * * *

Shelves and bins containing wires and electrical equipment lined the walls in the change room. Bunched in the center were lockers and benches. A huge "Safety is Job #1" poster covered the inside of the door. Guys changed in and out of steel-toed shoes, Carhartt bibs and coveralls while Jon introduced me. Too bad no one immediately confessed.

The only question when Jon was finished was from a short, baby-faced guy. "We done here?"

Glen and I hopped into his Silverado. "Learn anything interesting?" Glen asked.

"Safety is Job #1."

"So they say. Let's do them in the order they occurred. Used to be five separate lakes on this property," Glen said as we drove to the first accident site. "Pumped them dry, like we do with the big hole. All we got left is the evaporation pond."

The "pond" turned out to cover over a thousand acres, larger than most Upper Peninsula lakes. Our arrival startled a flock of mergansers, which skittered across the cerulean water. With a flash of white tail feathers, juncos flitted from the road into tag alders growing near the edge of the pond. Across the road a stand of aspen grew, mute testimony to a self-seeded clear-cut from years ago.

"This one was labeled a hunting accident?" I asked. "Isn't the mining property posted?"

"No legal hunting, which is why Arnold was here. The deer love this grove. Lots of browse, close to water, coyotes but no wolves and no hunting . . . except for Arnold. Everyone knew he hunted this area. Hell, even management knew. They figured it was better that Arnold thinned the population and gave the meat to charity than to let the deer starve. Arnold got a processor in Marquette to make steaks and sausage from his kills and gave them to a food bank. All under the table, eh? See the road past the gate?"

In the distance, I made out a fence and gate. "He parked there and walked in?"

"Yeah, that's a public road. Cops figure he tripped, discharged his twenty-gauge into his left shoulder—not fatal—and fell into the pond. Hit his head and drowned in six inches of water."

"Tough way to go," I said. "This was during last year's deer season?"

"Yep. What was Arnold doing by the water? He warn't huntin' no mergansers. You ever taste them? Fishy. Warn't fishing. Nothing but guppies and fingerlings in this pond. Hunting, he'd be in the trees. It's starting to drizzle again. If this had all been snow, we'd have three feet. You done here?"

I surveyed the area, tried to picture Arnold's death. The accident didn't make sense, but to outsiders how many of our actions do? Everyone knew Arnold poached, so if someone killed him, the list of suspects was endless.

Caws from a murder of crows cruising toward their evening roost brought me back to the present. Were they a sign? Only in a Bergman movie. I shook the rain off like a dog and got into Glen's truck. In the dusk, our headlights caught the scurry of hares at the side of the road and a coyote slipping into the brush.

"Slag heap's next," Glen said. After letting a gigantic truck pass, he turned onto the main drag. "A loaded dump truck developed an electrical problem with its lift mechanism at the top of the slag heap. Loaded, it was too heavy to tow, so Donny went up to work on it."

We turned onto a narrow road and serpentined up a hill. Eighteen-inch berms provided the only protection from dropping hundreds of feet into the mine pit. The outsized equipment below looked like matchbox toys. Butterflies tickled my stomach. I focused straight ahead, ignoring the increasing chasm out my window. We caught up to a three-story truck lumbering up the hill.

"Here's how it works," Glen said. "The engineers know the iron content of each face they're excavating, so if a truck's load contains enough iron, they cart it to the crusher. We'll visit that last. If the rock is overburden—not enough iron in it—the truck hauls it up here and adds it to the slag heap."

Partway up, Glen pulled so far to the right his tires rode slightly onto the berm. He yanked the emergency brake and hopped out. "Here we are."

I slithered onto the berm and inched around the front of the truck to join Glen. One slip and my next stop was a hundred feet lower. He pointed to the middle of the road. "Donny ended up here. Fell from up there." He waved vaguely toward the hill on our left. "Busted half the bones in his body. You be careful getting back into the truck now."

The top of the hill was flat, providing distant views of lights twinkling in the surrounding towns and, to the north, was the black void of Lake Superior.

"Can't build the slag heap no higher, otherwise we exceed the highest point in Michigan. Now *that* would cause a real stink."

The dump truck we followed proceeded to the far end of the plateau, deposited its load and a dozer pushed the slag over the far edge.

"If the trucks dump on the far side, why was Donny over here?"

"The accident inspectors found a cigarette butt nearby. Figure Donny took a break, slipped and met his maker."

"And you don't?"

"Probably happened that way. He liked the view from on top. Only other possibility is somebody took a chunk of ore and whapped him on the head, threw him over. Cops never found no motive."

I closed my eyes on the trip down and opened them once I felt the vehicle reach flat ground. Pale yellow light leaked from distant buildings growing harsher the closer we came. Glen stopped at the far end of the building where they made iron pellets.

"Got your earplugs, right?" He turned off his truck and screwed plugs into his ears. "We'll need them once we're inside. You know how we make the pellets?"

"Not so much," I said, raising my voice to accommodate the earplugs.

"First we crush the rock. Watch this guy."

We hopped out. The dump truck, with tires taller than our vehicle, backed toward the side of the building, the beep-beep-beep loud enough to warn off folks a county or two away. The truck backed until a light on the building turned from green to red. I felt the rumble of the huge truck's diesel engine through the soles of my feet. Nothing happened until a second light changed from red to green. The dump truck raised its box and a load of iron ore rumbled into a circular hole in the ground with the sound of Niagara tumbling over its falls. Even before the truck's box returned to level, the dump truck had pulled out and a second truck maneuvered to back in.

"Not your mother's blender," Glen said. "Those big chunks of rock all end up as powder. Let's get in out of the rain."

We walked through a narrow door, down a corridor and into a control room where the operator monitored the crusher.

"See them gauges?" Glen pointed to a row of displays along one wall. "Show what's happening in the crusher. Only two things stop this operation. A rock jams up the works, and they gotta knock it loose. Or a gauge goes kerflooey. Then they call us."

The operator, half-listening to Glen's narration, shot me a "who-the-hell-are-you?" look.

Glen continued his narrative. "When a jam occurs, the sensors automatically trip a circuit breaker. The operator resets it once they clear the jam. It's different for electrical problems. The electrician cuts all the power to the crusher. See the red switch?" He pointed high on a wall in a dark corner. "Four hundred eighty volts. He turns off the power, tapes it down and signs his name. The operator's gotta leave the room. Only the signing electrician can remove the tape."

The operator was now paying more attention to Glen than to the gauges.

"Paul grabbed a live wire. Cops decided he didn't totally disconnect the power. Least it was quick."

The operator yelled to Glen. "More OSHA? Man, I'm glad it wasn't my shift. Stunk to high . . . never mind." He turned around and stared at the gauges.

We backed out of the room and Glen shut the door. "You want to see the exact location?"

I shook my head. "You think someone flipped the switch?"

"This is why Jon thinks if there's a killer, he's an electrician. You saw where the switch was located? Only people who know are electricians, a few managers and the operators in that booth. If he didn't screw up, it had to be one of us."

"Your tone of voice says you think he did screw up."

"That's what everyone except Margie believes."

* * * *

I spent hours talking to the electricians, alternately soaked in the rain outside the plant and steamed like a lobster inside. Nobody knew anything more than what Glen had told me.

Using my coat for a pillow, I fell asleep on a bench in the change room. Jon woke me in the morning. "Got the information." In his office he handed me a cup of steaming coffee. I don't drink the stuff, but it warmed my hands and maybe the caffeine reached me by osmosis.

Using the electrician seniority list, he marked those who had worked during each shift the "accidents" occurred. Only three guys were on the premises during all the events, and all three were currently on vacation.

"Guys choose vacation based on seniority?" I asked.

"We only let six guys off at a time. At the beginning of each year the first six put in for their vacation and then the next six and so on. First week of deer season . . ."

He nattered on, but I was in my own little world. The first six guys were out at deer camp, and numbers seven, eight and ten were buried six feet under. Glen was number nine. Maybe Margie wasn't so paranoid. Jon stopped talking and looked at me curiously.

"Sorry, wool gathering," I said. "How frequently do guys retire?"

"Depends. The top two announced awhile back that this was their last year. They'll both have thirty-five years in and get full retirement pay."

"So next year—" I forgot and took a sip of the coffee and had to stop myself from spitting it out. I tapped the list to buy time. "Glen and this guy, number eleven—Reginald Drum—will be eligible for vacation during the first week of deer season? How long will the next guys have to wait?"

He curled his bottom lip in concentration. "Hard to say . . . maybe four, five years."

"Wait a minute," I said. "We got one wrong. Arnold died while he was off-duty. How easily could someone sneak down to those holding ponds? Isn't it more likely someone off-duty killed him?"

He scratched the top of his head with both hands. "Could be. That would mean . . ." He trailed a pencil down the list. Now only one guy could have done it: Reginald Drum.

"Tell me about him," I said.

"Moose?" He slapped the metal desk. Made me jump. "You think he killed three people so he could go deer hunting on opening day? That's crazy." He paused, tilted his head and stared at the ceiling. "Of course killing three guys ain't exactly normal, is it?"

He turned to a file cabinet, ran his finger down the drawers, reading labels aloud. "Here we are," he said and opened a manila file. "Let's see what Moose was working on when Donny fell." He flipped through some pages. "According to this, both Moose and Donny were working truck maintenance. Donny went up. Moose stayed."

"But it's possible," I said, "that Drum also went to the top of the slag heap to help Donny?"

"Not according to this file, but . . ." Jon rooted through the cabinets again, pulled another folder. "At the time of the crusher accident everyone was on break. Before and after the break most of the guys were relocating sodium lamps over the separation room. Moose was by himself replacing three-way plugs about fifty feet from the crusher control booth. I can't believe . . . when the crusher ain't running, this place loses that low thrum you hear and feel. Everyone woulda known the crusher was down. If he used his break to see what was happening and found Paul working inside the crusher, he coulda tripped the breaker and no one knows the better."

I pictured all the guys I had met the evening before. Several were sized double or triple X. "Moose a volatile kind of guy?"

"When he gets a few under his belt." Jon scratched his head again. "You saw him at the meeting. Little guy—the one that stormed out after the meeting?"

"He's Moose?"

"It had something to do with Moosehead beer when he was a kid."

Only in the Northwoods. "We don't have near enough to go to the cops," I said, "but tell me what you think of this idea."

* * * *

Jon parked me in the back stall of the men's room where I could overhear his prepared speech. He gathered the first shift at lunch break. "Sorry, guys, for another meeting. I got two quick announcements. Seamus McCree thinks Donny, Arnold and Paul were murdered. He's filling the manager in now and plans to head to Negaunee and talk with the State Troopers.

"I was gonna hold off the second thing until we're done with hunting season, but since I got you together now, I'll get it over with. Looks like next year management'll only let four of our guys off at a time—supposedly worried we'll be working twelves again and spread too thin during deer season. I checked: there's nothing in the contract says they can't do it. Questions?"

Guys grumbled and, Jon said, mostly stared at their shoes, except for Moose whose voice penetrated the bathroom wall.

"This sucks," he yelled. "If you think I'm waiting for two more guys to retire before I get that week—"

A slammed door cut off his tirade.

* * * *

After waiting ten minutes, I walked deliberately to my vehicle. I wanted to look over my shoulder and see who was watching. I wanted to shout, "I don't have any proof. I'm trying to smoke you out." My bright idea no longer seemed so bright. I placed one foot in front of the other until I got to my camp truck, an old Ford Ranger. Had Glen succeeded at the task Jon set him to before lunchtime? Would Moose take the bait? Had I surmised wrong and hooked someone else? I scanned the lot. Moose's black Tundra was missing.

I eased onto the mine's main road. At the four-way stop I looked right and left. No Moose. I surrendered my pass when I exited the mine property, a little surprised Moose hadn't taken a run at me while I was inside. Glen was supposed to remove the ammunition from Moose's rifle and follow him if he took his truck. I guessed I'd find out what happened from Glen when he was next at camp. At US-41 I turned away from the State Police in Negaunee, and headed home. At Michigamme, I entered the woods. The rain had stopped, but the roads were sloppy.

Halfway home, shortly before a one-lane bridge, a truck roared out of an abandoned two-track and slammed into the passenger side of my Ranger, toppling it into the creek. Water rushed into the upside down cab through the passenger door, which had sprung open from the impact. Elbowing aside the airbag, I released the seatbelt. Fighting the rush of water, I squeezed out the passenger door. The storm-swelled current swept me through the culvert, banged me on the rocky bottom and spit me into an eddy on the other side of the road.

Shock from the collision and the near-freezing water kept me from making any noise. A heavy engine idled on the bridge, spewing out fumes. I peered through weeds and spotted a pair of legs on the other side of Moose's truck. Glen had screwed up.

Shivering so hard I had to keep my mouth wide open so my teeth didn't chatter, I crawled out of the water, staying below the truck's profile. While Moose continued to scan the Ranger's wreckage, I used an ancient trick and tossed pebbles onto the bank where I had exited the creek. The legs inched around the side of the truck and paused at the front. I held my breath for a millennium or two. Finally, he rushed to the far side of the road and pointed a rifle toward the creek. I followed and drove my shoulders into his legs, slamming him into the ground. My brain flashed that something was wrong. Momentum carried me up his body and my weight pounded his head into an underwater rock. It wasn't Moose; it was Glen.

The justice of letting him drown flashed through my thoughts. Instead, I dragged his limp body and the rifle to the road and checked the truck. Under a tarp I found Moose—dead from a crushed head. Glen was stirring and I couldn't find anything to bind him with. I covered him with the rifle.

When Glen came to, his justifications flowed like an artesian well from built up pressure. "If Arnold hadn't tripped and shot himself, none of this would have happened. What was I going to do? He knocked himself unconscious and I was in trouble 'cause I'd boogied from work early. Then this thought came to me: Hell, if I can't get the first week of deer season off, at least I can take over Arnold's poaching. So he drowned, and you know . . . I was okay with that. Accidents happen.

"Those guys got ahead of me in seniority only 'cause I did my duty in Nam and they didn't. Now that's not fair, is it? The day Donny went to the slag heap to fix the truck, he and I came to work together. After the shift, I drove up to the top of the slag to pick him up. He razzed me about next opening day: him being in his blind with a 24-pack while I was stuck at work. Before I knew it, I whaled his head with a chunk of ore. Pitched him off the side and planted that cigarette butt."

"Why Paul?" I said. "He was behind you in the seniority."

"I never did like him and if anyone got suspicious, it might point the finger at someone else. Made you suspect Moose, eh? Everything was going fine until Margie got you involved. No one else tied it to deer season.

"When I got to Moose's truck, he was already there. I figured if you was both dead, they'd pin everything on him." He stood up. "Now Seamus, you got yourself a problem. Hypothermia will set in soon. I know you. You ain't gonna shoot me, gun's wet anyway. And you got no proof. I wore gloves, see?" He turned and took a step toward Moose's truck.

He was right, I wouldn't kill him.

I slammed the rifle butt into his knee. He crumpled to the ground wailing in agony. I thought about the victims and Margie's concern for his welfare and what this was going to do to her. I slammed the rifle into his other knee.

Accidents happen.

James Montgomery Jackson *lives with his life partner, Jan Rubens, on a remote lake in Michigan's Upper Peninsula. They winter in Georgia. Besides mystery short stories and novels, Jim's writing credits include short memoir and non-fiction pieces. He is sometimes master to their dog and always servant to their cat.*

IDENTITY CRISIS

BY DIANE VALLERE

"I want to buy a fish."

"Are you sure? Looks like you want a kitten."

Five rambunctious balls of fur climbed over each other in their attempt to paw at me through the glass. The loudest, a puff of gray, crouched over a newspaper article about a body found at the lake half a mile away. His wet spot distorted the already blurry photo.

It was the fifth time in as many days I'd stood here. Surprising I hadn't left a nose print on the glass. "No. I want a fish. A mean one." *One that I'm not going to start to love. I don't want to get attached.*

How was I supposed to explain that my shrink—I mean, therapist—suggested I get a pet? After watching me break down repeatedly after my cat of fifteen years left to rub ankles with a higher power, she—the therapist, not the cat—thought having something to care for would allow me to understand the circle of life. She—the cat, not the therapist—had seen me through two career changes and three breakups, but those I'd gotten over. I'd suggested a cactus. My shrink suggested a fish.

"Miss, what's your name?"

I adjusted my white patent-leather headband in the reflection of the glass and answered, even though the grey kitten with the litter box problem had been calling it out since I'd walked into the store. "Mia."

"Mia, I am Andrew." He answered in a stilted Armenian accent. He shifted his weight back and forth and stepped slightly away from me. "I help you find fish."

"A mean fish."

A lanky man in a wrinkled Hawaiian shirt and half-crushed straw hat eased past me as Andrew mopped his brow with an already discolored hanky. Didn't help that, in this unseasonably hot weather, the industrial fans in the corners of the store did little more than exchange the scent of animals from one side to the other. It also didn't help that my vintage sixties dress was 100% polyester. Looked cute, though.

The front door bell chimed and two men entered. The first man was straight from the pages of GQ, with his pocket square tucked into an expensive pinstriped suit and the sort of casually unkempt longish hair that came courtesy of a stylist. His friend was the opposite, with a loose tie, rumpled shirt, and perspiration circles under his arms.

They stood by the register, watching us. I cleared my throat to draw attention back to me. "My mean fish? And I'll need a bowl, too."

"I have just the fish in mind." He waved me towards a tank where a feisty bluish-green blob swam agitated laps. "He swims alone."

He glanced toward the men loitering by the register, mopped his brow again, and then refocused his attention on me. "I have special tank. Wait here. I keep spring water out back. Good for betta fish." He disappeared out the back door.

I stood by the kittens, because it was the only place to stand, mind you. A crackly voice on the transistor radio tucked alongside the register sputtered about the heat wave. Pinstripes squeezed past the aquariums filled with snakes and lizards and bent next to me, peering at the cats.

"You getting a kitten?"

"No, a fish."

He eyed me up and down. "You sure? You look more like the kitten type."

"Looks can deceive." I glanced over my shoulder. Sweat Stains rested against the front counter. The guy in the hat ignored us, leaning against a terrarium, head buried in a dog-eared paperback. His straw fedora shadowed his face. Or was it a homburg? I always get those confused.

Andrew returned carrying the fish equivalent of Wayne Manor, halfway filled. The bottom was covered in small pink rocks. The fish swam mad dashes back and forth. "He is fighting fish. Very mean. You will like him."

"I can't afford that aquarium!"

"Special price for you. Twenty dollars includes fish and tank. This is better for him to transport." He set the tank on the counter and punched keys on the register. I pulled a twenty from my beaded coin purse. Andrew looked at me, then at the men loitering by the reptile cages. "Take food, too. Special promotion. Complimentary." He thrust a small vial of fish food into my handbag. Pinstripes approached us.

"That's too heavy for you to carry. I'll get it."

"I can make it." I slung my handbag across my chest and wrapped my arms around the tank, then balanced it with my knee. He was right—it was heavy. I struggled to get a better grip.

"A pretty thing like you shouldn't have to carry that." He tugged on the tank until I was forced to let go. Andrew had disappeared to the back of the store. Sweat Stains was gone, too. Fedora squinted at us and tucked his book in his back pocket. Pinstripes turned towards the door and tipped his head for me to follow him. Fedora trailed a few steps behind.

"Which one's your car?"

I hesitated.

"Lemme guess," he said, with a backwards glance at my white patent-leather boots. "The Union Jack Mini." He headed towards my car, not waiting for confirmation. Maybe there was such a thing as too much personal expression?

"You maybe wanna get a drink after we drop this off?"

"No—no thank you." His unexpected proposition unnerved me.

The lot was speckled with cars but no people. I glanced at the store where I worked, hoping Carolyn, my manager, was out front on a break. Of course she wasn't. She was manning the store while I was buying a fish, no doubt restocking bloody knives or fishnets. NEW IDENTITY, her costume-slash-vintage store, was in the same strip mall as the pet store, which explains why I was able to visit the kittens five days in a row. I mean, fish. Her assortment of thrift store fashions came via flea markets and estate sales and kept me in scooter dresses and sixties attire for less than I'd pay on eBay. Plus, it was fun. Most of the time.

Pinstripes reached my convertible first and set the tank on the passenger seat. He picked up something from inside. I didn't want to leave my fish alone for one more second. He—the stranger, not the fish—looked at the item in his hands. My nametag. I'd been looking for that for a week. He scanned the row of stores, pausing on NEW IDENTITY, then nodded my direction and dropped the tag back into my car. With hands in the pockets of his suit he walked towards a Mustang parked in the far corner of the lot. I gave him a nice lead, tossed my handbag on the floor, and peeled out. My handbag tipped and the contents spilled. Water splashed from the tank.

"That was weird, right?" I said to the fish. He didn't answer. I scooped up my cell phone and plunked it in the cup holder. Then I turned on the radio and caught a reporter calmly talking about the only thing anyone was talking about these days, the town's recent homicide and law enforcements lack of leads.

"Any information leading to the arrest and or capture of the Stone Lake Killers should immediately be called in to the police on this hotline number . . ." He rattled off a series of digits while I shuddered.

A killing in my hometown. That's what had finally convinced me to listen to my shrink. Because some poor shlub had gotten stabbed and dumped at Stone Lake, halfway between the store and my apartment. No one had noticed that the guy had gone missing. He didn't have a wife. He didn't have a girlfriend. He didn't have a pet. Nobody had cared that he didn't show up for work. When the cops found his body, he'd been dead for days and the trail had been left cold. They determined his identity, and the multiple stab wounds must have told them a thing or two about how he'd died, but other than that, no leads. I didn't know what had gotten him killed, but I didn't want to end up like him.

That's when Dr. Clark suggested I get a pet. A pet, she reasoned, would make me feel less vulnerable and alone. Just a thought, she'd said. I glanced at the tank on my passenger seat. The fish had his back to me and was staring at the door. I asked for mean, not antisocial. Would it kill him to make an effort?

Back home, I struggled with the heavy tank until it was finally parked on the dining room table. Dinner for one happened in front of the TV. For the past year and a half, the table had been a place for me to throw the mail and set the dirty dishes when the dishwasher was full. Now it was living quarters for my new roommate.

Out of breath, I slumped into a chair and peered at the fish. He stared me down, fins flapping, gills puffed up. "I want you to stay mean, so I'm naming you Jaws."

He dove towards the bottom of the tank. It was out of scale with the rest of my small apartment. I found an old Barbie, already pockmarked by water adventure from when I was a kid, and anchored her feet under the pink rocks. Jaws circled her. I would have stayed to watch him—curiosity, not getting attached, mind you—but I had to get back to work. I already knew I wouldn't get one of the three designated employee parking spaces out front, which meant I'd have to leave my car around back or risk another ticket.

When I pulled into a space close to the front door of NEW IDENTITY, Carolyn stood, hands on hips, chin jutting out.

"You gonna get another ticket if you park there."

Working at a costume-slash-vintage store can have an unfortunate effect on your life. Carolyn was going through her Foxy Brown phase. I suspected it had more to do with the heat, her natural enormous 'fro, and a surplus of hip-huggers in our inventory, than her self-professed rage against society. But, committed to the persona as she was, she'd studied the whole catalog of blaxploitation movies and occasionally kept a fake pistol in her hair. And hey, if she refrained from commenting on my close approximation of *That Girl*, who was I to question her?

We'd boiled our lives down to a series of six month-long character sketches, dressing the parts and spouting off recycled dialog originally written by someone in Hollywood. People knew me by my costumes, not my personality. Nobody actually knew who Mia Thomas was. Some days even I wasn't sure. And on the really dark days, I wondered if anyone would care enough to find out. Or if they'd even noticed that I existed at all. That's largely the reason I'm in therapy.

"I don't want to park around back. I like my car where I can see it." Plus, the Mustang was still in the corner. I followed her inside.

"I forgot to tell you," she called out while straightening some hangers. "Some guys were in here asking about you."

"What guys?"

"Corporate-money looking. Like Donald Trump but without the hair."

"You mean they were bald?"

"No, I mean without the Donald Trump hair. Cute, too. Well, one was, but the other was sweating a lot."

Hmmmmm. "What did they want to know?"

"When you were coming in next. And where you lived."

I whipped around to look at her. "You didn't tell them anything, did you?"

"Of course not! But—"

"But what?"

"Remember those parking tickets you wedged between the register and the catalogs?"

I nodded.

"They're gone."

Besides Jaws, there was something fishy about the situation. I left NEW IDENTITY and headed towards the pet store to ask Andrew about the men that had been asking about me.

The chimes above his door announced my arrival, but Andrew wasn't going to answer my questions. His body lay on the floor, surrounded by a crimson stream of blood pooling on the uneven concrete at the foot of the reptile cages.

I raced out the door and back to NEW IDENTITY.

"Call the cops!"

"What's wrong?"

I squeezed my eyes shut but the image remained. "Andrew—dead—blood—" I clung to the counter to offset my spinning head.

Carolyn made the phone call and within minutes red and blue lights pulsated across the scene like a Fourth of July disco. Black-and-whites exploded with boys in blue and yellow crime scene tape. I told the cops about the three men who had been in the store—Sweat Stains, Pinstripes, and Fedora. There was no sight of them now. It took every ounce of energy to get to my car. Carolyn closed the store, too shaken up to care about peddling neon fishnets to the trannies in the neighborhood—the only customers we had these days.

I drove home and stared at Jaws. He swam in quick, jerky circles around Barbie, checking her out. Slowly she tilted and glided to the bottom of the tank where her hair fanned out around her face. A few stones shifted out of place from her tiny stiletto-molded feet, revealing an ebony handle with rivets and a steel blade running through the middle.

A knife. Buried in the rocks of my new free aquarium, given to me by a pet store owner whose shop was less than a mile from a lake where someone had been found. Dead. And now Andrew, the pet store owner, was dead, too. Murdered, probably.

That can't be good.

Suddenly scared by what I had, I turned off the lights and huddled next to the tank. The blinds were shut and the ancient air conditioner chugged and spit enough to drown out the neighbor's TV. The only light came from the base of the aquarium, an eerie green glow that illuminated Jaws, Barbie, and the knife.

Someone pounded on my front door. "Mia? Mia Thomas, are you in there?"

I crouched in the shadows on the side of the tank. It was a man's voice, and had an unsettling resemblance to Pinstripes'.

Muffled voices floated into the apartment. "Her car's in the lot. Should we go in?" The doorknob jiggled.

"Not yet. Let's figure out her patterns first." Footsteps receded down the hall.

Those men probably had something to do with Andrew's murder, and the knife in my fish tank, and now they were coming for me. I had to get out of there. I dug through my handbag in a futile search for my cell phone. I'd turned off my home phone a month ago in an attempt to save money, and, as usual, had left my phone in my car. There was no way to call for help. But if I was being watched, how was I ever going to leave?

I plunged my hand into the cool water. Jaws dove to the bottom and hid behind Barbie's flaxen hair. I pulled the knife out and put it in a Ziploc bag, then replaced it with an old rubber knife left behind from a Halloween costume. I taped the Ziploc-bagged knife to the inside of my calf with electrical tape and covered it with a pair of legwarmers from my *Flashdance* phase. A glance out the window showed the Mustang parked a few spaces from my Mini. No getting the cell phone now. I changed into shorts and a slashed sweatshirt and ducked under the strap of my handbag. I ran to the bedroom, and climbed out a window that faced the alley out back.

I kept a barely running scooter in the alley. It leaked oil like there was no tomorrow, but I was only worried about today. I pulled on the helmet and cranked the key until it sputtered to life—with the gas gauge on E. I needed a close, safe haven with a phone. I drove to my shrink's office.

The curbside parking in front of Dr. Clark's office was full. I parked on the street in front of a minivan and locked the helmet to the seat, then started toward the office door. Inside the minivan, a man peered over a newspaper at me. I dropped my head and hurried past, increasing the length of my stride. Dr. Clark's security-coded door wasn't far, but I wasn't there yet.

A car door shut behind me. My walk became a jog. Footsteps sounded. My jog turned to a sprint. At the front door I punched the four-digit code into the keypad and yanked the metal handle the second it buzzed. The hydraulic arm kept the door from slamming, though I threw my weight against it. After it clicked shut I raced up the stairs, and then turned to look behind me. Fedora's unshaven face stared up at me through the glass door, one floor below.

I ran down the hall and pounded on Dr. Clark's door. She didn't answer. I tried the knob, but the door was locked.

A lab technician poked her head out of an adjoining office. "Is something wrong?"

"I'm being followed."

She looked at the poster on the wall. *Experiencing feelings of depression or paranoia? You can get help.* "Maybe you should make an appointment."

"Can I use your phone?" My hands shook. I glanced over my shoulder.

She pointed inside her office. "Right there."

I called Carolyn and told her about the knife and the fish tank and the men at the store and the stalker outside.

"Why you calling me? You gotta call the cops!"

"But the cops—those tickets—"

"I'm comin' to get you. Don't do anything stupid." She hung up the phone.

I ran down the back staircase and watched through the door's smudged four-inch window until her brown Coupe de Ville blazed into the alley. I jumped into her car and slunk down onto the torn vinyl seat.

She didn't ask questions. Next thing I knew we were back at NEW IDENTITY.

She unlocked the store and pushed me toward the phone. "This is no time to be a punk-ass chicken about those parking tickets. Call the cops," she said, hands on hips.

When she got all Foxy Brown, I did as I was told.

The door chimed as I was begging dispatch to send some help. Sweat Stains pushed through the door carrying my fish tank. He plunked it on a sale table filled with beaded handbags. Pinstripes followed behind him.

I dropped the phone. Jaws hung very still in the tank, staring at Pinstripes, who stared at me. He leveled a pistol at my chest.

"We know the knife in the tank was fake. Now give us the real one."

"The money, too," added Sweat Stains, leaning against a bookcase filled with cheap shoes. Pinstripes stood six feet in front of me. Carolyn was to my left, and there was no sign of the cops.

"I don't know what you're talking about," I bluffed.

Wait.

Did they say 'money'? I guess I wasn't bluffing after all.

I heard tires and looked out the window. A minivan pulled into the lot. Time was running out.

"You want us to believe you just wandered into Andrew's store yesterday and picked up a five-gallon aquarium for one little fishie? Nice try. Now give us the money or somebody else is gonna get hurt," said Sweat Stains, taking a step toward me.

"I don't have it," I said. Nobody else knew the real knife was taped to my calf under my legwarmer. I had to buy time until the cops arrived. "The money's still in the tank."

Pinstripes reached his hand into the water, and Jaws twitched. The sudden movement surprised us. On instinct, I yelled.

It wasn't the high-pitched shriek of a teen in a slasher movie or the piercing scream of women in monster flicks who always wear red lipstick. It was a guttural, throaty, primal scream that tore at my uvula and left me gasping for breath. I grabbed the wooden fixture of shoes and tilted it toward my assailants. Lucite wedge sandals and gold Wonder Woman boots pelted Sweat Stains. The bookcase pinned him to the floor. Pinstripes ran toward the door.

A gun fired and the aquarium exploded in a burst of glass and water that flooded the table. Jaws surfed on a wave that spilled onto the floor and soaked a bin of discount Daisy Dukes. The rubber knife landed on the waterlogged hot pants with a *thwud*.

Pinstripes clutched his thigh. Blood seeped through his flat-front pants and mingled with the water-soaked garments, pooling by the rubber knife, making it almost look real—the knife, not the blood. The blood, I knew, wasn't fake.

"Police! You're under arrest!" Fedora shouted from the doorway, a gun in his grip. My hands shot up in the air. "Wait over there." He waved Carolyn and me toward the register while uniformed officers flooded the room. This time I barely noticed the hullabaloo. Injuries were tended to, handcuffs were clamped on, and bad guys were taken away.

Carolyn sank onto a beanbag chair, her 'fro disheveled. "I didn't know you had that in you."

Neither did I.

Pink rocks covered the floor of the store and Jaws limp body glistened against them. Fedora supervised the scene while the wall held me up. It seemed like hours until he approached me.

"I'm Dan—Detective Noh. I've been working undercover trying to get a lead on these guys. Last month we pulled a body out of the lake." He nodded his head toward the back of the store. "They left him for fish food."

"And they killed the pet store owner?" I shuddered, remembering Andrew's body.

"Probably knew something about the homicide. I thought they hid the weapon in his store but couldn't risk blowing my cover for a search." He scratched his beard. "You kept going in and looking at those cats. I started wondering if you were working with them."

"I'm not working with anybody except my shrink—I mean, therapist," I muttered half-under my breath.

He continued as though I hadn't said a word. "Word on the street is they extorted fifty grand from the first guy we found. They stabbed him and tossed the body in the lake. But we're out of leads. Can't find the money, can't find the weapon. And we can't book them for murder without evidence."

"I think I can help you with that."

I pushed my legwarmer down to my ankle, revealing the plastic bag taped to my calf. I unwound the electrical tape and extended the bag to the detective. He raised his eyebrows.

Next, I pulled the fish food container out of my handbag and popped off the plastic top. Nestled inside was a roll of money. "Is this what you're looking for?"

He looked surprised. "How'd you know?"

"You said they left him for fish food. They didn't realize the money was *in* the fish food."

"You knew all along?"

"No. The pet store owner gave me this when I got the fish. Only I forgot to feed him. The fish, not the pet store owner." I wiped the back of my hand across my forehead.

"You seem more like a cat person, anyway."

I stared at Jaws, dead on the store's floor. Detective Noh studied me. "You know, those kittens are down at the station. You should come down and pick one out."

So I did. And I named him Jaws 2.

Diane Vallere *is a fashion insider with a taste for murder. A 2009 winner of the Get Your Stiletto in the Door contest, (Chick Thrill), she started her own detective agency at age ten and has maintained a passion for shoes, clues, and clothes ever since. Find her at www.dianevallere.blogspot.com.*

SLEEPING WITH THE FISH

BY KB INGLEE

Autumn 1737

The woman was . . . had been . . . beautiful. She appeared to be of marriageable age but was not wearing a wedding ring. Fine golden hair peeked out from under her heavily starched white linen cap. Her left shoulder and hip rested among the ferns at the edge of the water while her right side rose and fell with the gentle undulations of the mill pond. Two fish nibbled at the edge of her red and gold striped petticoat. Her dull empty eyes stared past the tops of the old trees and on to the heavens. Her hands were folded upon her breast.

The cool autumn weather and the chilly water made it look as if only a few minutes before she had settled herself and died. The body was cold to the touch. The yellowed leaves of the chestnut tree had blown across her short gown and under her apron. The stiffness of the dead had already passed from her limbs. She had been dead for more than a day.

Clarissa Dillon ran all the way to the house, spilling nuts from her basket as she sped along the mill race. "Father, there is a woman dead just above the mill dam. I've never seen her before."

Without question or comment, Miller Dillon called his journeyman, William Cooper, from the mill and they headed toward the pond, leaving Clarissa standing by the mill door.

Shaken, she carried her basket with the few remaining nuts toward the house.

"Morning, Miss Clarissa," said Isaiah Cooper, William's brother, cheerful as he always was. He was washing his hands in the basin she had set by the back door early that morning.

"Did thee see thy sister yesterday?" she asked, pretending this was an ordinary morning, despite the fact her hands shook.

Half a day's journey had been far to go for a load of late summer hay, but Isaiah had delivered a box of tools Friend Price had bought from the Dillons at the last Monthly Meeting. And Isaiah had been able to visit his sister and brother who worked for the Prices.

"Yes, miss. She is getting ready for her wedding. The gift thy mother sent was happily received. Hope thy father will let me and William go. It's only a fortnight away." Clarissa's mother had sent a fine linen shift as a wedding gift for Isaiah's sister.

"I'm sure he will."

"Is thee ill, Miss Clarissa? Thee is pale and sickly."

"I am well. I found something disturbing in the woods. A body."

"Yes, miss. I know thee to be of tender feeling about the deer and the birds. I can see thee might be disturbed by coming upon one unexpected like."

She opened her mouth to correct him but thought better of it. Nodding, she turned and went into the house.

"Did anyone come in with Isaiah yesterday?" she asked her mother. "There is a dead woman in the woods."

"A dead woman? Is that why the men are off in such a rush?"

"I found her under the chestnut tree on the edge of the mill pond."

Clarissa's mother looked up from her work with a worried expression. "Drowned? Who is it?"

"I don't know who she is, but she didn't drown. She was laid out with care. I know Father was out there yesterday. He would have found her if she had been there then. He and William have gone to fetch to her."

"Where are thy brothers? Why didn't he take them?"

"Father sent them off early to have some smithing done and to see if the Miller Jones had the estimate for adding a third grindstone. They will be back by dark."

"It takes both of them to do that? Who is running the mill?"

"No one. William and Isaiah were cleaning until Father called William away. Isaiah was headed toward the barn as I came in."

Isaiah and William had worked for the Dillons since last summer. William was bright and industrious and would go far. Isaiah was illiterate, in spite of Clarissa's attempts to teach him to read. The family knew that William would move on to a better position soon, but they could do worse than to keep Isaiah if he stayed on.

He was none too bright, but he was hard working and once he learned a chore he did it well.

Father and William brought back the body and laid it on a board in the barn. Clarissa had a better look at the woman while Isaiah went for Constable Cobb.

The young woman's wheat colored short gown was splattered with what looked like dried mud, or perhaps blood, but when Clarissa stripped the body to wash it she saw no trace of a wound. Unlike her other clothing, her cap and apron were spotless. The cap . . . . Clarissa looked more closely. She recognized the tiny stitches, the ruffle that was longer in the back. It was her own cap, washed, starched, and ironed two days ago. A shudder ran down her spine.

Her mother brought a wooden tub of hot water, some clean rags and soap. "Has thee found anything?"

"Mother, this is my cap. Why is it on this stranger?"

Clarissa pulled it off. The hair under the cap was matted with dried blood. Someone had covered the evidence of a dreadful wound with the clean cap. She closed her eyes to block out the sight.

"The apron, as well." Mother lifted the hem to look at the careful stitching. Nothing else on the body was from the Dillon household. Someone who had access to Clarissa's things had dressed this woman and laid her reverently on the edge of the pond.

"Look at this," said her mother, indicating the single earring in her left ear. Dark metal with garnet beads.

"She must have lost its mate in the accident that had killed her. How sad this is. Someone cared for her and now she is to be buried where no one knows her." Clarissa slipped the earring into her pocket.

Clarissa and her mother washed the body and laid it out with the same respect as it had been at the pond and covered it with a bed sheet. Later they would wash her clothing and dress the body for burial.

When they were finished, they closed the barn door on the lonely woman. They scrubbed their own hands and arms until they were red and went to finish dinner. They worked silently for some time before Clarissa called the men to the meal.

Besides Father, five men from the farm and the mill joined them at the table. Constable Cobb, never one to miss food, especially at someone else's expense, arrived as soon as they began eating.

The talk was all of the woman by the mill pond. No one knew who she was. No one knew how she had come to be there. Cobb asked questions of each of them and received unsatisfactory answers. Isaiah had been away all the previous day. William had been working in the mill; Clarissa's brothers had been sowing winter wheat in a field on the other side of the farm. Any one of them could have laid out the woman. It would have taken only a few minutes.

"I followed the track of a wheelbarrow out along the millrace. I forgot about it until now," Clarissa told Cobb.

"I'll check for footprints after this fine meal."

Clarissa was standing at the table under the window when he said this, and she could see everyone's face but her mother's. There was no marked response on any of them except Isaiah, who looked puzzled.

"Someone pushed the wheelbarrow, so there must be footprints," she explained to him. "Unless it was a ghost."

Cobb laughed. "No ghosts."

Clarissa knew that each person's footprint is his own. She herself had a wide foot with the left turning out more than the right. She was sure he would find and recognize her prints. She could not remember seeing any footprints near the track of the single wheel, yet she had not been looking for them before she found the body and had been too upset to look for them afterwards.

"Perhaps someone at Monthly Meeting will know who she is," said Mother.

After dinner Father and Constable Cobb went off to the barn and the others returned to their tasks.

Late in the afternoon Isaiah found her by the hen house. "Miss Clarissa, I found something I thought thee would like." He handed her a trinket made of metal with dark red beads attached. She had the mate, from the woman's left ear, in her pocket. The loop at the top which held the ear wire was broken. She had not found the wire in the woman's hair or the borrowed cap.

"Where did thee find this?" she asked.

"One of the sheep had it in her wool. I didn't think sheep wore such things and I thought it would look better on thee." He smiled shyly.

* * * *

On First Day, the family piled into farm wagons and mounted every rideable horse on the property and headed for Kennett Monthly Meeting. Clarissa had tucked the pair of earrings in her pocket in hopes that someone would recognize them.

The morning was spent in quiet contemplation but the afternoon was social and everyone used the opportunity to catch up on news. The woman on the Dillon property was a big topic.

Amy Cooper had come with her brother Darby and was happy to see William and Isaiah. Darby found William and pulled him aside at once and they spoke privately until the four of them went off by themselves to trade family gossip. Amy's intended was there, as well, and he was properly introduced to the Dillon family. Miller Dillon found other millers to discuss the ups and downs of business. The biggest topic was finding laborers. Monthly Meeting would be where William would find a new employer and where Father would replace him.

Near the end of the afternoon a young man Clarissa had never seen before came up to her. "Is thee Clarissa Dillon?" he asked.

"Yes, I am." He took her arm and led her away from the crowd.

"My name is Nathaniel Foster. I'm told thee has an earring from the woman thee found. May I see it?"

"Does thee know who she might be?" She pulled the delight from her pocket.

He didn't answer. He took the pendant from her hand and sighed. "It's hers. I made them myself. Tell me what this woman looked like."

"I'm sorry." She handed him the twin Isaac had given her. "Here is the mate." His face grew sadder and sadder as Clarissa described the woman. "I washed and wrapped her and she was buried in the Meeting burial ground. I'd be happy to add her name to the marker. Perhaps thee could come visit her grave."

"Her name is Hannah Price. She lived with her aunt and uncle. We were to be married in the spring but a month ago she said she had other interests. I was certain she would change her mind after a while. Then one day she was gone."

Clarissa rested her hand on Nathaniel's arm. "I'm sorry. Whoever put her by our pond laid her out with reverence and care. That's not much consolation for the loss of a loved one."

"Thanks," he muttered as he turned away.

* * * *

Clarissa rode back home on the chestnut mare, seated behind William.

"I know what happened, mostly," she told him.

It had been her intention to confront him in the presence of others, but at a distance so their conversation was private.

He was silent for a bit, then he urged the mare to a trot, leaving the others behind. Clarissa tightened her arms around his waist as he turned into a farm lane. She had not counted on this.

"What is it thee knows?" he asked, pulling the horse up.

She glanced back at the road.

"I know that the woman, Hannah, was killed elsewhere and came back with Isaac in the load of hay. I think he knew nothing of the actions taken by either thee or Darby. He is too open and truthful. He was truly puzzled by the gewgaw that turned up in the wool. The earring must have fallen off on the wagon and been swept up when the hay was unloaded. Thee pulled her bloodstained cap off and disposed of it, and replaced it with mine, along with my apron."

William turned in the saddle and met her eyes with a warmth she had never seen in them before. She drew back in fear as he reached out and touched her cheek.

"I won't hurt thee." She knew he spoke the truth. "Her apron was torn and dirty. If she was to have a new cap, she should have a clean apron to go with it."

He drew a letter from his pocket and handed it to her. "When we Coopers find love, we are possessive of it."

My Brother William,
I am sending my treasure under the hay. Isaiah doesn't know. Take utmost care.
Darby

"I asked Darby about it at Meeting and he said he had loved her and she had encouraged him. Then it turned out she did it to impress this other fellow."

"I met Nathaniel Foster at Meeting. He seemed grief stricken."

William nodded. "Darby said he had carved her a ring from maple and brought it to her that morning in the barn, the morning Isaiah came for hay. She laughed at him and as she turned away, she caught her foot and fell down the steps onto the stone flagging."

"If it was an accident, why did he hide her? Why not run for help?"

William was silent, but she knew the answer. The Dillons, the Fosters and the Pierces employed people like the Coopers and would never be made to understand it was an accident. If in fact it was.

"I told Nathaniel Foster where she was buried and offered to have her name put on the grave," she said. "Thee will not be able to keep this a secret much longer. What will thee do?"

He took the letter back and pocketed it. "I subverted my own hopes and dreams to help my brother. As soon as I deliver thee safely home, I will tell Constable Cobb."

KB Inglee *writes historical fiction and interprets the Colonial and New Republic periods at historical sites in Delaware and Pennsylvania. She cares for a flock of heritage sheep, spins, and knits. She lives with her family in northern Delaware. She is past president of the Delaware Valley Chapter Sisters in Crime.*

FEEDING FRENZY

BY PATRICIA WINTON

One rarely thinks of fish as a murder weapon, and Caroline Woodlock certainly didn't have murder on her mind as she surveyed the vast piscine assortment spread out at the market near Piazza Vittorio in Rome. A display of fresh anchovies; flat flounder; a swordfish, complete with its sword; four types of clams and three of squid; little octopuses scarcely two inches long; and fat slices from large octopus tentacles, their suckers gleaming in the light, rose at a 45 degree angle before her. The briny air smelled like a day at the seashore.

A journalist now covering the international culinary scene, Caroline worked on an Italian cookbook for Americans in her spare time. She planned to adapt the recipe for *caciucco*, the stout fish soup of Livorno that her grandmother had carefully written in her tight, Tuscan hand years ago. Today, Caroline searched for a substitute for "cicada of the sea," something that she didn't think she would find in America and something she didn't think Americans would eat if she could.

The market echoed with its usual din of noises. An old woman selling vegetables called out *"Ecco belli. Guardate ai miei peperoni freschi. Colore di scarlatto e d'oro. Scegliere."* Here, beautiful people, look at my fresh peppers, scarlet and golden. Take your choice.

The butcher hoped to lure the Friday fish-eaters to his stall. *"Filetto di maiale. Sotto costo. È un regalo."* Pork tenderloin. Below cost. It's a gift.

A cacophony of voices clamoring for the fishmonger's attention swirled around Caroline. Suddenly, a voice at the adjacent stall rose above the others.

"Mi hai trattato a pesci in faccia!" The angry voice echoed throughout the suddenly quiet market.

Who had thrown fish in someone's face? At the next stall, two men argued, or at least one yelled at another. The screamer's left index finger wagged against the other's nose, magenta face reflecting his rage. No fish scales clung to his eyebrows; no octopus hung from his hair, but Caroline feared that the finger wagger risked a stroke or worse as he spewed his anger along with his spittle onto the other man's face.

The angry man wore a red knitted cap pulled close around his ears and a gray, nondescript jacket zipped up to his chin. The language that Caroline had learned at the knee of her prim Italian mother didn't allow her to decipher his expletives, but she understood the gist.

The object of his anger stood placidly, saying nothing. The calm man wore a multi-pocketed vest and a sardonic smile. His silence seemed to further enrage the screamer.

Fish in the face. I wonder what that expression means? And why is this man so angry?

A crowd gathered around the two, and as the decibel level lowered, Caroline turned back to the fishmonger to select more ingredients for her soup.

On the way home Caroline stopped at the supermarket for other supplies. She paused before the frozen foods case. There certainly were many differences between the offerings here and those in an American supermarket. The few ready-to-eat dishes required cooking in a frying pan or the oven. Nothing here for the microwave. Bags of grilled eggplant and roasted peppers lay beside little boxes of frozen basil and parsley. But she did not want frozen foods and hurried to find basic condiments like olive oil and salt.

* * * *

The sun had dipped low when she turned the corner into the Piazza di Trevi, the sound of water crashing over stone reaching her before she entered. She loved to stop here at the end of Via Stamperia and listen to the power of the sea that the fountain represented. The thunderous cascade drowned out the sounds of Japanese tourists shooting each other with their mobile phone cameras and the giggles of shy Swiss schoolgirls tossing coins over their shoulders into the fountain's grand central pool.

At the top of the fountain, Neptune looked down majestically onto it all from his shell-shaped cart. Caroline edged her way through the crowd to get a better look at the two winged seahorses pulling Neptune's chariot. The one on the right portrayed the benevolent sea, responding calmly to the gentle touch of the Triton driving it; its fishtail curled in repose. Beneath it she saw the coins thrown by those Swiss girls and thousands of other tourists glinting in the water, each one the symbol of a dream.

She descended the steps and turned left. Before her the second Triton strained to hold onto his raging seahorse, representing the fury of a stormy sea. The creature's nostrils flared, and its fishtail lashed against the rocks at its back. Caroline's gaze drifted to the small pool to the left of the truculent seahorse; something besides tourist coins shimmered in the water.

* * * *

"Nino." Caroline's breath came in quick puffs as she raced up the stairs leading to the National Graphic Arts Gallery in the building behind the fountain. "I saw fish swimming in the Trevi Fountain!"

A short, balding man with a fringe of white hair floating along his collar line drew her towards him, kissing first the left cheek and then the right in the traditional Italian greeting.

"Impossible," he said. "You just saw the reflection of coins thrown in by the tourists." Nino took her by the elbow and guided her into the exhibition.

Caroline rolled her caramel-colored eyes. She needed Nino Nardo's help with the cookbook project, but *porca miseria*, being a professor of Italian culinary history and traditions at the 700-year-old La Sapienza University did make him haughty.

"A couple of years ago, a prankster threw red dye into the fountain. It gushed through Neptune's basin and made quite a spectacle," Nino continued as he gently steered Caroline to the left toward a man as hairy as Nino was bald. "The police keep a sharp lookout now. You didn't see fish in the fountain. It's impossible. Isn't that true, *Commissario*?" He winked at the hairy man.

"May I present Caroline Woodlock?" he added.

"My brother's quite correct," the man said, taking her hand. "I'm Aldo, the more handsome of the Nardo brothers. And yes, I'm a police commissioner." He pretended to plant a kiss on her palm. Caroline stammered hello, and she forgot to tell Nino about the bizarre scene at the fish market.

Nino had invited her to the opening reception of a photography exhibit by Giorgio Delfino to introduce her to Rome's culinary elite. Now he guided her through a gallery lined with photos of chefs at work. Defino was known for choosing props that revealed secrets about his subjects.

Caroline glanced at a photo showing a fat, balding chef, sitting with his legs splayed; a massive bowl of water with cleaned artichokes and lemons floating in it stood on the table beside him. He clutched a paring knife and stripped off the outer leaves of yet another artichoke.

Her gasp echoed through the gallery. For a moment she froze, her eyes riveted upon the chef in the photo—her cousin, victim of a brutal murder less than a year ago. He had been stabbed with his own knife. The knife in the photo?

"I didn't mean for you to see that one, Caroline," Nino said. He propelled her forward, and she looked over her shoulder at Edoardo's sweet smile.

The professor guided her into the midst of a *prosecco*-sipping clump of people, but her thoughts remained with Edoardo. She drew a deep breath and looked around.

A ruddy-faced man in crisp white chef's jacket stood in the middle of an admiring crowd.

"Who is that man?" asked Caroline.

"Oh, that's Paolo Ricci. *È in gamba*. I'll introduce you."

"He's in the leg," repeated Caroline. "Nino, what does that mean?"

"It means he's an expert. And he is. He knows as much about fish and the Italian table as anyone in the country, aside from myself, of course. He grew up as the son of a Livorno fisherman, and he knows the sea as well as the kitchen. He's one of Rome's best chefs."

The man's shiny bald head glittered like a halo; he spoke with soft, measured words and smiled politely. Caroline closed her eyes to conjure up the man she had seen screaming in the market on Friday. His head had been covered with a knitted cap, but she recognized this bald chef as the crazed man who had waggled his finger and screamed about fish in his face. What a startling transformation from maniacal madman to elegant chef!

Nino introduced them and Paolo Ricci shook her hand. "Nino has told me you want to know more about *caciucco*. It's the specialty of my hometown. I'm sure I can help. Shall we meet tomorrow? My restaurant is nearby." He gave a stiff little bow and released her hand. No kisses here; she sighed with relief.

After chatting with a number of other impressive people, Caroline returned to the photos. She saw several of the chefs she had just met. Marco, the pastry chef, licked a dollop of whipped cream from his finger and twinkled at the camera. Pippo, the vegetarian specialist, smiled shyly as he carved a fennel bulb into an elaborate flower. Fennel is Italian slang for homosexual. How had the photographer convinced Pippo to pose holding *finocchio*? In his photo, Paolo masterfully wielded an enormous knife with his left hand, chopping parsley.

Caroline looked around for the photographer, but everyone she asked said, "I saw him a minute ago. Try the next gallery." She wandered through the galleries and glanced through an open curtain. The piazza spread before her. She leaned out, looking down onto the Trevi Fountain. The water gushed over the rocks, and coins sparkled through the foam.

But there beneath the window, in the smaller pool at the feet of the bellicose seahorse, fish darted in the water. She looked round for Nino. Where had he gone? She found him at the far end of the last gallery and they returned to the window. She looked down onto the fountain again.

As the water flowed into the small basin, it changed from crystal clear to a brilliant red. She could no longer see the fish. Then a human arm rose from the water, blood streaming from ripped flesh.

* * * *

In the kitchen of her rented apartment, Caroline stood before a pot of her latest version of *caciucco*. She peered in, stirring briskly. The red tomato base swirled around and pieces of fish flesh and shells roiled to the surface. Caroline stared into the pot, and for a moment she looked down on the piranhas and blood in the Trevi Fountain from the gallery window as she had the night before. She quickly covered the pot and turned away.

Those deadly fish had masticated the dead man's softest parts, cheeks and eyes, buttocks and thighs. No one could recognize the poor creature. Aldo Nardo, who had taken charge of the investigation, said it appeared that the fall on the rocks had done as much damage as the fish. But the presence of piranhas meant murder, not accident, he had said.

Caroline gave herself a shake. She didn't want to dwell on that image, so she turned off the burner and left the kitchen. She wandered around the apartment, picking up a book here, rearranging a chair there. The sight of blood, albeit diluted by the Trevi, brought back the image of Edoardo's blood-soaked body that she had discovered in his restaurant kitchen. Perhaps it was simply coming upon his photo so unexpectedly, followed by the sight of blood in the fountain. At least this corpse was a stranger, and she wouldn't come face-to-face with the killer as she had with Edoardo's.

She collected her notebook and recorder for her meeting with Paolo, still mystified by the finger-waving, screaming maniac at the market who turned into the super polite chef at the reception. What did he mean when he accused the other man of throwing fish in his face?

With a sigh, she reached for an Italian-English dictionary. She hated admitting that she needed it. *Pesci in faccia.* A grave insult. Hmmm. Caroline tried to remember the man Paolo had screamed at. What could he have said to insult the chef, causing him to lose control that way?

She played with this puzzle as she left the apartment. She had plenty of time before the appointment with Paolo, but she needed fresh air. Each time her thoughts turned to the blood in the fountain or even the tomatoes in the pot, she shivered. She wanted a clear head for the interview with the chef.

* * * *

Caroline skirted the edge of the Trevi Fountain. A remnant of red and white striped police tape fluttered from the railing around the fountain, but the tourists knew nothing about the death in the water and happily tossed their coins and snapped their photos.

She ordered an espresso at a nearby bar and sat down to review her notes before her meeting. A cloud passed over the piazza, casting a shadow over the fountain in the distance. The second hand on Caroline's watch crept along. She reached for a newspaper lying on an adjacent table. As usual, the headlines focused on a scandal first. Today, they described in lurid detail the latest sexual escapade of a government official. An image of the Pope saying mass during his current trip abroad provided balance.

Caroline unfurled the paper. Paolo's unknown adversary stared out at her from the lower half of the page. The police had dragged his body from the Trevi last night and now identified him as Giorgio Delfino, the photographer! The cloud over the fountain grew darker. Caroline shivered again.

Had Giorgio insulted Paolo in some way with his photo? Caroline closed her eyes. She remembered the knife and the parsley but nothing remotely suggestive like Pippo's photo. Caroline had to look again. She grabbed her bag and raced to the gallery.

Like Delfino's other photos, the one of Paolo exuded atmosphere. The chef's left hand grasped the glistening knife. The crisp photo captured the tilt of the blade as it cut the parsley. One could almost hear it hit the wooden board. Caroline examined every inch of the picture, trying to find a trace of insult. The shallow depth of field had the chef and the knife in clear focus, but the background blurred. On the counter behind Paolo some small rectangular boxes stood in a row. They looked vaguely familiar, but she couldn't identify them and nor read the labels.

On her way to Paolo's restaurant, she phoned Nino to tell him about the market incident and how her idiom deficiency had led her to misunderstand the exchange.

"Caroline, don't tell Paolo what you heard," Nino warned her. "And don't roll those big *caramelle*. He could be dangerous." She held the phone in her outstretched hand for a moment before clicking off.

* * * *

Paolo stood in his kitchen manipulating a flexible-bladed knife, deftly deconstructing a swordfish.

"*Caciucco*, like many great dishes, is essentially a peasant dish. The legend says that a poor fisherman's widow with many children to feed sent them out to beg from the other fisherman." Paolo separated the swordfish from its sword with one blow.

"Each fisherman gave the children the last, unsold fish from the day's catch, small unwanted fish that they would have tossed back into the sea." With staccato whacks, Paolo began cutting the swordfish into steaks. "From this motley mix," he continued, "the woman made a nourishing stew that kept her family alive."

Paolo offered much advice for her article. "You need lots of garlic for *caciucco*. And don't use fancy fish. You need some octopus and mussels. Plain fish."

Caroline switched off the recorder and closed her notebook.

"Thanks a lot for your help. You've been really kind." Packing up her tools, Caroline ventured one more question.

"What do you think of the market at Piazza Vittorio? I thought I saw you there on Friday."

Paolo suck in a breath.

"I like most Roman markets, but now I must get back to work." His brusque response signaled goodbye.

"I saw you talking with Giorgio Delfino," she said. "How did he insult you?"

The question transformed the gentlemanly Paolo into the lunatic she had seen on Friday. His face once again darkened, and he began spitting his words.

"Have you seen my photo? He stacked boxes of frozen parsley behind me. It made me look like an amateur. A professional chef never uses frozen ingredients—especially not frozen herbs! He wanted to belittle me."

Caroline recalled the little boxes of frozen parsley and basil that she had seen in the supermarket. All this anger over a box of parsley?

"It's just a photo. You look very professional, masterful even, the way you use the knife. He showed you as the great chef that you are."

Paolo grabbed the knife he'd used to filet the swordfish and turned toward her. "*Puttana!* You don't understand anything." Caroline felt his spittle hitting her face. She dodged around the island in the center of the kitchen. He jabbed at her with the knife, but she danced out of reach.

His breath came in sharp bursts. A fine line of moisture beaded on his upper lip.

"He had to die. It was so easy. I carried the piranhas in an insulated bag, much like the ones old women use to go to the market." He jabbed again, and warmed to his topic. Caroline's pulse beat against her eardrums.

"I rested the bag on a stone at the edge of the fountain." Paolo continued. "The policeman on duty often comes to my restaurant, and we chatted a minute. Then I pointed to a teenaged tourist."

Jab.

"Taking off her shoes to climb into the fountain."

Jab.

"The policeman ran to shoo her, and I dumped the fish. Easy."

He continued to thrust the knife with rhythmic strokes. She needed something to deflect the blade. Paolo made another lunge around a corner of the island. She grabbed the fish's sword and planted her feet firmly in a fighter's stance.

Like the Ancient Mariner, Paolo continued his tale. "Those windows in the gallery form a little alcove behind the curtains. I called Giorgio over to look at the fish below. One shove and out he went."

Paolo jabbed again, but Caroline blocked his knife with the swordfish sword.

"I must have pushed the curtain open when I fled," he said. "Otherwise it would have been tourists who saw the body first and not you."

Paolo raised his left arm high. As he began a downward strike, Caroline thrust upward with her fishy weapon, piercing the flesh of his bicep. He howled and dropped the knife.

At that moment, Nino and Aldo barged into the kitchen. Blood dripped from Paolo's arm, and once more he spewed obscenities and spittle. Caroline laid the swordfish sword on the counter. Her heart thumped against her ribcage, and she looked at Nino.

"After Edoardo's murder last year," she said, "I thought all chefs faced danger. Now, it's the chef who's the murderer."

Aldo restrained the belligerent Paolo and radioed for assistance. To Nino he said, "Bring Caroline to the *Questura* in an hour. She'll have to make a *denuncia*." A sergeant handcuffed Paolo and led him away. A stream of expletives hovered in the air behind him.

Together Nino and Caroline walked to the Trevi. He silently handed her a small coin. She descended the steps and the mist cooled her face. She gazed for a moment at the benevolent sea-horse and its Triton blowing gently into a conch. Then she turned her back on the fountain, raised her right arm and tossed the coin over her left shoulder, uttering a small prayer.

Patricia Winton *writes and reads, cooks and eats in Rome. She fell in love with the Bobbsey Twins at eight and has been hooked on mysteries since. She's been a college instructor, food writer, cooking teacher, book seller, politico, perfume purveyor, pencil sharpener, and both a bean counter and server. Visit her at www. patriciawinton.com.*

SASE

BY KAREN PULLEN

Headachy, constipated, and guilt-ridden: a morning like every other. On the table, a ragged stack of paper: early drafts, comments from beta reader, vacation ideas folder (as if), bills awaiting payment. The cat is napping next to the dead printer. Dead. The writer is a deadbeat parent, at a dead end, brain in deadlock, approaching deadline.

The writer needs a break and browses Facebook. Reheats cold coffee. Picks nose, sits, stares at screen. Cannot go on like this. Nevermore, quoth the raven. How to quit, that is the question. According to the lawyer, the writer cannot quit: child support, IRS, contract, lawsuit. Over-priced lawyer. *How does he justify $285 an hour?* Loathes lawyer. Feels used. Loathes publisher, agent, editor, ex-spouse. Each wants a piece but pie plate is empty. Wants to be happy. *What would make me happy?* Easy. An alternate existence. The writer envisions a stone cottage on the coast of Maine, cat dozing by blazing fire, a plate of fried trout, champagne. Weight of obligations has crushed the writer's spirit and creativity but not will. The writer Googles "arsenic."

* * * *

The famous literary agent awakens to synchronized ice picks jabbing into her skull. Her mouth is full of old carpet and her guts are as tremulous as Jell-O. She screws her eyes shut but the skull stabs and internal quivering don't stop so she creeps to the bathroom for a BC powder, her favorite hangover treatment. There, top shelf, one envelope left. She drops it into water and sips the fizzy concoction slowly. She gags a little but it stays down.

I will never have another drink as long as I live. She can't remember the last time she felt this sick; forty-five is too old to chug White Russians. It was a fun boozy evening with her ex-husband, still her best friend. She divorced him after he confessed his penchant for dressing in chiffon, heels and lipstick—and dating men—but he was still the most fun ever. They drank Pernod over ice at his apartment, then Rob Roys and Cab with dinner; so far so good, all under control, until the drinks at the club where her ex-husband's new friend Stan was performing. She isn't a music critic, but she formed an opinion of the new friend anyway—too much vamping and attitude to cover up his off-key crooning. Nonetheless she and her ex-husband applauded enthusiastically, and after his set, Stan joined them. He was an electric jazzy guy, a writer of gay sci fi erotica, and she remembers laughing too much at his stories. Her ex-husband ordered them all White Russians. The drink was delicious, like coffee ice cream. She ordered another one, and perhaps a third. She doesn't remember the trip back to her apartment. Her ex-husband must have put her in a cab.

The BC powder does its work and she begins to feel better. She makes coffee and takes a mug into the far end of her living room, stopping to feed the tank of betas. They dart to the top as she drops in a pinch of fish food. Snails have taken over the tank and it needs cleaning, but she can't abide the smell. It will wait until tomorrow.

Along the wall is the Pile; a stack of thousands of query letters and manuscripts. Each day's mail brings fifty letters or so, almost twice as many as she can process on a good day. Which today is not.

Two hours later the famous literary agent has made her way through seventeen envelopes. She has stuffed and licked fifteen SASEs, thirteen with form rejection letters and two with a request for a partial. Two queries didn't include an SASE—those she throws away.

At noon she gets dressed and leaves the apartment. She has projects to pitch to a senior fiction editor from The Press over lunch. She'll just have a salad because she still feels queasy. *And no alcohol.*

The famous literary agent makes it as far as the mail box. As she slips the letters into the slot, she's gripped by a sharp cramp in her gut. Her legs turn to jelly, the world spins, and she collapses to the sidewalk. A pimply kid in baggy jeans and a Mets ball cap leans over her. "You OK?" She moans, helpless, as he slides her wallet out of her purse and jogs down the street. She's never had a hangover this bad. *I am never going to drink again.*

And she never does.

* * * *

The senior fiction editor of The Press removes the lid from the purple box containing *Magical Fire*, Quincy Quaid's latest manuscript, its pages emitting the faint bug spray fumes of the author's perfume. For the past thirteen years it has been the senior fiction editor's job to turn Quincy's sludgy prose into readable books. She knows what she'll find: untethered participles, extraneous talky characters, confusing POV shifts. She scans page one. The word "actually" leaps out at her. She actually, really hates that word. She makes a purple dot in the margin.

Quincy Quaid's books are virtual heaving seas of emotion: longing, despair, lust, pain, humiliation, joy. Writing-wise, Quincy has slacked off in recent years, each new manuscript a half-ream of clichéd descriptions, flat characters and unresolved plot threads. Whole passages are copied from earlier books, as though her readers won't remember. But of course they will; they are eagle-eyed spotters of lazy writing and sloppy editing. Obsessed fans have created Quincy Quaid websites where they post the mistakes and errors the senior fiction editor has overlooked, relatively few for over a hundred books but nonetheless embarrassing.

The senior fiction editor sighs and looks at her watch. Thirty minutes to lunch; enough time to reject a batch of queries, a mindless activity that will give her the illusion that she is, actually, working. She pushes aside the purple box and starts opening envelopes. By noon, three dozen SASEs are stuffed with a photocopied rejection letter, licked, sealed, and dropped into the mail slot. She sets aside the non-fiction queries to give to her boss, the publisher of The Press (and ex-husband of a famous literary agent) and then wanders down the hall to the break room. Some generous soul has sent a gift box of fruit. She selects a pear and bites into it. Crisp, juicy, an almost citrusy flavor. Very good.

Feeling refreshed, the senior fiction editor pours herself a cup of decaf and walks back to her office to tackle *Magical Fire*. She sits down and picks up the purple felt-tip pen. The first time through she always reads for story, making dots in the margin as errors catch her attention. Dot, dot, dot. Rachelle, an innkeeper, encounters Damon, a sexy brooding ghost who time-transports her to his Wales castle and the year 833. The senior fiction editor scans Chapter 2 several times; something is missing. Rachelle zips back to the ninth century whenever Damon summons her. But why does

Damon pick *her*, out of all the women available to him throughout the span of human history? Oh God, this is going to be a real slog. She feels a little nauseated. Nine more years until retirement, she thinks. Maybe earlier if I cut back, move somewhere cheaper, someplace warm. Lower taxes. She turns on her computer and begins to search real estate prices in Raleigh. Suddenly, saliva fills her mouth and she retches. A godawful cramp seizes her gut and she feels faint and clammy. Quite ill, then even worse, actually.

* * * *

The publisher slides his feet into the pair of red Marabou slip-ons, women's size 14, that he keeps hidden under his desk. He waggles his toes, feeling the feathers brush against his instep. The shoes calm him. They are a source of solace in difficult times, a bit of contentment. He isn't hung over, exactly, just exhausted; after they left the club last night, and he sent his ex-wife home, he spent the rest of the night trying to appease his new friend Stan, the club performer, who was turning out to be a jealous control freak, threatening suicide if the publisher doesn't end it with his ex-wife for good. The publisher's sour love life is a perfect book-end to the seemingly inevitable demise of The Press, sinking like the Titanic punctured by an iceberg of relentlessly bad sales.

Is it time to find a therapist, someone to listen empathetically? A therapist might be able to help him prioritize, give him some action verbs, such as "vanish." Jumping from a cruise ship might be easy to fake; they hardly ever recover the body, do they? He could buy a balcony room on a ten-day cruise, drink mai-tais for a week, and then disappear. Leave a note in case no one notices he's missing, then hide out in the life boats or under a buffet table; there must be lots of good hiding places on those twelve-story floating cities. Stroll off the ship in Cozumel and never look back.

He gingerly rolls his head from left to right, bothered by a persistent ache in his neck. He tries to focus on the quarterly sales report. The Press's historical romance titles only broke even; it's impossible to compete with Harlequin, Random and Penguin in that category. Erotica did better; smutty sells. Quincy Quaid's revenues were a bit down, he notices, swallowing hard. If it weren't for her four books a year, The Press would have closed down years ago. Problem is, Quincy's advances deplete their capital, and where once he could borrow to keep the business running, now the banks act like every day is Sunday. If banks quit loaning money, how do they keep their buildings heated and all those vice-presidents paid? Oh, that's right—lifeblood-sucking extortionate credit card fees. The Cozumel cruise could go onto his Master Card, hee hee, soak up the last dollar of his credit limit.

Sighing deeply, the publisher speed-dials his ex-wife. He'll have to meet with her (without telling his new friend Stan) and renegotiate Quincy's contract. No one answers, so he leaves a message.

He picks up a handful of non-fiction query letters. The Press has a psychology "how-to" imprint, mostly books about codependency, of the "women-who-love-(fill in the blank)" variety. They published a blockbuster five years ago when sex addiction became such a, ahem, hot topic, and since then the publisher has read the best non-fiction queries, looking for the next big book. Alas, none of these is it. He slips a standard rejection into each of the SASEs and seals them.

His stomach growls. He never eats breakfast. It's a waste of good calories, better used on something tasty, something to lift his mood, like chocolate or smoked salmon. He takes off the slippers and walks down the hall to the break room for some coffee. He sees the pears but the publisher avoids fruit unless it's baked in a pie. He pours himself a cup of coffee, adds cream and takes a sip; it tastes metallic and he feels a bit shivery all of a sudden. Then dizziness tips his world sideways and clobbers him to the gritty floor. He groans loudly, clutching his chest, feeling his heart pound like an off-balance washer in spin cycle.

Not long after, his worries about Stan's jealousy and The Press's finances become, in effect, irrelevant.

* * * *

Thanks to the Internet, within hours the news sweeps over the publishing community like a tsunami: a famous literary agent, a senior fiction editor, and a publisher have died from apparent poisoning. The literary agent's clients frantically dig out their contracts looking for a death clause (there isn't one). The editor's friends blog tearful eulogies recalling their common love of scrap booking and Chihuahuas. The publisher's death seals the suspicion that the entire industry is under siege from terrorists.

Then the rumor spreads: the three victims ingested arsenic from the *glue of a self-addressed stamped envelope.* Traces of the poisoned glue have been found on their tongues. Hundreds of fragile agent-author relationships dissolve from mistrust. Paranoid editors view each query like a live grenade. Interns refuse to lick, ever again. The more astute writers run out and buy self-sealing self-addressed stamped envelopes, or SSSASEs, to improve their chances in the slush pile.

* * * *

NYPD Detective Mike McIntyre is assigned to investigate the three homicides. He scans the lab report on the doctored envelopes, which have been returned, "address unknown," to their three (dead) senders. Their sticky edges were laden with arsenic trioxide.

Mike begins with the apartment of the famous literary agent. He pulls aside the yellow tape and surveys her living room. The first thing he notices is the mountain of unanswered mail. He imagines his own query letter is buried in there somewhere. He wrote a police procedural, a story of gangs, drugs, and corruption á la Joseph Wambaugh. He spent three years writing and revising, then another year fruitlessly looking for an agent before abandoning his dream of early retirement and a beach house in the Outer Banks. He knows he queried the famous literary agent but doesn't think she responded. He sniffs in disapproval, knowing each letter represents a person who'd reached out to the famous literary agent in vain, begging for a kind word of validation. The mountain of letters represents a pile of broken dreams and broken hearts. A pile of suspects? *Did a writer commit this murder?*

Mike sifts, reads, and speculates that highly offended writers would come in three flavors: ignored, rejected, and mistreated. He calls for assistance and a uniformed cop shows up; together they go through every scrap of paper in the pile, logging names and addresses.

Next, he sorts through her project files. Mike recognizes the name of her star client, Quincy Quaid, author of over a hundred romance novels, many of them best-sellers. Quaid's folders fill an entire file drawer, with contracts for foreign rights and movie options and even merchandise deals. Whew, lookee that: a promotions budget that exceeds his detective's salary. Nice. He shoves the folder back into the cabinet and goes out to pay a visit to the offices of The Press.

* * * *

"Everyone's been murdered, how do you think I feel?" The Press's only remaining employee—an editorial assistant—wears excessive eyeliner and a silver stud in her slightly inflamed upper lip. A tattoo of a dolphin leaps out of her cleavage.

Mike feels repelled and confused. And old. "Can I get a list of Press authors?"

She leans onto one curvy haunch as she paints her nails a shiny black, probably not in mourning. "Going back how long?"

He shrugs. "Ten years?"

She waves her talons in the air to dry them, then turns to her computer and begins typing, the clicks of her fingernails hitting the keys like corn popping. "My question is, like, will I get a paycheck this week? Cause I have, like, bills. And I haven't been paid in a month." The printer spits out three pages, and she hands them to Mike.

"Who would want to cause . . ." (he almost says "like") ". . . harm to The Press?"

She pushes silky hair behind her curled-shell-like ears and taps the stud in her lip. It looks painful. "Omigod. It was high drama around here 24-7. New boyfriends, old boyfriends, bill collectors, banks cutting us off, writers wanting their money. Better than a soap opera. But murder? I don't *think* so."

Mike scans the list of Press authors. Three of them are also clients of the famous literary agent.

* * * *

Quincy Quaid's apartment smells like Raid and cat. The source of the latter odor, a yellow kitty with fur as fluffy as a dandelion, drapes itself at Mike's feet and begins a rumbly purring as he rubs its head. Quincy Quaid is a delicate petite woman with a writhing mass of blonde hair, too much make-up, and a fluttering manner.

"You're a big strapping fellow, aren't you? My, yes, nothing wussy about you. You may call me Quincy." She gives his knee a flirtatious squeeze but he senses that her heart isn't in it; her face is ashen, her eyes bloodshot.

"It's almost as though your career was a target," he says.

A tear slides down her cheek, carrying a speck of mascara with it. "I can't go on. My creative spirit is broken."

He feels a stab of sympathy; she seems fragile and vulnerable. "That would be a shame. I've enjoyed your books."

"Detective, I'm terrified. I keep thinking they died because of me! Meanwhile, I'm not licking any envelopes!" She half-laughs, half-shudders.

* * * *

He takes the subway to the address of the next author, a disheveled man reeking of bourbon, never a good sign at 10 AM. The writer shoos a tuxedo cat off the couch then clears a space by pushing aside an accumulation of unread newspapers, mail, beer cans, and pizza boxes. "Sit here. Want a drink?"

Mike declines. The writer picks up a glass of something that looks like water, but isn't, and takes a goodly swallow. "I'll confess to an abiding, deep, permanent hatred for all three of them."

"*I* confess I haven't read your book."

"You and the rest of the English-speaking world. Does literary scandal sell books? The question wasn't answered, because The Press pulled back all copies and burned them."

"A memoir?"

"It was fiction, baby, utter fiction. I'm a great writer, and it was a great story. But I'm a bald dork from Ohio and nobody wanted it. So screw 'em, I rewrote it as memoir, sent it to the dead agent who sold it in an auction to the dead publisher, to be edited by the dead editor. All three well aware it was fiction."

Mike knows the book's premise: a married couple, parents of four kids, find out they are siblings. The writer had written it as the story of his parents, a tragic yet vaguely icky tale. "So it wasn't true? Your parents weren't brother and sister?"

"You're sharp, Sherlock. That's what I said. Fiction. And those three left me nailed to a cross to die for their sins."

"So you hated them."

"Makes me a suspect, right?" He holds out trembling hands as if to be cuffed.

"Did you kill them?"

"No. But I'll shake the hand of the sorry bastard who did it."

Mike isn't sure he is telling the truth. "I'll be in touch," he says. Should he come back with a search warrant? Somewhere in this sad clutter, would they find traces of arsenic trioxide?

* * * *

He phones the third writer on both lists, a child psychologist from Charleston, the author of five books of advice for parents, starting with *Baby Your Baby* and ending with *Talk to Your Teen.* She has a breathy sexy voice with an accent marinated in grits, collards, and 'que. "Ah'm devastated. Ah'm readin' galleys and suddenly the rug's yanked and bam, Ah'm flat on ma ass with no agent and no publisher."

Envisioning a pissed-off Daisy Mae in horn-rims, Mike apologizes for the intrusion and asks if she knows of any conflicts involving the victims.

"Absolutely not. We were a team, Detective. Teamwork is what Ah'm preaching in ma new book, *Families That Flourish.* But now ma team is gone and ma book with it." She whispers, "Ah cain't talk about it now, darlin'. Ah have to take ma kitty to the vet." Mike hears a mournful piercing howl that gives him chills. What is it with writers and cats?

* * * *

Stan, the club performer and new friend of the now-dead publisher, isn't surprised that the detective wants to talk with him. He has *mad* ideas for who might have murdered his sweetheart and is *dying* to share them with a professional.

The detective is a bit overweight but in a firm not flabby way, with a nice face, kind of chiseled and Roman. Stan's tortie cat likes him too; she weaves around his legs.

"The neighbors heard you arguing," the detective says.

Stan jumps to his feet in horrified astonishment. "We were arguing? Discussing our feelings! That's what people do who care about each other!" He can't believe he might be a suspect.

"Furthermore, I never even met that editor. Why would I kill someone I didn't know?"

The detective shrugs his broad shoulders. "Accident, maybe. What were you two arguing about all night?"

Stan almost forgets his loss for a moment, so wrought up by the unfairness of it all. Also, he is sidetracked by the detective's pecs and quads. Yummy. Too bad the fellow is a *cop*; Stan could get arrested, he supposes, for the slightest insinuation of a proposition. This dating thing is damned tricky, like traveling a pot-holed rutted highway, a dangerous bumpy journey almost not worth the effort. So when he'd met the publisher (now dead) and they'd hit it off so well (except for the intrusive presence of the publisher's ex-wife, also now dead), he'd been so relieved, so glad to have someone who'd understand his emotional needs, assuage his fear of abandonment, tolerate his moodiness and outbursts. In return he had complimented the publisher's gowns and make-up, suggesting in the most gently tactful way styles that flattered, that disguised the publisher's burly body and stumpy legs. Now the detective is asking *him* about the deaths, as though he's Snow White's stepmom slipping poisoned apple slices into everyone's lunchbox.

"I loved him," Stan says, "we were like that," waggling his crossed fingers. "You can't possibly believe I would do anything violent."

"Poisoning isn't violent, actually. It's indirect, removed," the dreamy cop says.

"Semantics. I could never murder anyone." He closes his eyes to shut out the distracting man in a well-cut suit—clothes are *so* important—and thinks about his friend the publisher, now dead, gone forever. He is alone, again. Tears well up in his eyes and he pinches his nose to stop them.

* * * *

The writer notices new tremor in hands. Must taper Xanax. One more letter to prepare, difficult with shaking hands. The cat jumps on the counter, almost spills little jar of powder. Writer shrieks, "Get away!" and then feels bad for yelling at the cat. Lick & stick glue is a great invention. The writer feels stressed.

Doorbell rings and the writer opens door to the hot detective and a uniformed cop pointing a gun. Detective doesn't miss a trick.

The writer is afraid that what is to come will be horrible. The writer runs into kitchen, picks up little jar of powder and throws a good bit down throat. Curious how arsenic trioxide is tasteless.

The detective calls for an ambulance, takes writer in his arms and asks why? The writer explains, enjoys the snuggle, for a little while.

* * * *

They watch the ambulance take the body away, and then the uniformed cop begins to cordon off the apartment with yellow tape. "It looked like she was preparing another envelope," he says.

"For her ex-husband," Mike says. "She told me she was empty, she had to get off the treadmill of four books a year. But she owed so much money she couldn't afford to get out of her contracts. Somehow, she thought that murdering her publishing team would end her problems."

The uniformed cop, who wants to be a homicide detective some day, has been following the case. "What made you suspect Quincy Quaid?"

"The lab found yellow cat hairs on one of the doctored envelopes. I obtained cat hairs from the most likely suspects, and only Quincy's cat was a match." Mike reaches down to pat the cat's thick golden fur.

"One of the writers lived in Charleston, didn't she? You didn't go there."

"I heard her cat yowl and that was enough—it was a Siamese."

Seriously impressed, the uniformed cop realizes there is more to detecting than wearing a well-cut suit.

Karen Pullen *owns a bed & breakfast inn in North Carolina and teaches memoir writing at Duke and Central Carolina Community College. She has an MFA in Popular Fiction from the Stonecoast program at the University of Southern Maine. "SASE" is her first and last story featuring cats.*

NEW AGE OLD STORY

BY SARAH E. GLENN

When I was a child, I used to visit the rich ducks in Biltmore Forest. My father and I called them that because they lived in the very heart of the exclusive neighborhood: the pond of the country club's golf course. I threw bread to the ducks and said hello; they ate the bread, but snubbed me.

The Forest, originally part of the Vanderbilt estate, was incorporated as a town within a town: it was completely surrounded by the Asheville metropolitan area. The residents, the wealthiest in North Carolina per capita, resided in half-timbered manors set back from pine-lined roads.

Driving through Biltmore Forest today, still out of place in my dad's old Taurus, I saw that the houses were as secluded as ever. I wondered if the ducks were still as cold-hearted.

* * * *

Sophia Farris was the reason for this drive into my past. She'd phoned Fisher Investigations to say that she urgently needed my help. I had no pressing work, but even if I had I would have made the time. The last time I'd seen Sophia, I'd confirmed her girlfriend's infidelity and broken her heart. Maybe she was ready to let in someone new.

One wall of her studio was nothing but a huge aquarium, full of tropical fish. The slanted ceiling above the tank displayed a fresco of a woman, naked except for an old-fashioned diving helmet and lying on a bed of seaweed. I realized I was staring, and turned back to the figure pacing in front of me. Hair a sheet of black glass, face resolute as a nun's, Sophia was just the way I remembered her.

"I'm so glad you came, Lana," she said. "I called on behalf of Ananda. She's been arrested."

"Ananda?"

"Her mundane name is Amanda Calder. She's charged with killing Henry, her husband."

"Oh . . . my." Henry Calder, city council member, had died suddenly last week. The *Citizen-Times* had reported the death as a suspected heart attack. "It's murder, then?"

"Ananda called me from the jail. The police say Henry died from some type of poison. They think she put it in his food."

I could not, for the life of me, figure out why Henry Calder's wife would ask someone who did goddess paintings for legal help. "How do you know her?"

"Ananda runs the Ladyvisions Gallery—off Haywood near Malaprop's—and she shows my paintings. She's also a neighbor."

Asheville had changed since my childhood, becoming a mountainous Mecca for New Agers. Crystal workers, soi-disant shamans, and aura readers had flooded in from Sedona, Berkeley, and all points weird. Crystal shops dotted Buncombe County, and alternative medicine newsletters could be found in most grocery stores.

I'd seen the gallery, sandwiched between artsy jewelry shops and atmospheric music stores in the Art Deco section of downtown Asheville. Its ballyhooed opening had been about a year ago. "She wants me to investigate her husband's death?"

"*I* want you to investigate it." She shifted, giving me a glimpse of perfect calf below her dirndl skirt. "They're saying Ananda argued with Henry, that she was having an affair. But I know she didn't kill him. That sort of act would leave karmic traces in her aura, and I would see them."

Sophia wanted me to help someone accused of killing a city council member, based on a psychic impression (or lack thereof). I would have no leverage at all except with Amanda's friends and family, which would help very little if Calder's political allies closed ranks. I opened my mouth to say as much, and Sophia moved closer. She smelled like honeysuckle.

"Please? I'll do anything I can to help."

I found myself nodding.

* * * *

Amanda Calder, dba Ananda Calling of Ladyvisions, held her head high as she entered the visitors' room. She sat gracefully across the table from us, instinctively smoothing the jumpsuit as if it were a silk dress. "Sophia! I'm so glad you're here. Thank you for coming, Miss—is it Miss? —Fisher. My friend recommends you highly."

My heart warmed at the thought of inspiring such confidence in Sophia, even if she had no other detectives for comparison. "Miss Fisher is fine. Let me warn you that despite Sophia's good opinion, I can't guarantee that I'll find anything that the police haven't. I was an officer myself for several years—" I mentally flinched at the memory "—and they are intelligent people."

"Certainly. They're just wrong. I was shocked when my attorney told me they suspected poisoning. I thought Henry's bad dietary habits had finally caught up with him."

"What did he eat for his last m—what did he eat last?"

"Free-range chicken, parsley potatoes, corn, blueberry cobbler," she recited. She'd obviously given the list several times. "And a salad of wild greens, at my insistence. With fat-free vinaigrette dressing, from the co-op."

"Which dish do they think was poisoned?"

She looked down at her hands, revealing gray roots in her layered blonde hair. "I gave him herbal capsules to clear his body of toxins. Jim Bearcat sells them in his shop. I take them all the time. The capsules can be opened, though, and the police think I put something else inside."

"Maybe it was an accident," Sophia said. "Jim orders some of his herbs by mail. The supplier could have made a mistake."

"If there'd been a mix-up, other people would have died, too. Besides, Jim is careful."

I interrupted them. "You have to be straight with me, ma'am. Any evidence I find will have to be turned over to the police. Did you kill your husband?"

"No." Patrician lines formed around her mouth. "I did not."

"I'll take the case based on your word, then. I need you to sign a contract, plus a release giving me permission to visit your house, look into records, and so on." I produced the documents my cousin Allie had copied at the law library in the Buncombe County courthouse and modified for my needs. Allie worked for the pittance my budget permitted, because I let her keep her toddler in the office. I hoped there were no small fingerprints on the forms this time.

"Certainly. Oh! If you're going to the house, there's something I'd like you to do."

"Yes?"

"Check on PawPaw." The name was incongruous on those cultured lips. "Henry's father. He has a night nurse, but my son won't be flying in till tomorrow and PawPaw's been alone."

"Certainly, ma'am. Perhaps he even knows something that will help."

* * * *

We returned to the Forest. Sophia pointed out the proper turns to me, and we approached one of the Tudor-style houses.

PawPaw smiled toothlessly at Sophia and let us in. We followed with baby steps as the old man crept along the edge of the carpet to a recliner. Most of the furniture came from the days before outlets popped up everywhere along I-40. The recliner was new. He carefully lowered himself into the seat. "Sorry, gotta keep my legs raised. So, you're a detective, eh? Never met a detective before, man or lady. Hold on a sec while I put this in." He fumbled with his hearing aid and nearly dropped it.

When he was situated, I began the interview. "Mrs. Calder hired me to investigate the death of her husband. Do you have any opinions on what happened?"

"No need for opinions. We had dinner, Henry died. Didn't see anybody poisoning anything." His hand trembled on the recliner's arm.

"You may not have seen the substitution made, but your son received something poisonous. The police think it was administered to him in one of his herbal capsules."

"My, what big words you use. Slow down, why don't you? Amanda had nothing to do with it." His bleary blue eyes fixed on me. "You have to help her, Miss Fisher. She's all I have here. My grandson is coming down, but he'll have to get back to his wife and family. Don't know where I'll end up if Amanda goes to prison."

Sophia, who had wandered off, returned to tap my arm. "Come to the patio and see what I've found."

I let her lead me out the French doors into a small courtyard. A faun poured a steady stream of water into a pool of water lilies near the center. The azaleas omnipresent in Southern gardens cupped several small geometric plots with blooming flowers.

Sophia pointed. "Look. That's foxglove, and there's monkshood. Both of them are poisonous."

"That doesn't sound good for Amanda."

"Perhaps Henry wanted to get rid of her. She's the one with the money. He could have put some cuttings in the capsules. Only he got them mixed up and took the bad ones himself."

I had no faith in villains getting hoisted on their own petards. "Like I said, that doesn't sound good for Amanda."

"She's innocent; we just have to prove it. Maybe PawPaw saw Henry in the garden."

We returned to the living room and questioned the old man. His response was guarded. "Only one went in the garden was Amanda. Her house, her garden."

My companion sighed.

* * * *

After we left the Calder house, Sophia insisted I take her to an acupuncture clinic on Merrimon Drive. She patted my shoulder before she got out of the car. I vowed to never wash it again. "You're going to be wonderful. Come back at noon, and I'll take you to lunch."

I got out of the boutique shop zone and located a strip mall where I could park and make a few phone calls. The first call I made was to the detective handling the Calder case. I was forwarded to the voice mail of a man whose name I didn't recognize. After leaving a message identifying myself and my client, my second call was to a friend I still had in Asheville's Finest. We were beat partners back when my world was young. These days, he focused on auto theft. That wasn't in the Major Crimes Unit, but maybe he could give me some information.

"Hoo boy," Jess Davenport said when he heard my voice. "You stepped in it this time, Fisher, working for a homeopathic black widow."

"Word gets around fast. I need information."

"Of course you do. When else do you call? Not this time, though."

"I just need to know why they suspect poisoning. Any chance they found a poisonous herb?"

"Captain Vickers is in charge of Criminal Investigations these days. Word gets back to him, it's my butt."

I remembered my former commanding officer too well. His continuous insinuations about 'my kind' were a large reason why I had left the Department.

"C'mon, Jess. Mrs. Calder could be innocent."

"Or guilty. Those crystal clinkers have impure thoughts just like us earthbound types. Call the coroner."

Click.

Damn.

* * * *

Sophia was wearing a lavender fedora when I picked her up.

"What's this?"

She smiled mysteriously. "I decided to accessorize. Let's go to lunch, and I'll tell you what I detected."

"What *you* detected?"

We ate at Richmond Hill on a patio overlooking the French Broad River. The twitter of birds and tourists faded into background music for my admiration of Sophia's small chin, the delicate notch at the base of her throat, and her tiny adorable ears.

I was startled when my paragon said, "Ananda was definitely having an affair."

"What?"

"Ananda was having an affair with Jim Bearcat. I told you I'd help. Yukio hears all sorts of things when she's working with people."

"Why didn't you include me in that interview?"

She moved closer. I didn't know eucalyptus could smell so sexy.

"Well, Lana, I really don't look that attractive with needles stuck in me. Besides, she wouldn't have talked in front of a stranger."

She wanted to be attractive for me. Yippee!

* * * *

Before we headed for Bearcat's place, I tried the coroner's office and got a recording. We left Asheville on Hendersonville Road, passing small strip malls, barbecue eateries, and used car lots.

When we arrived, we were in the middle of nowhere. I wasn't even certain we were still in Buncombe County. The 'shop' was a refurbished trailer with a rich man's view of the mountains. A small sign at the mailbox advertised healing herbs.

With a name like Bearcat, I'd expected a Native American. Instead, a small man with thinning blond hair greeted us at the door. He recognized Sophia, and was delighted to hear I was helping Amanda. He shoved a pair of cats off the sofa and offered us a seat. Racks of smudge sticks, incense, and small plastic bags filled with capsules faced us. A bookcase housing jars of dried plant shreds sloped against the back wall.

I indicated the racks. "Tell me about these capsules you sell. 'Heart Health,' 'Spring Tonic,' "Detoxifying,' and so on."

"Everyone wants to know about them now, and not in a good way. There's nothing much to tell, though. None of these herbs are harmful."

"Maybe not, but anyone could reopen one of those capsules."

"Yeah, I know. I keep hearing that." He rubbed his chin. "Now the paper says they want to make the sale of homemade capsules illegal."

"You know how it is. Someone dies from something, they make it illegal."

"Don't kid yourself. They want to get rid of us, Miss Fisher. The herbalists, the Pagans, the crystal healers. The residents of La-La Land."

"Who are 'they?'"

"Folks like the ones at Lake Junaluska and Woodridge. The religious establishment."

I had no dog in that fight. "Then it's in your best interest to help me. I hear that you and Amanda had a shared interest in more than herbs. Is that true?"

"Ananda is a beautiful woman. Lots of people would like to put her together with me because she visited often."

"That's not an answer."

"It's all you're going to get, same as the police. If I say yes, then they claim motive. If I say no, they assume I'm lying, and claim motive anyway."

Smart man. "Did you make up something special for Henry Calder?"

"I sold her my standard detoxifying preparation. She thought it might help his constipation."

He and Sophia both snickered; I forged on. "Did she take any of them herself?"

"No, she preferred 'Menopause Mollifier.'" With a grin, he added, "I suppose I'm breaking herbalist-client confidentiality."

Sophia broke in. "What if the capsules were mistaken for one another?"

"Guess he would get in touch with his inner woman. The capsules are different, though." He indicated the column of empty capsules. "I do the Detoxifier in size 000, the Mollifier in 00."

* * * *

My phone chirped on the drive back.

"Fisher."

"This is Bob Levin. I got your message."

"Hang on." I took the Holiday exit and pulled into a parking lot. "Thank you for returning my call. I know you're busy."

"Thank Jess Davenport. He called me at home. I understand you're interested in the cause of death. I will warn you that they haven't finished the full tox screen yet. That can take a while."

I silently blessed my old partner. "Yes. How did they conclude it was poison?"

"There were pills inside the capsules. They'd started to dissolve, but they resembled the digoxin your client's husband was already taking. An overdose would definitely explain the death."

Pills. I thanked him and put the phone away. So anyone could have done it, even the night nurse. I needed to learn more about the Calder family, and not from Amanda's current clientele.

I turned to Sophia, who obviously expected an update. "The garden and the herbs were distractions. Can you give me the names of some of Amanda's older friends?"

* * * *

Cornelia Platts volunteered at the Mountain Arts Center and was one of Amanda's bridge partners. "Or at least I was, until she started inhaling too much incense."

I was doing this interview alone, over Sophia's objections. I didn't think she'd mix well with the blue hairs. "So you hadn't seen her recently?"

"Oh, we still serve on a few committees together. She's a part of the arts scene, even if she doesn't sell landscapes anymore."

"Landscapes?" I couldn't imagine 'Ananda Calling' doing anything that pedestrian.

"Amanda always wanted to support local artists, provide a venue for their work. One day, she came into the Center, all atwitter. She'd gone to a show in Hendersonville with her crazy neighbor and saw all the New Age 'art.'" I could hear the quote marks. "She said it was a new style, like Cubism. Next thing I knew, she'd reinvented the store. Herself, too. You can't talk to her nowadays without wondering what's in those capsules she takes."

I ignored the 'crazy neighbor' remark. "When was the last time you heard from her? Or from Mr. Calder?"

"About two weeks ago, both of them. First he called, wanting to know about the place I'd put Mother when she got sick. It sounded like his dad was having problems. Is PawPaw still at home?"

"Yes, he's still there."

One withered cheek quivered as she smiled. "Amanda must have won that one. She called me the next day, telling me not to encourage Henry."

"Mr. Calder was looking into assisted living for his father, then?"

"Something more than that. They'd hired a nurse, but Henry was concerned that he might need more care."

* * * *

When I returned to my suite in the Rhododendron Shopping Center, I closed my office door to block out young Ava's gurgling and rebooted my laptop. Time to review my notes and do some heavy thinking, not something I could easily do near Sophia.

PawPaw had been headed to a nursing home before the murder, whether he knew it or not. But why? As far as I could tell, the Calders had enough money to hire full-time nursing if the old man needed it.

The thought brought back bad memories. When my grandmother got too feeble—and addled—to live without a keeper, we didn't have as many choices. My parents and I tried sleeping in shifts, but somehow Gran managed to get out of eyeshot and fall down, put food on the stove to burn, or leave the tap running to flood the bathroom. After several arguments, we surrendered and put her in senior care. I would never forget the smell, the sounds—disoriented old people shrieking—or the warehoused patients, waiting for Death to drop in along with the relatives.

PawPaw wasn't nearly that bad off, though. I could understand the night nurse, but why round-the-clock care? Maybe something else was going on. Mrs. Platts said Calder had never taken an interest in his father's upkeep. Perhaps his sudden change of heart was due to another change . . . of address.

* * * *

When I returned to the Calder house, a fellow about my age opened the door.

"You must be the grandson," I said. His face was grooved with the same lines I had noticed in Amanda's face. The resemblance would be even greater in another decade.

"Ted. And you are . . ."

"Lana Fisher. Your mother hired me to—"

"Come in!" He stepped back from the door. "PawPaw was telling me about you. Did you learn anything yet?"

"A few things. May I speak to PawPaw? Privately, if possible?"

* * * *

The old man was in a wheelchair. He must be having more trouble today. I sat on an antique love seat and faced him.

"I finally figured it out. Your daughter-in-law didn't kill your son. She planned to divorce him. She was keeping the house, since it was hers to begin with. Jim Bearcat would have been hers and the store would be hers. The only thing she would no longer have would be you."

The old man shifted in the chair and turned his bad ear towards me. I leaned closer and raised my voice, although I was certain he heard me quite clearly.

"Mrs. Calder hired you a night nurse, but your son thought that was too expensive. Especially since you would soon be entirely his responsibility. I spoke to her friends at the craft center. Henry asked about recommendations for your relocation. You knew that, didn't you?"

"Relocation is one way of putting it." PawPaw didn't look me in the face. "Nursing home."

"With him dead, you knew you could live here until the end of your natural life. Even in jail, she worried about your welfare." I thought of my grandmother, restrained in that aluminum bed, and sighed. "Some things are worth risking prison for, aren't they?"

I got a flash of denture. "You know, even if Amanda is into that New Age stuff, she's more old fashioned than Henry. She knew it was wrong to treat your parents like that. Not if you have a choice. They thought I couldn't hear them, but I hear real well when it's about me."

"You were fine until they told you they were getting divorced. You probably hated Jim Bearcat for that. Was that why you used the capsules? So the blame would fall on him?"

"Oh, I don't blame him for the divorce. It was me they argued about the most." His hand trembled, and he stilled it with the other one. "The doc says I might be getting Parkinson's. Henry wasn't going to hire no full-time nurse, he was going to put me away. I took those capsules and opened them up while I still could. Damned if my heart pills weren't a custom fit. I never thought they'd blame her. I am sorry for that."

His story sounded right, but that didn't mean it was true. Amanda had clearly been on PawPaw's side, and the old man could be agreeing with me to save her. "Weren't you afraid she might accidentally take the pills instead?"

"No, she kept those herbal thingies separate. Beside, the capsules were different sizes."

Good enough for me. "Mr. Calder, you know I have to tell the police. It would really be best if you told them yourself, though. I'm sorry."

"I am too, but I'm not sorry I did it, Missy. I hoped they'd think it was a heart attack. I was his age when I had my first. But prison or a nursing home, it won't make much difference to me. Not for very long. If I need to talk to the police, though, you'd better take me to the jail. I'm too old to make any more stops than I need to."

* * * *

After I took PawPaw downtown, with a bewildered Ted following me in his own car, I had to break the news to my client. I brought Sophia in case Mrs. Calder needed support. When I told the story, though, Sophia was the one to cry.

"That poor man," she said. "So afraid he'd be put away."

Amanda was more practical. "What happens now? What will they do to him?"

"Your attorney would know better than me. His illness may be a consideration."

"You think that he wasn't himself anymore? Dementia, perhaps?"

"No, I think he knew exactly what he was doing."

* * * *

I'd hoped to speak to Sophia after the case was over, suggest that we get to know one another better, but the situation made that grossly inappropriate. I thought about calling her several times during the next week, but was afraid to punch in her number (which, I confess, I had optimistically put on speed dial). Maybe Sophia had some psychic sensitivity after all, though. She called me.

"Hello," she sang into the phone, as if nothing had happened. "How are you?"

"Um . . . I'm fine. And you?"

"I was thinking . . . Ananda paid your expenses, but I'm the one that really engaged you. And I didn't pay anything."

"Consider the lunch your payment."

"Still, I thought I should do something . . . so, I was wondering. How would you feel about sitting for a portrait?"

"A . . . portrait?"

"Yes. I think you have a really nice aura. I'd love to capture it on canvas. Perhaps we could discuss the best approach . . . over dinner?"

My faith in her perceptions immediately took an upturn. "Sure."

Sarah E. Glenn was born in Asheville, North Carolina, and her family has deep roots there. She now lives in Lexington, Kentucky, where she has befriended ducks of lower income. Information on her first novel, All This and Family, Too, *can be found at sarahglenn.com.*

THE SHADOW OF THE RIVER

BY GIGI PANDIAN

I arrived ten minutes early outside the office of Dr. Omar Khan, professor of history at the university. That's when everything started to go wrong.

My knock was greeted with silence. That surprised me. In spite of my early arrival, I had been confident Omar would be there.

I knocked again.

"Omar? It's Tarek. I'm here for our appointment."

A faint groan sounded from behind the door.

"Omar?"

I hadn't imagined that sound.

Omar was getting on in years. I knew he took medication for his heart. He'd made a big discovery earlier this week. An ancient map depicting three sacred rivers in India. It was a huge find. Could the excitement have been too much for him?

I tried the door handle. Locked.

Calling out again, I pressed my ear to the door. Nothing. But I was sure of what I'd heard.

I ran down the hallway. Skidding to a stop, I pounded on the door of the corner office. It gave way, swinging open to reveal Dr. Lydia Reynolds, Chair of the History Department. She looked up from her desk.

"Tarek, what on earth—"

"Do you have keys to the department offices?" I asked. "I think Omar is having a heart attack."

Lydia sprang up from her chair. "No. With those manuscripts of his, only the campus police have keys."

"But—"

"I know." Lydia rushed past. "There's no time." She disappeared into the office next to hers.

Lydia emerged from the office moments later with a young professor, Bradley Atkins, who was new to the department. Lydia's gray hair bounced as she trotted down the hall with her colleague jogging after her—all 6-and-a-half feet and 250 pounds of him. Watching his sturdy frame, I realized what Lydia had in mind. I sprinted after them.

"You sure?" Bradley said to her, stopping in front of Omar's office.

"You're certain what you heard?" Lydia asked, turning to me.

"Positive." I hoped.

"I take full responsibility," Lydia said.

Bradley shrugged helplessly, which under other circumstances would have been amusing coming from a man who looked more like a linebacker than a history professor. He breathed deeply, and then took a few steps back from the door. He ran towards it, lifting his foot just in time to make contact with the edge of the door. A loud thwack echoed down the hallway. The door didn't budge.

At the noise, several heads poked out of doorways. One was that of my friend Jaya Jones.

Bradley hurried several paces further back, allowing for a bigger running start. This time the door splintered. He faltered, almost falling onto his hefty back, which would surely have broken several bones of whomever he landed on. Based on my location, they would probably have been mine.

Luckily for me, a stocky professor who'd emerged from one of the offices steadied Bradley. With one more heave, the two of them together broke down the door and spilled inside the office. The other man landed on the floor at Omar's feet.

Jaya and Lydia stood at my side, but as soon as the door was broken open, the three of us rushed inside. We stopped just inside the doorway.

Omar lay on the floor of his office. But the problem wasn't his heart. A large patch of blood covered his thinning hair. His large green eyes stared up at the ceiling, unmoving. There was no life left in Omar Khan.

A thick wooden figure lay next to the floor next to his body.

The statue of a smiling Buddha.

A shrill voice screamed. A deep one did, too. Somebody shouted about calling 911. It might have been me, but I honestly can't quite recall.

Jaya squeezed my hand.

"I thought he'd had a heart attack," I said. "I heard him cry out. That's why we needed to get in."

"Wait," Jaya said. "He doesn't look like he could have—"

"What's all this?"

I started at the deep voice next to my ear. Jaya jumped a little as well. She relaxed when she saw the man in the tweed jacket.

"I didn't see you, Isaac," I said.

"Sorry, didn't mean to scare you," the university's museum director said. "What happened? Are Lydia and Bradley standing over Omar?"

I nodded.

"I wonder . . ." Jaya murmured, and let go of my hand. Her lips continued to move almost imperceptibly. I'd seen her look like that before, at the university library, late one night the previous year. I'd walked up to her table and said hello, but she hadn't responded. She wasn't being rude; she hadn't heard me. She was so wrapped up in the volume of bound journals in front of her that the rest of the world had been invisible.

"Jaya?" As I expected, she didn't seem to hear me.

Lydia knelt next to Omar's body. She reached out, but Bradley stopped her.

"I'm telling you," Bradley said into his cell phone. "He doesn't need an ambulance. Just the police."

Jaya wasn't paying attention to any of them. Her olive complexion had paled, but her eyes scanned the room before stopping on one particular spot. She seemed to be looking at the plant on Omar's desk.

I studied the plant myself. At first I thought the object next to the plant was only a shadow, but it was a dried leaf. Jaya took a step towards it, then stopped.

Why was Jaya so interested in a dead leaf?

"I understand," Bradley said, his face grave. He closed his phone. "There isn't anything we can do for Omar. The police want us to wait in the hall. Nobody leave."

Omar wasn't only dead. He had been *murdered*.

Jaya pulled me into the hallway. She didn't stop there. She's stronger than she looks for her petite five-foot frame. I've seen her flip a six-foot man over her shoulder when he didn't believe she could take care of herself. I nearly tripped as she pulled my elbow until we were around the corner.

"What's going on, Tarek?"

She glanced around the corner before I had a chance to answer.

"It's okay," she said. "Nobody followed us. They're all still outside Omar's office."

"What do you mean what's—"

"The leaf," Jaya said. "Didn't you see it?"

Why was she so concerned about a leaf?

"Didn't you see what was in that room?" Jaya continued. "I saw you looking at it, too. We have to tell the police, you know."

I stared blankly at her.

"Next to the plant on his desk," she said.

"A dried leaf?"

"Exactly."

"Why does it matter that Omar forgot to water his plant?"

Jaya threw up her hands. I thought nobody actually did that, but Jaya never ceased to amaze me with her varied gestures. She'd been raised in both India and the United States, the respective countries of each of her parents, and had consciously or unconsciously picked up a jumble of body language as well as the spoken languages.

"A scrap of *palm leaf* was on the edge of his desk," she said. "It looked like a leaf because it *was* a leaf. Just not the kind that came from Omar's plant."

I groaned to myself, finally beginning to understand.

"His great discovery," Jaya said. "It was a torn edge of *that map*."

"How do you know? I thought he hadn't shown it to anybody yet."

"You've been studying Western history too long, Tarek. You were thinking about Western maps on inked parchment when Omar told you about it. But in India, they often used dried palm leaves for paper. We need to tell the police that Omar was killed over the map."

Jaya poked her head around the corner again, and then motioned for me to follow her back to the rest of the solemn group of professors and graduate students. She paced the hall, as if she was full of nervous energy. Nobody seemed to know what to do.

It was a welcome change when the police arrived and wanted to talk to us. Two unsmiling detectives led us down the hall to Lydia's large corner office. They closed the door behind them.

"There's a fragment of an historic map on his desk," Jaya began. "That's why he was killed. Someone has stolen the rest of that map."

"You saw it happen?" the older of the two detectives asked. He raised a gray eyebrow.

"No," she admitted. "But when a mild-mannered professor of Middle Eastern and South Asian history discovers a priceless map earlier this week, and is bludgeoned to death today—"

"Wait a sec—*priceless* map?"

"Maybe we should start at the beginning," I cut in. "Two days ago, Omar Khan discovered a very valuable map. It was a last minute gift for the university museum's collection. It's a map of the Triveni Sangam in India, the meeting point of three sacred rivers: the Ganges, the Yumana, and the 'invisible' Saraswati."

"Why is it so valuable?" The detective looked interested.

"In this map," I said, "the Saraswati *isn't* invisible."

"So it's a fake?" The detective rubbed his hand across the deep creases in his forehead. "The forger got it wrong? Then why is it so valu—"

"No, there's a river there. Four thousand years ago, a great earthquake struck India. The river Saraswati was swallowed up and became an underground river, said to be bestowed with mystic powers. The site where the two grand rivers converge with this legendary one in Allahabad, northern India, is a sacred place for Hindus. Such an ancient, unique map would be worth a lot of money."

"And a piece of the map is on his desk," Jaya said. "Somebody must have torn it from his hands before hitting him with his Buddha statue."

"Who would want to hurt the professor?" The detective's face was impassive.

Jaya frowned. "But I just told you why—"

"If they didn't want to hurt him, they could have stolen this map from his office when he wasn't there." The detective's voice was quiet.

"They couldn't have gotten in," I said. "Only Omar and the campus police have keys to his office. He keeps too many valuables in there to give the key to anyone else."

"Well, somebody else had a key," said the detective. "The dead bolt was locked from the inside. And we're three flights up. No fire escape next to his office."

"Tarek is right," Jaya said. "Nobody else had a key."

"The professor's keys were still in his pocket." The younger detective spoke for the first time. "We tried them in the lock, and they're the right keys. Someone else must have made a copy. We'll find them."

"Thanks for your help." The detective held out a business card. "Here's my phone number if you think of anything else."

Jaya opened her mouth, but it was my turn to pull her away. I led her back to the group in the hallway, a scowl on her face.

Bradley came from the opposite direction and stopped next to Isaac and Lydia. He handed Lydia a cup of coffee, probably from the vending machine down the hall. Lydia looked as if she'd aged ten years in the past half hour. Her usually sleek gray hair stood out in all directions, and deep wrinkles creased her forehead. She and Omar were two of the old guard in the department and had been at the university for decades. It seemed they had a special bond from their status as a woman and a minority years ago when neither was the norm.

"Do they know anything?" Lydia asked.

I shook my head. "Who would want to hurt Omar?"

"It was clearly an intruder," Isaac said. "Someone who didn't realize he was here and who wanted to steal one of his valuable historical manuscripts—"

"It was that damn map," Jaya said. "That's what they were after."

"You don't know that," Isaac said.

"There was a piece of it on his desk."

Lydia looked on the verge of tears. "Why didn't he just give it to them? It wasn't worth his life."

Isaac gasped. "If you're right, Jaya, I wish I'd never showed him that map . . ."

"You didn't actually show it to him, did you?" I said. "Omar told me he was visiting the storage room of the museum when your latest shipment arrived. He took the initiative himself to look at the latest items. There's no need for you to feel guilty, Isaac."

A peculiar expression came over Jaya's face.

Isaac was usually so composed. He would never be seen without a pressed handkerchief in his tweed jacket pocket as he stood confidently with perfect posture. Now, he slumped against the wall, fidgeting incessantly with his jacket, as if he didn't quite know what to do with his hands. He'd been close to Omar, too, since Omar had been quite involved with the university museum.

Bradley couldn't stand still either. His shoulder and leg were probably stiffening up after his door-breaking adventure. In broad sweeps, he stretched his arms across his chest. After a few swings, he bent his right knee towards his chest in a leg stretch.

"You're making me nervous," Isaac said to Bradley. "What's the matter with you?"

"Sorry." Bradley's face flushed. "I'm not used to breaking down doors. My shoulder is killing me."

"What?" Isaac said. "Oh, yes." But he hesitated a second too long.

I heard a sharp intake of breath. It was Jaya.

"You weren't there." She looked at Isaac, her eyes wide. "In the hallway. You weren't there to see Bradley break the door down."

"Oh, of course." Isaac tugged at his jacket. "Yes, you're correct, Jaya. I came upon the scene late. I had to infer who would have—"

"No, you didn't." Jaya spoke calmly, but a subtle vibration in her voice hinted at her excitement.

"Of course I—"

"You were there when the rest of us were there," Jaya said. "You spoke to Tarek right away. We rushed into the office at the same time, all of us after Grant. He was ahead of Bradley, so that's why you thought Grant was the one who broke the door down. The only way you could have *not* seen that Bradley was one of the men who kicked in the door was if you were inside the room already."

"Jaya." Isaac's voice was cold. "I know we're all upset—"

"Isaac?" Lydia whispered.

"It explains how someone got out of the room," Jaya said. "You *didn't* get out of the room. Not until we came in. All you had to do was blend in."

"Have you gone mad?" Isaac was no longer calm. "Why would I want to hurt Omar? You were the one who said a thief wanted the Sangam map. Why would I want to steal my own map, for Christ's sake?"

"Tarek already explained that," Jaya said. "Without knowing he'd done so."

"This is ridiculous." Isaac turned away.

Bradley put his hand on Isaac's shoulder. "I want to hear what she has to say."

Isaac looked up at Bradley. Or rather, at Bradley's girth.

Jaya's hands shook, but she continued in a measured voice. I could almost see the gears turning in her mind, putting the pieces together as she spoke.

"You didn't want to show the map to Omar," Jaya said. "Tarek said Omar happened by when you were unloading a shipment for the museum. He *wasn't supposed to be there*."

Isaac opened his mouth and drew breath, but didn't speak.

"Our little university museum isn't like the Met," Jaya said. "There isn't much to keep track of. Omar would have known ahead of time if we were receiving something so amazing. Did he find it strange that this amazing piece was included with no advance notice? Is that why he took it? To look into it further?"

"Is it true, Isaac?" Lydia whispered. "Why were you keeping it a secret? Why would you—" She broke off in a stifled sob.

"You never meant the map to be part of our collection," Jaya said. "A reputable university would serve as a great cover to bring valuable antiquities into the country without strict scrutiny. Only you didn't have time to remove anything from this shipment before Omar saw it."

"What have you got under your jacket?" Bradley asked Isaac, flexing his arm muscle as he did so.

Isaac swallowed hard.

"Oh, lord." He closed his eyes as he pulled out the broken piece of palm leaf from inside his jacket.

The intricate markings of the three rivers seemed to curl around his finger tips. The map was intact except for the broken edge.

Jaya squeezed my shoulder as I carefully took the palm leaf map. Would the shadow of this day eventually pass?

Gigi Pandian *is a graphic designer, photographer, and mystery writer in the San Francisco Bay Area. After discovering National Novel Writing Month, Gigi was awarded a Malice Domestic grant for her first mystery novel. Find her at a Sisters in Crime Nor-Cal chapter meeting, or online at www.gigipandian.com and www. pensfatales.com.*

THE TURKEY HILL AFFAIR

BY WARREN BULL

Turkey Hill, Iowa was a big disappointment until I bumped into Bennie. He was robbing the Farm and Business Bank. I was daydreaming, looking out the front window at a cute farmer boy walking by. So, when I say I bumped into Bennie, I mean I actually collided with him.

He dropped his gun and a sack stuffed with money. He reached for one and then for the other, but when he saw me, he stopped and stared. Ever since I was fourteen I've had that effect on men, even when they expect to see me. And Bennie, the big lug, has never been the sharpest pencil in the box.

Pop Thomas, the bank guard, looked back and forth between Bennie and the ancient pistol on his own hip, the one he had lugged across the muddy battlefields of France during the First World War. I'd have to take charge or somebody was going to get damaged.

"No, don't hurt me," I yelled. I scooped up the gun and handed it to Bennie. Then I retrieved the bag of money and handed it over, too. "Don't make me go with you," I shouted as I pushed Bennie toward the door. Luckily, Bennie was used to doing what other people told him to do.

I spoke softly. "Meet me outside the bank at ten tonight."

"Won't people see us, Roxie? Is that safe?"

"This isn't New York. They roll up the sidewalk at eight. Now shove me away and get out of town."

Bennie gave me a little push. I twisted around and grabbed the bank guard. I started sobbing. "Don't let him hurt me." I pulled Pop Thomas's head to my chest. Thomas hugged me back. His body responded to my closeness. Who would have thought there was so much life left in the old codger? When the sheriff arrived a few minutes later, he had to practically pry us apart.

Sheriff Allen was a dreamboat redhead with a wide chest and muscular shoulders. He sent me to wait in his office at the court house while he interviewed people at the bank. I flashed him a bright smile when he came into the office.

"Miss Terry, I know this has to be a difficult time for you. I'll try to keep my questions as short as possible."

Oops. I dropped the smile and put on a teary-but-trying-to-be-brave expression.

"The witnesses said that the robber just gave you a little nudge as he left the building, but you spun around and latched onto Pop Thomas like you were drowning. Can you explain that?"

I'd practiced the story in my head, starting from the time when I entered the bank and ending when the sheriff came in. Beginning the story at the end left me a little off balance.

"I was terrified, Sheriff. I saw Pop and hung on for dear life."

"By grabbing Pop, you made sure he didn't follow the robber out of the bank. If it was on purpose, I'd like to thank you."

"You would?"

"Sure. Pop shouldn't be chasing bank robbers at his age. He'd only get himself shot. This way he's a hero and nobody got hurt."

Allen smiled and continued. "He's been explaining why fighting in the trenches was tougher than landing on the beach on D-Day. From the way he's strutting around, I figure Mom Thomas might want to thank you tomorrow."

"I'm glad nobody got hurt," I said.

"The witnesses also told me that you and the bank robber chatted like old friends while he held you hostage. They said they couldn't hear well because you were talking so softly. What was it that you two talked about? Why did you talk so softly?"

I looked down at the floor before answering. "I was so scared that my mouth was dry. I don't know why the robber talked quietly. I begged him not to hurt me. He told me to do what he said."

Sheriff Allen nodded. "I wondered if it might be something like that, but the witnesses insisted that you two were gabbing away like you'd known each other for years. You know they're not big city people, but they're still pretty sharp."

I looked at him. Like you.

"One odd thing is that you seemed to know what to do during a robbery better than he did. You bumped into him. He dropped his gun and the money. You picked up the gun first. You handed it to him instead of pointing it at him."

"He, uh, he was too close. He could have taken it from me. Somebody might have gotten shot in the process. Maybe me."

"I agree. That was good thinking. It's best to keep everybody safe. Next you picked up the money and handed that to him."

"He threatened me."

"There's another odd thing," said the sheriff. "Nobody heard him say a word to you right then."

Then my mouth really got dry. I shrugged. "Maybe it was the expression on his face."

"The witnesses thought you started pushing him toward the door instead of the other way around."

I didn't like the implication of the questions.

"I swear to you on my life that I had no idea the bank was being robbed until I ran into that man. I had nothing to do with planning the robbery. I wasn't part of it. I did what I had to do and then I collapsed on the guard."

Sheriff Allen narrowed his eyes. He questioned me over and over again. At last he said, "It doesn't seem likely that you'd go waltzing into the bank to rob it dressed in high heels, a short skirt and a low-cut blouse. Even if you wore a mask, everybody would have known that you were the one who did it. No other woman in Lincoln County dresses like you do."

I smiled, although I wasn't sure that was a compliment.

"I know Bob Tatum brought you back from New York to meet his parents. I took one look at you and I knew why. I've known Bob all his life. He's a fine man. I know he volunteered to be a medic the same day I volunteered to fight the Nazis. What I don't know is why you would come here with him."

The sheriff was pretty sharp. I'd be better off sticking to the facts. I sighed. "I have a loving nature. My boyfriend in New York, Frank, was not a nice man. To tell the truth, he ran a mob, and made money from politics, loan sharking and blackmail. Frank took advantage of my loving nature and snapped some photos of me loving some well-known people. He planned on hitting them up for dough, which, in the long run, didn't look good for me. Frank could take care of himself, but some heavy hitters might get it in their heads that they'd be safer if I was out of the picture, so to speak. So I hired a P.I. Somehow he got the negatives. I knew Frank would be upset, and that could be really bad for my health. The P.I. worked faster than I expected, so I needed to get away quickly and quietly. I knew I could trust Bob. He would never sell me out. I let him take me out of town."

"And Iowa isn't quite what you thought it would be."

I looked at my hands. As a combat veteran, the sheriff had seen plenty of things in Europe that his neighbors would never even dream about. He might have a more sophisticated attitude than most people in the area.

"Don't get me wrong," I said. "The Tatums are fine people and Bob is a real gentleman. I just don't know if I was cut out for living here. I've talked it over with Bob and he agrees that it would be best for both of us to just be friends. I expect to go back to New York pretty soon. As nice as this town is, the only ones here wearing tassels are ears of corn."

"We don't have that many strippers," admitted Allen.

"I got excited when I heard about swap meets, but it's not where you meet and swap partners."

"The only stud fees we pay around here are for pure-bred bulls," he added.

I batted my lashes. "Once I got really got my hopes up when Bob suggested that we sneak out to be together late at night. He said if I brought the bait, he'd bring the pole."

"Let me guess. He took you to his favorite fishing hole."

I nodded and stepped closer to him. "You know, Sheriff, I haven't lost that loving nature. I could show you sometime. You probably know where the haystacks are. We could go for a roll in the hay."

"I don't know if my wife would go along with that."

"Tell her she's invited, too."

Sheriff Allen smiled. "I might just do that. I wonder what she'd say."

"Take it from me, Sheriff, you'll never know until you ask."

"Miss Terry, I promise I will give that my full consideration. Let me get back to you on that."

I lowered my eyelids and looked at him through my lashes. I sighed. It was time to get back to business.

"Sheriff, can I ask you a question?"

"Sure thing."

"Do you think you can find the robber?"

"If he's anywhere in the area, I can."

"Why do you say that?"

"Miss Terry, there aren't many people in this part of the state. We take quite an interest in whoever is around, especially a stranger. I already put out bulletins. Unless the robber high-tailed it out of here, sooner or later somebody will tell me where he is."

* * * *

As planned, I met Bennie at ten on the deserted street outside the bank.

"The last time I saw you before the bank job, you were collecting debts for Frank," I said. "What are you doing here?"

"When you disappeared from New York, Frank got real mad. We looked all over for you. I came into his office early one morning and found the door to the safe wide open. It was empty. Right then the cops busted down the door and told me Frank was dead. Some of the boys thought I had cleaned out the strong box."

"Maybe the cops took the blackmail photos."

"Nah, they would've sold them back to us. Cops don't have the patience to do decent blackmail work."

I had to admit that was true.

"It got so hot for me in New York that I had to hop a train. I came out to my granny's farm. I hide in the barn all day so nobody sees me. I can't go anywhere without stepping in pig shit. You're a smart girl, Roxie. Help me out. I thought if I robbed the bank I might have enough money to get away, or they might send me to prison and I'd meet somebody who could tell me what to do. I met Frank in prison and he let me work for him."

"How much money did you get?" I asked.

"Almost eight hundred or almost nine hundred. I don't count so good. What should I do? I could leave here, but where would I go and what would I do when I got there?"

"First, you need to give me the money."

Bennie hesitated. I raised my eyebrows.

"Do you want to figure this out on your own?" I asked. Bennie handed over the sack. Why can't all my boyfriends act like Bennie?

"I'll talk to the sheriff. Maybe you can turn yourself in."

"I don't know," said Bennie. "I'm not a squealer, even on myself."

"Okay." I thought for a moment. "Maybe he could catch you."

"That's better."

"Bennie, meet me here at the same time in two days. Let me see what I can arrange."

I stopped by the sheriff's office the next day.

"Did you make any progress on the robbery?" I asked.

"I'm starting to get reports about strangers. So far, they're just hobos or folks passing through, but it won't take much longer. There is one more thing that's strange, though."

"What's that?"

"Carl Elkins, the bank president, estimates the robber made off with twenty thousand dollars."

My legs felt shaky. I looked for a chair and sat down.

"You picked up that bag," said the Sheriff. "Was it as big as the one Santa Claus carries?"

I shook my head.

"I didn't think so. That much money wouldn't fit in a regular bag. I know that weeks ago the bank auditors scheduled a visit for next Friday. It seems to me that the bank is in trouble."

"Do you think that the bank president set up the robbery?"

"No, but he's trying to take advantage of it. The bank records will sink him in the end. He's just stalling. My guess is that he's been making bad loans and taking a little out of the till for a long time. He's been on the phone all night, getting pledges from successful farmers and business owners. There's a reward of a thousand dollars for the capture of the robber."

"That's more than . . ."

The sheriff raised his eyebrows. "More than?"

"More than enough to get people out carrying guns and looking for the robber. It could turn dangerous."

"I know, but what can I do about it?"

"I have an idea."

* * * *

Thursday evening at five forty-two, Sarah Elkins left home to attend choir practice at Covenant Presbyterian Church. At five fifty, Bennie slipped through the back door of the banker's house with the sheriff and me close behind. Bennie walked quietly into the library while the sheriff and I waited in the hall. Carl Elkins sat at his desk staring at a ledger.

"Which set of books is that, Mr. Banker?" Bennie raised his gun. "Is that the one that shows how less than a thousand dollars becomes twenty thousand?"

Elkins pointed his finger at Bennie. "You're the robber."

"I'm one of the robbers," said Bennie. "I'm the one who used a gun. You're the one who cooked the books. As long as I'm on the hook for twenty thousand, I might as well have that much. Where is it?"

I was impressed that Bennie remembered what I told him to say.

"You fool," said Elkins. "It's long gone in bad loans and un-collectible bills."

Bennie laughed. "You're the fool if you think I believe that. The robbery gave you perfect cover to make another personal withdrawal. I'll take that money."

Elkins cursed.

"I could just kill you and search on my own," Bennie said.

"It's in the drawer to my right."

"Open the drawer slowly. Tell me now if there's a gun in there."

"Only money."

"Move away from the desk." Bennie walked to the desk and looked into the open drawer.

Elkins dived at Bennie, grabbed his wrist and wrenched the gun out of his hand. Panting, Elkins turned the gun on Bennie.

"That's enough, Carl." The sheriff stepped into the room.

"It's the bank robber," Elkins said. "I caught him sneaking into my house. He said he's already sent the money he took in the robbery to his friends out of state. He, he came here to kill me so I can't identify him."

"It won't work, Carl," said the sheriff. "I heard everything."

Elkins looked at the gun in his hand as if he'd never seen one before. He lifted it slowly.

"Carl, don't."

Elkins pointed the gun at Bennie. Then he swung it around toward Allen. His hand shook as he put the barrel in his mouth.

"Carl," said the sheriff.

Elkins pulled the trigger. The hammer landed with a click on an empty chamber. Elkins dropped the gun and stood without moving while the sheriff handcuffed him.

When I came into the sheriff's office the next day, Bennie was in one of the cells, whistling while he tried to teach Elkins how to play slap jack. I dropped the sack of money from the bank on the sheriff's desk.

"How much is it?"

"Eight hundred thirty seven dollars."

"A search of the house turned up less than that. I'll bet the audit will show that the bank didn't keep enough cash on hand. With the robbery solved, the FDIC will cover everybody's deposits. People will be okay. Thanks for talking Bennie into telling you where he hid the money. Thanks for bringing it in."

"I'll be satisfied with my half of the reward."

Sheriff Allen smiled at me. "Half? I'm not eligible for the reward, so you'll get the whole amount in the next couple of days. I expect you'll head back to New York after that."

"I suppose so. Bob is an awful nice guy, but I don't think I'm a small town girl. With my old boyfriend out of the picture, there's nothing keeping me from going back to New York."

"I'm glad you can stay or go as you please. Oh, my wife heard about the bank robbery. I'm sure it must be the talk of the county. She told me to invite you to dinner tonight."

I stepped closer to him and smiled. "And after dinner? For dessert?"

"As a beautiful, smart young woman from the big city once said to me, Roxie, you'll never know until you ask."

Warren Bull *is the award-winning author of* Abraham Lincoln for the Defense *(PublishAmerica 2003, SmashWords 2010), a short story collection,* Murder Manhattan Style *(Ninth Month Publihsing, 2010), and more than a 20 short stories. His web site is WarrenBull.com. He is proud to be a Mister in Crime.*

SOMETHING FISHY

BY PEGGY EHRHART

It's a perfect night for a moonlit cruise around Manhattan. Add a shipboard wedding and a wedding reception with some good blues, courtesy of yours truly and friends, and what could be nicer?

"How about some champagne?" Josh Bergman calls, raising a champagne flute. He's leaning against the ship's railing, elegant in a tux, cummerbund, bow tie, the whole works. I make my way toward him, swaying from the combination of the river's waves and my rhinestone-strap spike-heeled sandals. I pulled them out of the back of my closet this morning as soon as I hung up the phone. They go great with my silver lamé sheath dress from the Rescue Mission Thrift Shop.

"Thanks for filling in at the last minute," Josh says. The condos of northern New Jersey slip by as the ship heads south, lights on the shore just starting to come on as twilight deepens late on this June evening. We'll end up right back where we started though, Arianna and Karl having become man and wife on our circuit of the island.

Josh smiles and his eyes crinkle at the corners. He's been a fixture on the New York music scene forever, but he doesn't seem to age. His explanation is that the blues keep him young.

"No problem," I say. "But is Belle going to recover?" She's the singer who usually does wedding gigs with Josh's band.

He shrugs and looks pensive for a minute. "It's nothing physical, and she has good days and bad days. But she can't seem to pull herself out of it. Splitting up with Tom really wiped her out."

We're on the back deck setting up for the reception while the guests cluster around the bar inside, waiting for the bride to emerge from the master stateroom for the ceremony.

"All set," says the drummer, a guy named Robby. With a satisfied sigh, he gives a last twist to the bolt that connects his biggest cymbal to its stand, then climbs up onto his stool and tests the snare with an experimental tap. "What do you say we warm up? Somebody call one."

Josh sets the champagne flute on his amp and reaches for the gleaming black Stratocaster balanced in a stand nearby. "Blues?"

"Do you have to ask?" says Phil. He grabs his bass from its stand and ducks as he pulls the strap over his head.

"Got your harps, man?" Josh nods toward Tom, the fourth member of the combo, who's just rounded the corner with a champagne flute in one hand.

Tom rummages in a small black satchel and brings up a handful of harmonicas. "Ready to go."

"'Everyday I've Got the Blues.'" Josh settles his guitar strap around his neck and twitches his shoulders as he balances the guitar to his satisfaction. I adjust the mike stand to the height I need for my five feet nine inches plus the spike heels. When I look up, Josh catches my eye. "B flat okay for you, Maxx?"

"More than okay. It's the only key I can do it in."

"Can't do B flat," Tom says. "I just brought the harps I thought I'd need tonight."

"No big deal," Josh replies. "'Sweet Home Chicago' then. In E."

And we're off, Josh launching the tune with a classic blues turnaround, notes chiming in silvery pairs, ending up with a satisfying chord fingered one string at a time. I sing a couple of verses and the guys take solos, even Phil and Robby. As we wind down and Josh finishes things off with one last solo, the rear deck starts filling up with people, drifting back to take their places in the neat rows of seats that flank an aisle leading to a flower-bedecked arch against the back railing.

The guys play a bluesy version of the Wedding March while I settle into a seat in the back row and study the set list. Everything on it looks familiar except the tune that starts the second set, something called "Fish." But the bride's going to sit in with the band for that one so it doesn't matter that I don't have a clue what it is.

I look up when Arianna makes her grand entrance, solo, gliding up the aisle toward Karl, her waiting groom, tall and imposing in his perfectly tailored tux. Her dress is a strapless number, white of course, with an elegant skirt tucked up in little puffs and sweeping the deck of the ship. Her dark hair is arranged in a smooth updo, and a wreath of tiny white orchids holds a gauzy veil in place. It doesn't hide her face though—Arianna would never go for that.

The veil simply floats over her bare shoulders and all the way to the hem of her dress.

As soon as Arianna and Karl are pronounced man and wife, the party begins, with the caterers popping champagne corks and filling champagne flutes as we kick things off with "She's Into Something." In no time the chairs are folded and whisked away and the dancing starts with an abandon that soon has guys tossing their jackets aside and women stepping out of their fancy shoes.

Arianna is boogying as best she can in the elaborate dress, holding up the skirt with both hands as her feet sketch quick patterns in time to the beat. She's even left the veil on. The river breezes catch it from time to time and it billows aloft or drifts across her gorgeous face.

Karl can't take his eyes off her, and a lot of the other guys are watching her too, more closely than they're watching their own partners.

But as Josh steps up to the mike to report that the band's about to take a short break—and that Arianna's got the first song when we return, she tugs off the veil, taking the pretty little wreath of orchids with it, and announces that she's got to change into something she can actually *dance* in.

* * * *

The break stretches longer than I expect. The guests have all gone back inside to hang around the bar—unless you're dancing it's actually a little chilly. The other musicians have wandered off, too, except for Josh, who's noodling quietly on his guitar. It's dark now, as dark as it ever gets in New York with so much light radiating from the city. Along the shore, the city's workaday grunge has been transformed to twinkly magic, Brooklyn on one side and Manhattan on the other.

The bride's sister, Arlene, reels around the corner. "Is she back here hanging around with the musicians?" she says, hands on hips and a frown carved into her otherwise pretty brow. Beauty runs in the family.

"Who? There's nobody here but Maxx," says Josh, aiming his guitar neck at me.

"You haven't seen her?" The frown becomes deeper, for real now, not the mock exasperation it was before.

She whirls around and starts down the narrow aisle that leads along the side of the cabin to the forward deck. Then she stops and utters a startled cry, gazing down into the water. Her hand reaches for the railing as if she needs the support.

Josh and I hurry toward her, shooting puzzled glances at each other, and when we reach her side, we look into the water.

Arianna floats by, still dressed in her wedding finery. She's a pale blur poised beneath the surface of the Hudson, pulled down by the heavy dress, soaked through, as the veil spins out behind like a fragile net for some delicate fish.

Arleen cries out. We all edge backwards, staying even with the body as the ship moves past.

A few people stick their heads out of the door that leads to the bar, curious at first, then solemn and alarmed. They hurry toward us. Soon a panicked crowd is clustered at the railing.

"It's Arianna!" Shocked murmurs pass through the crowd. "Where's the captain?" A small woman hurries along the aisle that leads to the forward deck, calling for the captain.

The life preserver someone belatedly thinks to toss doesn't do any good. Arianna's not floundering. She's just floating, already gone.

The captain's call to 911 brings a police boat, speedy, and they retrieve her body. Then police are onboard, and when we reach the pier where we started we don't go ashore till we've each had an interview, not with the uniform guys but with some other cops in sports jackets that come aboard. The one I talk to gives me his card at the end and says to call him if I think of anything else. I put the card on my dresser when I get home.

* * * *

Lots of things keep me awake that night: I keep seeing people's faces, especially Karl's, puzzlement as he leans over the railing replaced by misery when he turns away. I finally sink into that state at the edge of consciousness when the real world and the dream world swirl together in a kind of gumbo.

The set list for the gig is part of the gumbo, especially the tune Arianna never got to sing. "Fish." An abbreviation, obviously. The set list was full of them, but I recognized the others. "Rooster" was "Little Red Rooster," "Chicago" was "Sweet Home Chicago," "Angel" was "Sweet Little Angel," and so on.

But what was "Fish"?

* * * *

The next afternoon, I'm almost happy to head off along Tonnelle Avenue for my day job at Aldo's Seafood Chalet. Taking orders for shrimp scampi and fried calamari will be a welcome distraction, not to mention gazing at the cowboy-themed murals left over from the restaurant's past as a barbecue joint.

I'm still in kind of a daze though.

"Hello-o-o?" The solitary woman hogging a table for four has craned her wrinkled neck to catch my eye.

I shake my head a few times to pull myself back to the present. And I notice Aldo bearing down on me, a disgusted expression twisting his mouth under his silly mustache.

"I asked you if the red snapper was fresh," the woman says.

Before I can answer, Aldo chimes in. "It was swimming just this morning, ma'am. I can assure you it couldn't be fresher." His disgusted expression has turned into a smarmy smile, but directed at her, not at me. He pulls me away for a lecture about daydreaming on the job.

I hardly listen. The red snapper was swimming just this morning. Fish swim, of course. Fish *got* to swim, like in the first line of "Can't Help Lovin' That Man of Mine." *That's* the tune Arianna was going to sing after the break. It's the perfect tune for a bride to sing to her husband on their wedding day.

Arianna had sung it to other guys before, even to Josh, though that romance had subsided into friendship long ago, which is how he got the wedding gig. And she'd sung it sitting in with my band at the Hot Spot. All the while, the satisfied expression on her face suggested she was counting the guys in the audience who looked like they wished she couldn't help loving *them*. No evil of the dead and all that, but Arianna was a shameless flirt. Only a guy as rich and self-confident as Karl would even have a chance to tame her.

Remembering that night at the Hot Spot triggers something—a vague thought that gradually takes form. A thought about something that happened at the wedding gig. A thought about something fishy.

* * * *

When I get back to my apartment at eleven p.m., I go through my usual homecoming ritual. The first step is to get rid of the fancy pushup bra. It's not the most comfortable bra in the world and I'm happy to take it off at the end of the day. But without it I wouldn't have a figure anybody would look twice at. Then I pull on my Red Bank Blues Festival T-shirt and a pair of biking shorts. Finally I grab a can of Bud out of the refrigerator. But tonight, before I put on a Big Mama Thornton CD and sag into the big chair, I dig out my copy of the Fake Book. It's the indispensable band reference, especially for jazz, filled with unofficial transcriptions of almost any tune you can name. I check one little detail then I set it by the door and get the Big Mama Thornton CD going.

Thursday night is band rehearsal at Feedback in Manhattan. It's a couple nights away, but I'll take the Fake Book to the copy place tomorrow and make some copies. The guys in my band might remember the changes to "Can't Help Lovin' That Man of Mine"— but they might not, and I want to do a little experiment.

* * * *

Thursday night, I luck into a parking spot on Thirtieth just as a van is pulling out. The spot is big enough for my old Bonneville and just a few doors from the building housing Feedback. I follow a couple of kids with gig bags slung over their shoulders down the crowded sidewalk and into the building's lobby. The elevator doors are closing, but one of the kids makes a dash for it and holds them with his arm. As I follow him and his friend into the elevator, I notice Josh in the corner.

"Change your schedule or what?" I ask. "I don't usually see you here on Thursdays."

"Belle's feeling better and she wants to work on some new tunes."

Josh looks more like himself tonight than he did in the fancy wedding duds. His white T-shirt sets off his swarthy skin, already tan though summer has barely started, and a pair of faded jeans skim his slender hips.

"Pretty horrible the other night," he says. "Are you okay?" I nod. The elevator shudders a few times, groans its way up to the sixth floor, and then jolts to a stop. "Cops give you one of their cards?"

I nod again. "You?"

"Yeah. Think of anything else to tell them?"

"I'm not sure."

* * * *

When we're about halfway through the set list for our next Hot Spot gig, I pull out the copies I made from the Fake Book.

Michael is retuning his bass, an intense expression on his thin face, and I know better than to interrupt him when he's concentrating. And Neil is staring straight ahead in a contented daze, probably thanks to a few tokes of marijuana in the Feedback bathroom before we got started. But Stan looks interested. And Mitzi's new enough to the band that she comes to rehearsal like an earnest student willing to do whatever the teacher wants, even though the drummer doesn't need to know the chord changes to play a tune. She holds out her hand for a copy.

"Oh, I remember this." Stan shakes his shaggy hair out of his eyes as I hand him his copy. He's wearing his favorite warm-weather outfit—a Fender Guitars T-shirt that manages to be huge even on his six and a half foot frame, and a pair of much-washed jeans with rips in the knees. "It was Arianna's song," he adds, his face suddenly grave. "Is that why we're doing it? Because she's dead?"

News travels fast through the Feedback grapevine.

"Something like that."

I lay a copy of the song on Neil's keyboard. He barely glances at it before his fingers get busy, improvising on the changes and coming up with something Bach might have played.

"Hang on a minute." I hold up my hands like I'm pushing the sound back, but with a smile.

Michael plucks his low E string and listens with a satisfied nod. He takes his copy of the tune and squints at it. "It's not really what I'd call blues." He frowns. "You don't want to add this to the set list do you? Because I don't think it goes with our style."

"No, I don't want to add it to the set list."

"Then why—"

"Please just humor me. I want to see something."

"I don't like spending time on tunes that aren't relevant to the band's future."

"*Please.*" I grit my teeth.

"You want to do it in E flat like it says here?" Stan asks.

"No. Let's try it in B flat."

"That's how Arianna did it," Stan says mournfully.

"I know."

We launch into it, Neil contributing a tasteful little intro, Mitzi pulling out a set of brushes in deference to the tune's jazz pedigree.

But I have to stop after the first verse. B flat might have been Arianna's key but it sure isn't mine. We try a couple other keys till we settle on D, and I manage to get all the way through without running out of voice on either the low notes or the high ones.

"Why are we messing around with this?" Michael asks with a more intense version of the frown that's his customary expression.

"We're done now," I say. "And I just learned something very important."

Some tunes give you a certain amount of wiggle room. If the melody uses a narrow range of notes, you have a choice of keys. But if the melody goes real high or real low—or both—you have to find the key where your voice can handle all the notes. "Can't Help Lovin' That Man of Mine" is kind of a workout. Arianna probably only had one good key for it, B flat, the key she sang it in with my band.

* * * *

Tony is manning the desk out front. His homely face creases into a smile when he sees me emerge from the long hall that leads to the rehearsal rooms.

"What room does Josh Bergman have tonight?" I ask him.

"G, I think." He crinkles his forehead and consults a schedule book on the counter in front of him, running a stubby finger down a page smudged with penciled notations of bands, rooms, and hours. "Yep." He looks up. "G it is."

I hate to interrupt Josh while he's practicing, but this is important. I can hear the music as I approach Studio G, and I recognize Josh's elegant blues lines, playful and intense at the same time. I tug open the outer door then push at the inner door. The double doors are supposed to make things soundproof but sound leaks out anyway. You can always hear what everybody else is doing unless your band is playing too, in which case you drown them out.

Belle is singing, caught up in the tune and looking almost like I remembered her, except she's so thin she looks frail. When they catch sight of me, Josh signals Robby to stop, and "Night Train" winds down, ending with a few hesitant taps on the snare.

"Glad you're better." I give Belle a quick hug, and then tug Josh toward the door.

"Sorry to bother you," I say when we're out in the hall, a version of "My Funny Valentine" leaking from the door to our left and some death-metal thing leaking from the door to our right.

"What's going on?"

"How did Tom end up at that gig the other night? He's not a usual member of your band, is he?"

Josh wipes his hand over his forehead. His skin is gleaming with a fine sheen of sweat. "He called me—out of nowhere. I hadn't seen the guy for months, even though he and Belle were living together till recently. Said he could use some work that paid better than bar gigs and asked me to keep him in mind. I'd just been talking to Arianna about the wedding gig, so I thought, okay—I'll throw it his way. He's a great harp player."

"That's the other thing I wanted to ask you. Do you know if he ever played "Can't Help Lovin' That Man of Mine" with Arianna?"

Josh blows out a little puff of breath. "Probably. At one time he was the man she couldn't help lovin'."

"I thought that was you."

"I recovered," he says with a grin. "I figured Tom had too, even though he took it hard when Arianna left him. I told him that's whose wedding it was going to be, but he said he was cool with it. It really knocked Belle low when he took off, but what goes around comes around. He didn't manage to hang on to Arianna very long. Karl's got money and money talks. Arianna may have thought it was fun to hang out with musicians, but deep down she knew what she really wanted."

What Josh just told me about Tom and Arianna confirms a rumor I'd heard, and it ties in with what I'm beginning to suspect. I go on. "Did you let that cop in on this stuff?"

"That Tom and Arianna were once an item?" Josh says. "No." He draws the word out and shakes his head. "I'd have had to admit she snared me once too . . . not to mention half the other guys on that boat."

"At the wedding gig, we wanted to do a tune in B flat to warm up," I say. "But Tom didn't have the right harmonica." Josh nods. "Arianna was going to do 'Can't Help Lovin' That Man of Mine' when she sat in with the band after the break—that's what the abbreviation 'Fish' meant in the set list. Right?"

"Right."

"Is Tom usually the kind of guy who keeps track of who does what tune in which key?"

Josh laughs. "I've been in bands with him where he was practically the band historian. Why?"

"Arianna did that tune with my band at the Hot Spot last year, and she did it in B flat. If Tom's played it with her before and he's so good at keeping track of things, how come he didn't bring the harmonica he'd need for a tune in B flat?"

Josh shrugs.

"Unless he knew she wouldn't be alive to sing it when the time came."

"She wouldn't be alive to sing it because he had something else in mind . . ."

The death-metal band behind the door to our right launches into a new tune and the barrage of howling guitars makes it hard to talk for a few minutes. Then the guitars give way to a foreboding bass riff.

"Do you have that cop's card on you?" I say. "I left mine at home."

_____

Peggy Ehrhart *is a former English professor with a Ph.D. in Medieval Literature. She is the author of the Maxx Maxwell mysteries, published by Five Star/Gale/Cengage and featuring blues-singer sleuth Elizabeth "Maxx" Maxwell. The audio version of the first Maxx Maxwell mystery,* Sweet Man Is Gone, *is available from Books in Motion as* Blue Murder. *Visit her at PeggyEhrhart.com.*

THE TRUCK CONTEST

BY KAYE GEORGE

The first time I saw it I assumed it was an accident. Assumed some poor schmuck had left a truck out on the ice just a little too late. Every morning on the way to work, I drove the winding road around Lake Minnetonka and followed the progress of the yellow pickup, sinking lower and lower as the early spring sun picked up strength.

That first winter in Minnesota, I had noticed right away how Lake Minnetonka becomes a huge playground. The natives use it for snowmobiling, ice skating, and ice fishing. They cavort outside in frigid weather as if it were summertime. I was most fascinated by the ice fishing, though. My dad had never taken me fishing when I was a boy. Hell, he'd never taken me anywhere, except to the track.

I'd done a lot of hard outdoor work in a hot climate recently and had no desire to repeat that sweaty experience. The cold weather did take some adjustment, but I had the Minnesotans' example to follow. And anything was better than being locked up. I bought a lot of new winter clothes, that helped me keep warm.

At the beginning of that first winter, I observed people driving their pickups onto the frozen lake. They unloaded dozens of one-room wooden fishing shacks, mostly homemade, and created a temporary village between Excelsior and Big Island. At work they told me it was called Ice Town. Some of the guys in shipping were avid ice fishers.

The little shacks really did look like a town out there on the frozen lake, with narrow streets laid out where guys drove back and forth to their houses. Some of them even spent the nights there. They hauled in carpeting, huge coolers full of beer, and satellite dishes to give them some of the comforts of home. It was mostly a guy thing—I never saw more than a couple of women. It looked like fun and I thought about giving it a go the next year.

When spring approached, the natives hauled off their fish houses and drove their trucks home. One lone pickup remained, however, that yellow one, parked in a widening puddle on the thinning ice. It was obviously too dangerous to go out and get it. I shook my head every time I saw it and felt sorry for the slob who had left his truck to sink into the lake.

One morning, I lingered on the way to work, watching that damn truck, and arrived a couple minutes late, not unusual for me. So why did Karen, my chubby little boss, give me the evil eye?

Get used to it, I thought. Some people don't live for this sorry job. Who would want to? I inhabited a cubicle, an invention of the devil himself, I'm sure, and processed orders for imported junk. Little plastic bracelets and gifts bags, shit they sold at the Dollar Store. I was as far from my previous address as I could get, and the company didn't do background checks. That's why I worked there. Karen as my boss lady I could handle. I even flirted with her some when I started there. The one who got to me, though, was Clark.

That day, in the break room, Clark mentioned the Truck Contest.

"What's that?" I asked, waiting for him to quit fiddling with the sugar packets so I could get some for my coffee.

Clark cleared his throat wetly, one of his least obnoxious mannerisms, raised his superior eyebrows almost up to his wig, a toupee that might have been a squirrel in its former life, and informed me that bets were placed on when the truck would sink.

"So that yellow pickup doesn't belong to some poor sap who just procrastinated too long?"

"Hell no. What a stupid thing to think." He picked his nose, stirred a small mountain of sugar in his Styrofoam coffee cup, and strolled off to his cube, the one next to mine.

Clark was not a desirable cubicle neighbor. Most mornings his radio blared stock market reports, and in the afternoon he listened to, as far as I could tell, the worst music ever recorded, big band and polkas. Where did he find those stations? My protests would prompt him to lower the volume for half a day, then he would twist the dial back up and dare me to say something. I decided I had to start raising my issues with Karen.

It really didn't bother me, working for a woman. I know a lot of guys couldn't do it. But I was just lucky to have a job, and, if I had to work for a broad, I could handle it. This broad, however, wasn't the one I'd pick. I think the feeling was mutual. She'd flirted back when I started, but was always too busy to meet me anywhere after work. I dropped the act eventually. I wasn't going to get any from her.

I rapped on the door to her office—she had an actual office, with a door—and entered when she told me to come in, after the second knock.

I walked up to her desk, remained standing. "You know Clark, in the cube next to me?"

She looked up from her paperwork and frowned. Those little plucked eyebrows were cute. "Jesus, Roy, how would I not know Clark? I'm his boss, or hadn't you noticed?"

"Yeah, sure."

"You have a problem with Clark?" She drew out his name, those fleshy lips caressed it. Not good.

"Well, not with Clark. With his radio. It's hard to work with it turned up so high, you know?"

"No, I don't know."

"Can you say something to him?"

"I'll see." She bent her head to the papers on her desk and I left, not hopeful.

I tried a few more times, but Karen barely listened to my complaints. She only mentioned the radio to Clark once and, when she began picking up the phone and dialing it as soon as I walked through her door, I gave up. Her office reeked of Obsession. Made me nauseated.

One day I grabbed my dictionary off the metal shelf above my monitor to check the spelling of a word for the report I was writing. The page was missing. I looked up and Clark stood in his cubicle, leering at me over the short wall that divided us.

"What are you so happy about?" I asked. He didn't answer, just kept smirking.

"Do you know anything about this page that's torn out of my book?" I asked him, trying to be as civil as possible.

"Oh that. Yeah." He scratched his armpit. "They were out of toilet paper in the john."

I stared. "You used my dictionary for toilet paper?"

"Worked pretty good." He turned away and plopped down into his chair.

I felt my sanity straining against its mooring, threatening to float off, out of my Cubicle From Hell. There was no way I was going to go through the job hunting process again. It had taken months to find this indoor position. Most other employers checked references more thoroughly than these people.

About a week later I saw that my company directory was missing pages. Clark stood and grinned over the partition when I riffled through the pages to find a number. I didn't say anything.

Something had to give and it wasn't going to be my mental health. I'd had some problems in that area in the past and didn't need to repeat the trial and the hospital stay. To say nothing of the prison sentence.

So I plotted all summer until I figured my plan was perfect.

I started buddying up to old Clark in the fall and it was pathetic how eagerly he joined me for our stag outings. One fine crisp afternoon I had him over to my apartment for a hockey game on television. He didn't seem to know much about it, asking me what "icing" and "off sides" meant. I took a deep breath and explained as much as I could to him.

Next I invited him to make the round of sports bars with me. I couldn't believe the idiot actually got a temporary tattoo, shaped like a hockey stick, just like one of mine. I guess he was trying to get into hockey. He didn't go for aping the skull on my other arm.

All winter I endured his poisonous company and things improved slightly at work, but not enough to make me want to abandon my plan. Some days in the office he would ignore me completely and go back to the old radio bit. More pages went missing from the new dictionary I had bought. I don't think he really wiped his ass with them, but couldn't be sure. I bought another one and kept it in my drawer.

Clark and Karen would sometimes disappear together for an hour or so. I refused to even think about that, not wanting to ruin my lunch.

Other days he would come over and sit with me during breaks, trying to talk about sports. Those days were worse than the blaring radio days. I don't know why he sometimes targeted me. Maybe he and Karen had occasional lovers' tiffs. Shudder.

The third dictionary, the one hidden in my drawer, disappeared.

I bought an ice house and set it up in Ice Town, but didn't drill my fishing hole. In fact, I didn't spend much time there, not wanting to become a familiar face to my neighbors on the lake. I invited

Clark out twice. He seemed impressed with my little shack, although I didn't have a television set, and had only a small ice chest for the beer—no gas-powered mini-fridge. Clark's pole looked as new as mine.

The first time, Clark offered to drill the hole inside the fish house, but stood in the middle of the circle of ice. If the hole were a little bigger, it would have put him into the water when he finished cutting, just like in a cartoon. I suppressed my laughter as I had been suppressing my contempt—no, my hatred—for the last several months, and finished up with the auger myself. I at least knew how to drill a hole in the ice. Afterwards I thought maybe I should have let him fall in. We fished and drank beer for awhile. It was obvious Clark knew as little about ice fishing as I did.

The second time out, what surprised me was the lingering scent of Obsession wafting from Clark's ragged rug. The boss and Clark must be really, really tight, I thought. Looks like someone will miss him. Good thing it's nobody I like.

Finally, it was zero hour—all the fishing houses had to be removed by the end of the day. The contest truck had been positioned, a green Dodge this year. I picked Clark up and we made our way out to Lake Minnetonka for the third time.

Killing Clark was easy. After all, I'd had good teachers in stir. Those bums had been caught, sure. But most of them had gotten away with three or four times as much stuff as the cops would ever know about. There's no better place to learn how to commit a crime than prison.

Since his body would never be found I just stabbed him with my fishing knife as he hunched over the hole, looking at his line as it disappeared into the inky water. After dark, I tossed the weapon into my trunk along with his body. I knew his corpse was leaving forensic evidence there, but why would anyone ever have reason to look for evidence in my trunk? Who would ever connect his disappearance with me?

A little later, when everyone had gone, I drove over to the contest truck and dragged his body out of my trunk. I didn't have to worry about leaving footprints or tire tracks in the thin layer of snow that lay on the surface of the ice, since it would turn to slush in the morning sun. I heaved his body into the cab, which was not that easy since rigor was just starting. His wig fell off and I tossed it back into the trunk of my car. The stench of Obsession hit me in the face as I slammed the trunk shut. I'd never be able to date anyone who used that scent. Hell, maybe I'd never open the damn trunk again.

After today, no one would be allowed onto the ice. And you'd have to be crazy to attempt it. It was cracking a little already that night. When the truck sank, his body would never be discovered. There was no reason to be extra careful about any of this.

Karen seemed distraught when Clark didn't come to work Monday. She called me into her office, something she'd never done before. I gagged at the reek of the perfume. She held a few sheets of paper in her hand so tightly they crinkled.

"Clark isn't here. That's not like him. He told me you guys were going ice fishing over the weekend. What happened?"

I shrugged. "He didn't show up."

A tear tried to fall down her cheek, but the cheek was too round and the teardrop trickled over in front of her ear.

She showed up for a couple of meetings with red-rimmed eyes, clutching damp tissues. The cops came to the office and talked to everyone and, after they'd left, Karen set up a howl in her office behind the closed door. She was too distracted to micro-manage anyone. I loved it.

She was back to her usual bitchy self in a few days, though, hovering and correcting every report I turned in.

I smiled every time I drove past the truck, morning and evening, and saw it had sunk another few inches. Down, down, Clark, down to hell, where you belong. Work was pretty peaceful without him. I even started keeping my new dictionary out on the open shelf where I could get to it a whole lot more easily.

Finally, one afternoon the truck's green roof disappeared and I had a little one-man celebration that night. I even continued it and called in sick the next day.

The winner of the contest was announced in the paper. I thought maybe I'd place a bet next year. What a great tradition. What wonderful people these Minnesotans were, to think up such a thing. First ice fishing, then the Truck Contest. Great place. Glad I found it.

Saturday after the contest ended, I decided to go out to the lake. I pulled into a parking area alongside the road, intending to gaze for awhile at the spot where the truck rested. I wanted to contemplate the place of my liberation. I had even brought a folding chair and a couple of brews.

The parking area was crammed with cars. A crowd stood along the edge of the lake. Something must be going on. Something to do with the truck?

I dragged the chair out of the trunk and carried it over to the edge of the crowd, where I could get a good view of the lake, unfolded the chair, sat, and popped a tab top.

Then did a double take.

The commotion centered around the spot where the truck had gone in. A winch was pulling it from the bottom of the lake.

"What's taking so long?" Karen said behind me. My beer can hit the ground. "I wonder why they've stopped. Gosh, they're all looking in the front seat."

"Why . . . why are they bringing the . . . the truck up?" I stammered.

"They always do, Roy. That's what we're all here to watch. You think they'd leave those rusty trucks in the lake?" Karen gave me an annoyed look. "What a stupid thing to think. You look pale, Roy."

I twisted around in my chair to get a good look at her.

Her smirk looked like Clark's. "You dropped something out of your trunk." She held Clark's wig, gingerly, between her chubby little thumb and forefinger.

Kaye George is an Agatha-nominated short story writer. Her comic mystery, Choke, *is available as of May 2011. She lives near Austin, Texas, having lived in most parts of the US. Some of her more interesting jobs have been tractor factory janitor and nurse's aide. Her webpage: www.kayegeorge.com.*

AMAZING GRACE

BY BETSY BITNER

I have been planning my husband's funeral for twelve years. No, he doesn't have a slow-acting terminal illness. And he's not some bigwig requiring a send-off befitting his stature in the community. It's just that, like the Scouts say, you've got to be prepared. Everyone has to go sooner or later and, with any luck, my husband's time will come sooner. Call me an optimist.

It started when I went to the funeral for one of my parents' long-time friends, an extremely large man who'd wasted away to nothing from cancer. At the end of the service, the wife followed her husband's casket out of the church as a lone bagpiper played *Amazing Grace*. While others reached for tissues to dab at their eyes and blow their noses, I was transported by the bagpipe's mournful sound. I glanced at the wife in her black boiled-wool suit and pearls, gripping the arm of her grown son for support, and I envied her. No, it was more than envy. I wanted to be her. I wanted that casket to contain my husband, Frank. And then a wave of emotion swept over me. Not grief, nor guilt for having had such a thought, but excitement. Did "widow" always have to have a negative connotation?

> *Amazing Grace, how sweet the sound,*
> *That saved a wretch like me.*
> *I once was lost but now am found,*
> *Was blind, but now I see.*

I haven't always felt this way. The early years were good. Frank was charming, polite, and attentive when we were dating. Nothing like he is now. I would never have married him if he'd been that way. I'm not stupid. And he wasn't that bad for the first few years. But as his job got to Frank, Frank took it out on me. He finally realized he was never going to get to be the plant manager, or a foreman, or even a shift supervisor. He was beaten down by years of thinking he would be someone and finding out, in the end, that he was just Frank.

He couldn't control things at work, so he controlled things at home. Including me. Our marriage deteriorated over the years as we slid slowly towards our current state of unhappiness. I never dared to imagine him dead while the kids were young. A child shouldn't grow up without a parent. I would never have wished that on them. What kind of mother would that make me?

Once the kids were grown and had moved out of the house, it was just the two of us again. We hadn't really been alone together since we were first married. It was pretty clear that this time the honeymoon was over. Frank would come home from work at the plant and take out his frustrations with the foreman or the weather or the traffic on me. He'd go on and on about my shortcomings.

But one day, while Frank was griping about how I'd put too many onions in the meatloaf and now he wasn't going to be able to sleep that night, my mind drifted to the sound of bagpipes playing *Amazing Grace*. The knot that had taken up permanent residence between my shoulder blades began to loosen. I pictured Frank inside a casket, in peaceful, eternal slumber, eyes closed, and more importantly, mouth shut. Frank's funeral could become my secret fantasy.

> *T'was Grace that taught my heart to fear,*
> *And Grace, my fears relieved.*
> *How precious did that Grace appear,*
> *The hour I first believed.*

Why did I put up with Frank if things were so bad? Why not just leave him? Because if I left him, I would have to leave the house, too, which had been my parents' house, on the shores of Lake Pleasant. It wasn't big, but it was mine. And it was full of memories. Memories were all I had left of happy times in my life. Frank may have taken the shine off what was supposed to be our golden years, but he wasn't going to take my memories.

My father loved to fish on the lake. He'd take me with him when I was a girl. We'd get up at the crack of dawn to fish for salmon, pike, or small-mouth bass. I never complained about the early hour because fishing on the lake was our special time together. My mother would make sandwiches for us the night before, and I happily carried our lunch basket as I tromped through the wet grass to the dock. My father would help me into the boat and get me settled before starting up the small outboard motor and setting off.

Once we'd reached his intended destination (always a secret to prevent others from homing in on that day's quarry), he would open his tackle box and ask me which fly he should use. The array of flies inside the box dazzled me and I took my time looking them over before I made my decision. I wanted to make sure I got it right. My father would wait patiently, as if we had all day. Eventually I would point to one, and he would smile and say "All right then, a *Maid of the Mill* it is," and he would pluck the fly from the box and tie it to his line. If I happened to pick a fly meant for bass and he was fishing for salmon that day, my father never let on. But after some time with no nibbles on the line, he'd smile and wink. "The fish must still be asleep," he's say. "Let's try something else and see if we can't wake them up." Then he'd tie on a *Minister's Dog* or a *Hairy Mary* and cast off. He valued my opinion, even when it was wrong. I never worried about making a mistake back then.

Now I won't get through a day without making a mistake. At least from Frank's point of view. He blames me for everything— big things, little things, things that can't possibly be my fault. Like last week when I told Frank to take an umbrella because it was supposed to rain. That afternoon his favorite ball team was ahead 2-0, when the game was called for rain. After the game resumed that evening, his team ended up losing 3-2. The next morning he yelled at me that I should've kept my stupid mouth shut because I jinxed the team. He went on and on about it.

After he left, I went to my closet. Way in the back I keep my black suits. I have several, in different sizes, to accommodate my ever-changing waistline. If I'd had to put one on that day, it would've been the wool gabardine double-breasted jacket and the skirt with the comfortable waistband. I pulled the hanger from the rod, examined the suit and used a lint brush to tidy up the shoulders. I fingered the brass buttons. They'd compliment the necklace that had belonged to my mother. I imagined how I'd look walking behind Frank's casket as it left the church, and I began to forget that morning's tirade.

Through many dangers, toils and snares
I have already come;
'Tis Grace that brought me safe thus far
and Grace will lead me home.

My father taught Frank to fly fish. Frank had fished before we met, but only with bait. Dad taught him the finer points of casting, as well as how to tie flies. After we were married, my father even showed Frank his best fishing spots. When my father died, he left the house to me and he left his fishing gear, including his fly-tying equipment, to Frank. Frank kept the gear, but he didn't wait long to trade in my dad's boat for a fancy new one with all the bells and whistles my father never needed.

I missed that boat and the happy times spent fishing when I was growing up. My fishing days are over, now. Oh, I'd tried to fish with Frank. But it wasn't the same. His self-centered pursuit was the opposite of my father's attentiveness. As far as Frank was concerned, when it came to fishing, my job was to provide the food, not the company.

* * * *

Frank did take the boys fishing when they were young. I would pack a lunch basket for them, just like my mother had. But Frank would come home grumbling that I'd put the wrong kind of pickle relish in the ham salad. Or complaining that I shouldn't have packed potato chips because they made too much noise and that's why they hadn't caught anything. Back then, when Frank would talk like that, I held it in and focused my attention on making the boys happy. I hadn't yet discovered the therapeutic power of funeral planning.

As I attended funerals over the years, I took mental notes of what I liked. I was drawn to a casket at one funeral, made of dark, polished mahogany with large silver-colored handles along the sides. It was beautiful—the perfect final resting place for Frank. I began researching caskets, always when Frank was out on the lake, of course, until I found a similar model that I could afford. It was solid walnut, with a gloss lacquer finish and an almond velvet interior. I thought that the praying hands embroidered on the head panel were lovely, but, in truth, I was more drawn to the fact that its highlights listed a state-of-the-art lid locking mechanism. At last I'd found a casket that was tasteful, affordable, and met all the criteria I required. Solid. Permanent. Soundproof.

Several years ago Frank retired from his job at the plant and took up fishing full-time. He even turned it into a fishing guide business. I wasn't sure, given Frank's personality, that his business would be successful. Fortunately for Frank, fishermen tend to be a taciturn bunch when they're on the water. Frank was smart enough to know when to keep his mouth shut. That ability proved to be a real business asset.

Unwilling to divulge his secret fishing spots on the lake, he took people to the Vissenkill River to fish for brown trout. Frank built quite a reputation through the years as a skilled angler and we had a mantle full of trophies to prove it. Brown trout are notoriously wary and harder to catch than other types of trout, especially with a fly. But fishermen love a challenge, and Frank was gifted at read-ing streams. He would take a group and hike in to a remote area of the Vissenkill, tell them what fly to use and show them where to cast their lines. Frank even developed a special fly, the *Blonde Bombshell*, which proved irresistible to trout. Between acting as a fishing guide and tying flies on my dad's old equipment in the basement, I saw less of Frank than I did when he was working fulltime at the plant.

The thought of Frank's retirement filled me with dread at first, but I began to think it might not be so bad. Then November rolled around and his guide business dropped off for the season. I won-dered if both of us would make it through the winter alive. Thank God for ice fishing. I spent many peaceful hours, cup of tea in hand, staring out our front window at Frank's shanty in the middle of the lake, planning the funeral of my dreams.

> *The Lord has promised good to me.*
> *His word my hope secures.*
> *He will my shield and portion be,*
> *As long as life endures.*

One morning my dreams nearly came to a crashing halt when Frank came into the kitchen with a handful of pamphlets on funer-al planning and a casket catalog. "I found these in the hall closet. What the hell are they doing there?"

I was afraid to look him in the eye for fear that he might be able to read my thoughts. "Oh, those? They must be from when I planned Dad's funeral," I lied.

Frank shoved the papers into the garbage can with disgust. "Maybe if you spent less time on your ass watching Oprah and more time picking up around here, this place wouldn't be such a pigsty."

He slammed the door and I watched him through the kitchen window as he got in his pickup and drove off to meet that day's fishing party. When I was sure he was gone, I retrieved my papers, brushing off the coffee grounds and carefully smoothing the crumpled pages. My hand caressed the top pamphlet, a glossy image of fluffy white clouds in a blue sky on the cover. Above the picture, fancy script lettering promised: "Your healing starts here." My heart wasn't beating as hard in my chest and the prickly feeling under my arms was gone. I poured myself another cup of coffee and turned on Oprah.

Selecting the flowers for Frank's funeral was the easy part. I inherited the gardens around my lake home, as well as my love of gardening, from my mother. From the moment the ground thawed in late spring until the first hard frost in the fall, I felt a sense of renewal from nurturing the life in the soil. During the winter, I stayed sane by pouring through garden catalogs, deciding what new flowers I would plant that coming season. It was a nice change of pace from thinking about planting Frank in the ground.

I envisioned a huge saddle of roses draped over Frank's casket. They would be red, of course. In the language of flowers, red roses symbolize strength of feeling. No one had to know my feelings weren't those of love. And lilies, there would be lots of lilies. A traditional flower of funerals, they quickly became my favorite. In summer, I grew them in my garden and brought bouquets of them inside. In winter, I used lily-scented candles and plug-in air fresheners to fill my house with their thick, sweet scent. My friend, Sally, couldn't understand my fascination with lilies.

"I hate them," she told me. "They're funeral flowers. When I smell them, I think of death."

Well, isn't that the point?

The years passed, and as my loathing for Frank solidified, so did my plans for his funeral. Every habit and quirk repulsed me, from the way he cleared his throat before turning on the television to the way he clicked the tines of his fork on his plate while he was chewing his food. I was particularly aggravated by the fact that my father's fishing gear, which was once a part of so many happy times on the lake, now belonged to Frank. He would sit in the basement, hunched over my father's workbench, using my father's fly-tying vice to tie his *Blonde Bombshells*. He'd lick his callused fingertips and then run them down the thread and then lick his fingers again, over and over, while tying his flies. Another one of his little quirks. It certainly wasn't one he picked up from my father. Or from any other fisherman, for that matter. At least I could derive some comfort from the fact that the money he earned from his fishing business would someday go to pay for his funeral.

Then, last winter, I attended my friend Nancy's funeral. She had died unexpectedly. I hugged her sister, Susan, saying that Nancy had gone too soon. Susan broke down and told me that Nancy's daughter was going to be married that summer. Nancy had been planning the wedding for years, even before her daughter got engaged. She'd kept a wedding file, clipping articles and pictures, taking notes of what she liked at other weddings, hoping to give her daughter the perfect wedding.

"I can't believe she didn't live to see that day," Susan sobbed.

Then it hit me. All this time I'd assumed that Frank would go first and his funeral would be my freedom. But what if I died first and never got to see the happiest day of my life? All my careful planning would have been for nothing. I wouldn't be able to give Frank the funeral of my dreams. If the roles were reversed, I was sure Frank wouldn't put much thought, or money, into my funeral. I'd be lucky if he bought a vase of carnations and a bag of chips. To add insult to injury, he'd get to spend the rest of his days on the lake. Alone. In my house.

> *Yea, when this flesh and heart shall fail,*
> *And mortal life shall cease,*
> *I shall possess within the veil,*
> *A life of joy and peace.*

Frank did not look well this morning when he left to meet his fishing party. Business always picks up in the spring. He works late into the night, tying flies for customers, and leaves early in the morning to meet fishing parties as their guide. Our phone rings almost nonstop this time of year. I do my part for the business, taking orders and messages. Yesterday, I slipped another order onto the pile on his workbench—a big rush job for his specialty, the *Blonde Bombshell*. Frank stayed up all last night trying to fill it. Fishermen, it seems, are the only ones Frank hates to disappoint. As the snows melt, they become impatient to cast their lines into the chilly mountain waters. I'm impatient, too. I want to host a funeral. From the way Frank looked this morning, he won't be disappointing me, either.

My garden is just starting to wake up from its winter nap, and the perennials are beginning to poke through the soil. I'm itching to sink my hands into the just-thawed dirt. The tulip and daffodil bulbs will flower soon, but the garden won't be truly spectacular until summer, when most of the flowers, including my lilies, will be in bloom. Mother Nature rewards the patient gardener. Everything has its time and season.

There's a patch of monkshood down by the dock I've been meaning to transplant. I dug it up yesterday, even though it's really too early in the season to do that. Fall would have been the better time, but I just couldn't wait. Monkshood will be much more deadly in a few months, but I need it now.

Luckily, I don't have to wait for its lovely blue blossoms. The roots of the monkshood plant are its most potent part. Was it my imagination that I felt its strength through my garden gloves as I carried it into the house? Or was it my own power I felt as I chopped the root and added it to the pot of water on the stove? Boiling the root and running the fly-tying thread through the solution was easy. I did it while watching Oprah. Frank's nasty habit of continuously licking his fingers and then the thread while tying his flies went from being disgusting to being incredibly convenient. He did it repeatedly last night while working feverishly to complete the rush order for the *Blonde Bombshells*. No one has to know that order came from me.

And I'm the only one who will know that Frank's poor state this morning was not due to fatigue. That's the beauty of monkshood. His condition will worsen as he hikes far into the woods with his customers to some remote location on the Vissenkill. First, Frank will begin sweating and he'll get a headache and become dizzy.

Then he'll have trouble breathing and his vision will blur. Finally, the tingling in his arms and legs will quickly lead to paralysis, which will cause him to collapse. Just like a heart attack or stroke.

No doubt the other fishermen will try to call for help. Unfortunately for Frank, cell phones don't work out there. They may even throw his considerable bulk in the back of his truck and drive him to the nearest town. But Frank will be dead before help can reach him. Not that a doctor could do anything for him. There's no antidote for monkshood poisoning, even if they knew what to look for. And they won't know to look for it because nothing will seem out of the ordinary. Men of Frank's age and physical condition drop dead every day.

I check the clock and listen for the sound of sirens, even though I know they'll be too far away for me to hear. Frank left over two hours ago. I wonder if someone will call me, or will they just come to the door. I really don't know what to expect. I've never done this sort of thing before.

My day in the sun is finally here. The thought gives me goose bumps. I put on some lipstick and check my hair in the mirror. I want to look my best when I get the news. I light a candle and breathe in the scent of lilies. It won't be long now. If I close my eyes and listen, I can hear the bagpipes playing.

Betsy Bitner is a former criminal defense attorney who gave up law to become a chef. She then gave up cooking, at least professionally, to become a mom. And while Betsy hasn't given up on her three kids, she's decided to try her hand at writing fiction. "Amazing Grace" is her first story.

A MURDER RUNS THROUGH IT

BY ANNETTE DASHOFY

Nothing ruins a romantic riverside picnic like a dead body. At first I thought someone had dumped a bag of trash in the water. But when it bobbed against the rock at the edge of the Youghiogheny, where Josh and I were breaking out the fried chicken and potato salad, I gasped. Choking, I waved a hand at the soggy mound crashing our party.

Josh scowled at me, but followed my gesture and swore under his breath. "Call 9-1-1." He grabbed for the tattered wet fabric still clinging to the corpse.

I can't recall what I said on the phone. I must have given adequate directions because before long, the Pennsylvania State Police and an ambulance rolled up.

The first thing the troopers and paramedics did when they arrived was assist Josh. They dragged the poor stiff onto dry land and rolled him over.

That's when the day went from lousy to seriously crappy.

I knew the dead guy.

"Isn't that . . ." Josh asked.

"Anthony."

"You know this guy?" one of the troopers asked.

"It's Anthony DeStephano. I work with him." Or used to. The two of us had closed up the Whitewater Café last night.

The trooper whipped out a notepad and pen and fired questions. "Had he seemed depressed recently?"

"No."

"Did he do drugs or drink?" I had no clue about the drugs. As for drinking? Yeah. He and his buddies liked to head up the hill to the Patio Bar after work. "Was he in any kind of trouble?"

Looking at him now, all gray and bloated, bearing no resemblance to the vibrant party boy with the toothy smile and infectious laugh, I guessed the answer had to be a resounding *yes*.

After the coroner and police did their thing, we followed the emergency vehicles back to Ohiopyle. Tourists continued to ride their bikes and bundle in life vests to take their whitewater rafting tours. Families with kids and dogs lined the river's edge and played in the water upstream from the falls. Life went on. For everyone except Anthony.

Josh and I headed for the Whitewater Café. Like most summer days, the line stretched out the front door onto the deck. Unlike most summer days, Marilee Weber sat on the deck with her face in her hands.

Marilee was Anthony's girl.

She spotted our approach and called out our names. "They said you were the ones who found him."

"Yeah," Josh said. "He was already gone. There wasn't anything we could do to save him."

Bob Taggart appeared at the door, wide-eyed and frazzled. "Hey, Nell. We're swamped in here. Don't suppose you're up to filling in for Marilee, are you?"

The last thing I felt like doing was looking at food. But Marilee wasn't going to snap out of it any time soon.

"I have to get to work, too," Josh said.

As Josh gave me quick good-bye kiss, a state police cruiser pulled up. The trooper we'd talked to earlier climbed out and barreled past us.

"Bob may not be as overworked as he thinks," Josh commented. "A cop asking questions about a dead employee will likely clear out the crowd."

"Or bring out the looky-lous," I said.

He shrugged. "Or that."

The trooper set up shop at picnic table on the deck and called us out of the Café one at a time to question us. He saved me for last. "Nell Parker, right?"

"Yes, Trooper Mason."

"I have a few more questions for you. What was the victim's relationship with his co-workers?"

"Okay, I guess. He and Marilee were dating. Everyone else liked him. He was a good guy."

"Apparently someone didn't like him. You mentioned earlier you didn't know anything about the victim's involvement with drugs. Are you sure about that?"

"Yeah. Why?"

The trooper kept his gaze on his notes. "Just following up on some allegations that have been made. Do you know of anyone who might have wanted Anthony DeStephano dead?"

I choked. "You think someone killed him?"

"I'm looking into all possibilities." Trooper Mason snapped his notebook shut and slipped it into his breast pocket. He handed me a business card with his name and number. "If you see, hear, or remember anything, call me."

He followed me back inside and asked if any of us had plans to be away the next few days. We all stared at each other.

Crap. Did he think one of us killed Anthony?

I thought the police presence and the buzz around town about the drowning might put a dent in the afternoon business. Wrong. Tourists still wanted to eat. They acted like Anthony's death was part of the entertainment. At least the volume of customers kept me too busy to think about what had happened.

* * * *

I strolled into the Café the following morning. Raul was firing up the grill and Bob sat at a table with a piece of cardboard and a marker. "Can you work today?" Bob showed me what he was writing.

Help Wanted.

What I really wanted to do was get the hell out of there. But I needed the money. "Yeah, I'll work."

Two college kids applied for the job. I spent the entire day training them while taking orders, running the cash register, making lemonade, scooping ice cream, and bussing tables. Bob and I agreed to close early.

I barely made it across the road and into my house before collapsing on my sofa. That's when I noticed the red light blinking on my answering machine.

"I've been trying to reach you for hours." It was Marilee's frantic voice. "Don't you answer your cell phone? Meet me at the bridge on Route 281 by the ice cream place in Confluence."

I dug my cell phone out of my purse. The screen indicated I had three voice messages. They were all from Marilee, variations of the one on my machine. My return call went straight to her voicemail.

Confluence was ten miles upriver. As I negotiated the rutted, winding road, my work-fogged brain started clicking. What did Marilee want with me? Why Confluence? Why a bridge?

Anthony lived in Confluence. Or had.

At the stop sign, I made a left and dropped down the hill, past the ice cream place and over the bridge leading into town. No Marilee. I eased my Toyota off the road and tried calling her on my cell phone again. Her voicemail kicked in.

"I'm in Confluence. Call me."

I wandered over to the ice cream shop and bought a shake. Then I sat on the concrete side of the bridge. Scrawls of spray paint tagged the structure. Bonnie Jean Forever. Class of '98. Apparently no one ever attempted to clean the graffiti. R.T. heart M.W. Marilee Loves Anthony.

That one caught my full attention. I had to lean back to get a good look at the flowery blue scrawl and tried not to look down at the river and the rocks beneath me. Vertigo's ugly fingers gripped my arm and tugged me backward, toward the river.

Shivering, I decided Marilee was on her own. I sprinted to my car and got out of there. By the time I arrived home, it was dark. The town was quiet except for the Patio Bar on the hill. I tried Marilee's number again. Her voicemail picked up and I left another message.

The next morning, I was awakened by someone beating on my door. I glanced out of my bedroom window. A police cruiser sat in the road. I headed down the stairs.

"Do you mind if I come in?" Trooper Mason asked. "I need to ask you a few questions."

I moved aside and he stepped into my living room.

"Have you spoken with Marilee Weber recently?" He pulled out his notebook and pen.

Had something happened to Marilee?

I told the trooper about our game of phone tag and my trip to Confluence.

"May I listen to those messages?"

I pressed buttons on my answering machine to locate them. "Has something happened to Marilee?"

"We don't know. That's what I'm trying to find out."

I played back Marilee's frazzled call. Then I let him listen to the messages on my cell phone.

"Where were you all day when Ms. Weber was trying to reach you?"

"Working at the Whitewater." At least I had an alibi. But for what?

"I'd appreciate a phone call if she tries to reach you again, okay?"

"Why all the questions?"

"Marilee Weber is missing." He headed for my door. "No one has seen her since yesterday around noon."

I watched the trooper climb into his car and spotted Josh strolling toward my house.

I opened the door and fell into his arms. Given my choice, I'd have hit the pause button and stayed there all day, but he sat me down at my kitchen table and proceeded to make coffee.

"I was up at the Patio last night," he said. "Everyone was talking about Anthony."

"Did you learn anything?"

"You first. What did the state cop want?"

I told him about Marilee's phone calls and my trip to Confluence. "And now Marilee's missing."

"Missing? What's going on around here?"

"Your turn. What were the guys saying up at the Patio Bar?"

"Apparently our boy Anthony was a popular dude and everyone misses him."

I'd hoped for a little more than that. "Why?" I asked, only slightly ashamed of my sarcasm. "More beer for everyone else?"

"Yeah, but less weed."

"What?"

"Apparently the late Mr. DeStephano kept the local boys well stocked in weed."

"Weed? As in marijuana?"

"That would be the stuff, yes."

"Is that state cop still out there?" I craned my neck to see out the window.

"I don't think so. Why?" Josh asked. Then, his eyes widened. "No. You can't say anything to the police."

"Why not?"

"Because everyone will know how they found out and I happen to like living here. The cops will probably find out anyway. Just let it go."

I couldn't just let it go. I didn't see state troopers paying early morning visits to any of my neighbors. "Did anyone say anything about Marilee?"

"Not a word." Josh poured two cups of coffee and set them on the table. He slid into the chair across from me and placed his hand on mine. "Let the police do their job. And for what it's worth, I don't believe any of those guys at the Patio had anything to do with Anthony's death. They truly miss him."

"They miss their source."

"That, too. But they definitely didn't seem glad he was gone."

I pondered the case through two cups of coffee and my shower. I didn't want Bob roping me into another daylong shift of dealing with rookie help and demanding tourists. I headed back to Confluence.

Marilee had wanted me to come to the bridge on Route 281 yesterday before she went missing. Why? Graffiti aside, I hadn't found anything remotely resembling a clue.

I parked my Toyota on Confluence's town square and wandered around, asking questions. Everyone knew Anthony and Marilee, but no one had seen the girl since Anthony died. She didn't live in town and no one knew where she was from.

The temperature soared. With sweat trickling down my face and my back, I found a spot along the Youghiogheny where I could stick my feet in the water.

"Nell?"

I spun and almost lost my footing on the rocks. Marilee stood on the bank. Her hair was pulled back in a disheveled ponytail. Her clothes were wrinkled. She wore no makeup.

"Marilee, where've you been? I've been leaving messages on your cell phone."

She scowled and patted her pockets. "I must've lost it."

I sloshed back to dry land and grabbed her by both arms. She was trembling. "What's going on, Marilee?"

"What are you doing here?" Her voice sounded strained.

"You called me. Yesterday. A bunch of times. You asked me to meet you here."

"Oh. You didn't come. You didn't answer your phone."

"I didn't get the message right away, but I did come."

"You did?" Marilee worked her fingers through her hair, loosening the ponytail.

"Yes. I did. What'd you want? Why'd you want to meet me here?"

"Not here," she said. Her voice sounded childlike and small. "At the bridge. I needed to show you the bridge. I know who killed Anthony." She turned and ambled away, moving like something out of an old zombie movie.

I hopped first on one foot, then the other, to get my shoes on. "Where're you going? Who killed Anthony?"

"You'll see."

We walked back to the bridge. She climbed onto the low concrete barrier edging the span and stood up, her arms slightly away from her body for balance.

"Hey, Marilee," I said. "Come down from there. It isn't safe."

"Anthony really loved me, you know?" she said, her head tilted to one side. A faint smile played on her lips. "The way you love Josh."

"Really, Marilee, you should come down. We can talk down here."

She acted like she hadn't heard me. "Do you think Josh loves you the way you love him?"

"Um, I hope so."

She gave a little knowing nod. "We do, don't we? Hope the person we love loves us back? But sometimes they don't. Sometimes they can't because they love someone else."

I didn't like the direction this rambling tale was taking. Josh loved someone else? And what did any of this have to with Anthony and Marilee?

"I never realized," she went on. "Never suspected a thing. I was so happy with Anthony. He was my soul mate." She took a few pointed-toe steps, moving like a gymnast on a balance beam. "But then *he* started leaving messages on my voicemail." Her voice turned bitter.

"He? Who?" I asked. Josh?

"Next he started leaving me notes and sending me e-mails. They were sweet and romantic at first. I admit I kind of liked it. I thought of it as a game. He flirted with me. I flirted back. Harmless stuff. You know?"

No, I didn't know. Marilee and Josh? *My* Josh?

She paused for a moment and struck a pose. Then she teetered and leaned precariously, waving her arms. I gasped. She regained her balance, both feet on the bridge's edge, arms extending to the side. "Ha," she said. To my horror, she started the routine all over again. "Where was I?" she asked. "Oh, yeah. I never thought anything of it, all of this flirting and love notes. I never took it seriously."

She stopped again, made a little flourish with her hands, and performed a 360 degree turn on one foot. This time she didn't wobble.

This was insane. "Marilee, stop it. Come down so we can talk."

"Anthony always loved it when I played around like this. He called me his little ballerina." Marilee performed a couple more slightly off-balance moves on her tiptoes.

I wanted to grab her, but was afraid she'd topple over the edge before I could get to her.

"So, as I was saying, I didn't realize he was serious. Until after." She stopped her antics and stared off at the distance. "He came to me and told me he'd done it for me. He'd gotten Anthony out of the way so we could be together. He told me everything. How he'd taken Anthony out drinking and then brought him here. To sit, he said, and just talk. Then he got Anthony to show him how I always do my gymnastics routine. And when Anthony was up here clowning around, he pushed him over."

I'd been so focused on Marilee, I hadn't noticed the approaching footsteps. But the flop, flop, flop of sneakers on the pavement grew fast and close.

"Oh, my god. Get down from there, Marilee." Josh's voice was frantic as he stopped at my side, panting.

He was a stranger. He looked like the man I'd lost my heart to, but that man was a lie. This man in front of me now was capable of deceptions and murder.

Marilee pivoted slowly and looked down on us. "Hey, Josh. How ya doin'?"

Was I in an episode of Twilight Zone? Or maybe I was being punked. But this wasn't some sick joke. Anthony was dead.

"You," I said, pointing an accusing finger at Josh, "need to get out of here. Now."

"What?" He seemed startled. Give the guy an Oscar. "Why? We need to get her down from there."

Yeah. Down the long way, to the rocks and water of the river below. "You should just leave."

"It's okay," Marilee said in her little girl voice. "He can stay."

She intended on jumping. In front of Josh. "No, Marilee. Don't do it."

"We've got to stop this," Josh whispered to me.

"This? This is all your doing," I said, keeping my voice low.

He frowned. "What are you talking about?"

Marilee picked up her "routine" where she'd left off, as if Anthony's killer and I weren't there. A car crested the hill and I stepped closer to the side of the bridge. Marilee walked to the end of the concrete edge. The car slowed as it reached us and then braked. Marilee paused. She bent her knees as if she were going to sit. Instead, she sprang into a series of back flips across the length of the bridge. Any other time or place, I'd have been impressed. My breath stuck in my throat right next to a scream.

She slipped. One foot landed too close to the edge and in less than a heartbeat, she was tumbling toward the river, arms flailing, fingers grabbing at the concrete. Josh and I leaped toward her. Behind us, a car door slammed. I caught one thin arm as Marilee dangled above the water. Josh had the other. Her face was frozen in a silent scream. The vertigo returned as I looked down at her and beyond to the rapids and the rocks.

"Don't let her go," Josh said.

"Don't *you* let go," I screamed.

"I won't."

Together we hauled up Marilee. Thank heavens she was so small. Josh reached down and caught her by the waist, hoisting her to the relative safety of the concrete edge. I kept my grip on her arm.

"How could you?" I asked him. "I thought you loved me. I thought—"

"I do love you, Nell." He sounded confused

"No, you don't." Tears dampened my face. "Marilee just told me everything."

Panting, Marilee gave me an odd look.

"She told me how you flirted with her and told her you loved her and killed Anthony for her." The words spilled out. I was helpless to stop them at that point.

"What?" Joshua said.

"What?" Marilee echoed. Her eyes shifted from him to me and then over my shoulder. She gave a little cry. "No. Not Josh. Him."

Josh and I both turned.

The car was parked in the center of the bridge, a familiar looking heap. Standing next to it was the driver.

Bob.

"You moron." Bob's face glowed red. "Why did you have to go and mess everything up? Why couldn't you keep your mouth shut? I had it all set up to look like Anthony was involved in a drug deal gone bad. You and I . . ." He extended his arms toward Marilee. "We could have been together, no questions asked."

Whoa. I owed Josh one major apology.

"Look what you've done," Bob went on. "Now I've got to do something with the two of you. And, my darling Marilee, since you obviously don't care for me the way I care for you . . ." An eerie smile crept over his face. "But you've all given me a prime opportunity here. Of course." He reached inside his car and came out with a wooden ball bat. "Poor distraught Marilee tries to jump. You two try to save her. But instead, she pulls you both over, too. Such a tragedy."

He charged us, cranking the bat back with one massive arm.

Josh still had an arm around Marilee's waist. He pulled her hard to one side and shoved her down, out of the arc of the swinging bat. I dived the other way and forward. The heavy wood caught Josh with a thud. I heard him grunt. Somehow, he managed to grab the bat and wrest it from Bob's hand. Bob caught me with his free arm, driving me back toward the barrier. I lost my footing. Then I was looking at sky and Bob's weight was on me. I heard a scream, but still don't know if it was mine or Marilee's.

This was it. I was going over the edge, backwards and head-first. Deep inside, a little survivalist voice cried, "No."

I clamped my heels down against the barrier and twisted. Just a little.

Just enough.

Bob's momentum shifted. The brute force intended to push the three of us over the edge, instead carried him over it.

Josh, still clutching the bat, lunged for him. He got a hand on Bob's shirt, but the fabric slipped through his fingers. With a scream that I remember to this day, Bob fell.

I don't know the sequence of events afterwards. My mind went blank. I think Josh called 911, because police and ambulances and fire trucks soon crowded the bridge and the hillside leading down to the river.

Marilee looked down, over the edge at the scene below. "He really thought he loved me."

"You don't need to watch," I told her.

"I'm not. He's gone anyway. Downstream somewhere."

I imagined Bob's body floating up to a rock, disturbing someone else's riverside picnic.

"See?" Marilee pointed.

I leaned over to see what she was indicating. She was pointing at the graffiti.

"Marilee loves Anthony," I read.

She gave a sad smile. "Yeah, I did that one. But look." She pointed again. "R.T. and M.W. in a heart. That was Bob."

It clicked. Bob. Robert Taggart and Marilee Weber. The vertigo hit me again and I sat down on the bridge deck. At what point, I wondered, had the simple sweetness of R.T. heart M. W. grown so unbalanced as to drive a man to murder and send him plummeting over the edge of sanity?

Josh appeared and joined me on the concrete. He held one arm around his ribs where the bat had caught him. He slipped the other around my shoulders.

"The cops want to ask you a couple questions. Then we can go home."

Had he really said 'we'? "Josh, I'm so sorry. I can't believe I thought she was talking about you."

Josh pressed his lips to my forehead. "Yeah, I'm really disappointed in you. But I have some ideas how you can make it up to me."

My vertigo melted away, replaced by a deep inner stillness. "I love you," I whispered.

But he'd better never expect me to put it in graffiti.

Annette Dashofy's *short fiction includes a finalist for the 2007 Derringer Award. She is vice-president of the Mary Roberts Rinehart chapter of Sisters in Crime and is the Pittsburgh area representative for Pennwriters. She lives in rural Washington County, Pennsylvania with her husband of 26 years and one spoiled cat.*

DEAD-EYE GRAVY

BY KRISTA DAVIS

Dana paid for her allergy medicine, shocked by the price. "Has it gone up?"

The pharmacy clerk smiled at her and winked. "I put your husband's medicine in there, too, dear."

Dana thanked her out of polite habit. A prescription for Jeff? She didn't even know he'd been to a doctor. She tore open the bag, but the not-so-discreet cough from the man behind her prompted her to move away from the cash register. She walked toward the door, pausing briefly in the privacy of an aisle to pull out Jeff's prescription. Viagra.

So that was why he'd been excited about their weekend away at the cabin. She couldn't help grinning. But now she wished she could stop for a pedicure and a leg wax. She glanced at her watch. She should have left town over an hour ago but the Flower Club luncheon she'd catered ran long. Which, in turn, made her late picking up her son, Mark, to take him to the airport. It seemed as if she was always running behind and playing catch-up these days.

She wondered if she should check on Mark yet. At twenty, her son was a fearless rascal at heart, but the poor kid hated flying because of the peanuts served on board. Not all airlines offered a peanut buffer zone and his peanut allergy caused him stress every time he flew. He even had to cover his seat with a plane sheet to protect himself from peanut crumbs. She made a quick call to be sure he was all right before putting the hybrid SUV into gear and heading for the highway.

Her cell phone rang and she glanced at the caller. Of course, Mr. Viagra himself. She didn't want to tell him she'd just left. She'd wait until she was at least an hour down the interstate before she called him back. As she expected, when she stopped for gas and called him, he wanted to know where she was. If she knew Jeff, she'd still manage to beat him to the cabin.

The three hour drive passed pleasantly as she shifted into day-dream mode. Maybe this weekend would be a turning point. Now that the kids were almost grown, she and Jeff could slow down a little, spend more time together. Hadn't he mentioned a possible promotion that would mean less travel? Maybe he was planning to tell her this weekend. She should stop to pick up a bottle of champagne.

As she pulled off onto the snaking country road, it dawned on her that she'd meant to pick up groceries before she left the city. The sun would set soon, and she wanted to get to the cabin in daylight. She could go out for real groceries tomorrow. For now, all she wanted were milk, eggs, champagne, and a couple of steaks for the grill.

She pulled into the parking lot of the old grocery store. Her grandparents had bought basic supplies there when she stayed with them as a child. The ramshackle place looked like it hadn't had a coat of paint since then. Hoping they carried something besides bait, Dana ventured inside. A little snack counter had been added, and the back was stocked like a convenience store. She found milk but sighed at the meager selection of fresh food. At least they offered packaged cheeses and fresh eggs. An omelet wasn't the kind of celebration fare she'd had in mind, but it would have to do. She gathered bread, inexpensive wine, and a few other items and brought them to the cash register. "Do you have any champagne or steaks?"

"Sorry, hon."

While the woman rang up her purchases, a little boy seated at the counter said, "Hi! My name's Jewemiah."

Dana said hello while a scrawny man looked on. She handed her credit card to the woman.

The gaunt man leaned against the counter and appraised her. "You some kind of fancy cook or something?"

"Something like that." Catering hardly counted as fancy cooking but she didn't want to go into details.

The man prodded Jeremiah with a bony hand. "Tell her your favorite food."

Pink-cheeked Jeremiah couldn't have been older than four. "Dead-eyed gwavy and bis-cuts."

From the way the couple beamed, Dana assumed they were his parents. "He's adorable. I bet he keeps you busy."

The woman filled a paper bag with the groceries, her face lined and weary beyond her years. She'd probably been attractive once, but she already wore the haggard face of someone who worked hard every day. "Both my boys keep me busy."

Dana looked at the man—he couldn't possibly be her son.

"Gabe there is my husband, but you know how it is. The women hold down the fort, while the men go fishing and take money out of the till."

"Watch your mouth or Jeremiah and I'll trade you in for a newer model."

Dana cringed.

"I bet you make great Red-Eye Gravy and biscuits," Gabe said.

Truth be known, she had never made it in her life. She didn't even have a clue what was in the gravy. "I'm afraid not."

"What kind of cook doesn't make Red-Eye Gravy?"

"I'll have to try it sometime since Jeremiah recommends it so highly." Nodding goodbye, Dana left in haste. She wasn't going to be put down by some man she didn't even know.

Minutes later, she pulled up at the cabin. The setting sun turned the sky orange over the distant mountains, and reflected in the windows of the old cabin. Everyday stresses washed away as she drank in the scent of pine, even if it did mingle with a hint of fish egg stink. Cheerful from the freedom of a mini-vacation, she unlocked the door, anticipating the musty scent of an unused house, but it smelled fine. Something wasn't right. She and Jeff had planned this weekend at the lake for months, anxious that the summer was slipping by while they were too busy to get away. The house had been closed up all winter and should smell funky.

She walked through the little cabin opening windows. The only thing amiss was the faint smell of a cloying perfume in one of the bedrooms. She sniffed carefully, certain she wasn't imagining the scent. Mark came to mind immediately. That stinker. She'd bet anything that he'd been bringing dates out to the cabin on weekends. Dana couldn't help smiling. She and Jeff had used the cabin as a romantic hideaway when they were young, too.

Satisfied that nothing was wrong, she opened the fuse box and flipped on the appliances. She brought in the groceries, stashed the eggs and cheese in the fridge, and decided that it was more important to shed her pantyhose than put away the rest of the groceries. Once she wore a sleeveless top, shorts and flip flops, she returned to the kitchen and stashed the bread in the deep closet they used as a pantry.

A spider had set up residence in the corner. She stepped inside for a roll of paper towels so she could get rid of him, and something crunched under her foot. She swiped at the web with a paper towel and looked at the bottom of her flip flop. Part of a pretzel nugget clung to it along with something that looked suspiciously like peanut butter. She pried it off and sniffed. Definitely peanut butter. Dana recoiled. She flushed the spider in the toilet and returned to the pantry. There weren't any other pretzels, nor did she see a bag of them, only the remnants of the one she'd stepped on. Everyone in her family knew better than to bring anything with peanuts into the house. Someone had been using the cabin, but it wasn't Mark. He would have had a fit if a girlfriend brought peanut butter-filled pretzel nuggets, and if she'd eaten any, he wouldn't have gone near her.

She scrubbed the pantry floor, now wondering if Jeff had loaned the cabin to one of his buddies.

Although a glass of wine was tempting after the drive and the difficult day, Dana decided to wait for Jeff. She left the front door unlocked for him, turned down the inside lights and, sipping a glass of sparkling water, wandered out to the deck.

The light of the moon danced on the water and a few fishing boats bobbed lazily. She yearned to go for a swim. She called Mark to be sure he'd made the trip without any ill effects and was happy to find he was already busy with friends. But where was Jeff? She was about to call him when her phone rang. He was on the way.

When she hung up, she clenched her teeth. After all, she'd rushed to the cabin. But the glimmer of the moon on the water reminded her that life was too short to be annoyed about little things. She changed into a bathing suit and switched on a light. Enjoying the solitude, she walked down to the dock and eased into the warm water. It enveloped her in a way no soothing spa treatment could match. She floated on her back, away from the shore, her eyes closed. She made leisurely figure eights with her hands as little sunfish nibbled at her fingers and toes.

She opened her eyes. The dark outline of the cabin stood on the hill, a few windows softly lighted. The rumble of a boat engine disturbed the glorious calm. Dana side-stroked as the roar grew louder. A fishing boat soared across the water toward her. What was wrong with those guys? Didn't they know the rules of the water? No wakes permitted near docks. Unsure if they would see her in the dark, she swam faster to reach the safety of the old dock.

The boat kept coming, far too fast. She expected them to cut the engine any second, and to swing the boat near the shore for fishing, but it continued on a path to the dock. It wasn't unusual for fishermen to be out all night, but there weren't many who would want to disturb the fish by roaring to shore. There was something menacing about the way it zoomed right at her, and she did something she hadn't done since she was a child. She swam under water and came up underneath the dock.

The boat finally slowed. Dana held her breath and tried not to hit her head on the lurching dock as the boat came alongside. She heard someone jump out, his feet heavy against the wood.

"There's a light on."

"She thinks Jeff's coming. Probably left it on for him and went to bed."

Dana's breath caught in her throat. They were talking about her! The second man's voice sounded so familiar. Where had she heard it before?

"You sure you want to do this?"

"Heck, yeah. It's easy money. Besides, he's got a forty-two inch plasma TV that I've got a hankering for. If we take it, the cops will think she got shot during a robbery."

"We're gonna steal from him?"

"Sure. What's he gonna do? Call the cops?"

"So what's the deal? His old lady spending too much money?"

"He's trading up. He said the new one wants a diamond, so he's ready to move things along. No big loss, the wife doesn't even know how to make Red-Eye Gravy."

Dana clamped a hand over her mouth. Gabe from the little store. Her head reeled, but she forced herself to focus. This had been planned. That's why Jeff hadn't arrived. He'd called to be sure she would be at the cabin. She shivered in the warm water. There must be some mistake. Jeff would never hire anyone to kill her. But Gabe had said Jeff's name, hadn't he?

Her head throbbed and she needed air, but she forced herself to breathe slowly and tried to process it all. The Viagra, the lingering scent of perfume, the peanut butter. Jeff's lover must not know about Mark's allergy. Or maybe the peanut butter pretzels were part of Jeff's rebellion, representative of the new life he coveted.

How could Jeff do this to her? The man she slept next to, the one she built her life around, the father of her children—he wanted to murder her? Woozy and nauseous, she held onto a beam under the dock to steady herself.

A heavy boot stepped on a loose board that thunked her on the head. A grunt escaped Dana's lips and turned into a gurgle as she dipped under water.

"You hear that?" asked Gabe.

"Must be one of those lake otters. They make some weird noises if you get too close to a nest."

"It sounded like a person," protested Gabe.

"Are you kidding? Look around. You see anybody? Now, hurry up."

Afraid Gabe would recklessly shoot into the water, Dana remained still, resisting the temptation to rub her head. A chill engulfed her as the gravity of the situation sank in. They would kill her if they found her.

Her hands shaking, she waited until their footsteps faded on the hill. Moving slowly, she ducked under the edge of the dock and emerged on the outside. The shadowy figures of the men headed toward the cabin. She clung to the weathered boards.

That had been close. They would be back soon. She had to pull herself together. What would they do when they didn't find her? She needed a phone.

Trying not to make any noise, she pulled herself onto the dock, untied Gabe's boat, and tossed the mooring lines into the water. As quietly as she could, she swam toward the middle of the lake, towing Gabe's boat behind her. When it was infuriatingly far from the dock, she let go and turned to look up at the cabin. It went dark. They'd cut the electricity.

Their voices grew louder. She didn't have much time left. Swimming as fast as she could, she headed for a neighboring cabin. She knocked on the door. There was no answer, so she heaved a concrete flower urn at the glass door and cringed at the sound of glass shattering. They'd hear that. She'd have to hurry.

She threw a doormat over tiny blocks of tempered glass to protect her bare feet, found the phone and called 911. Assured an officer would be on the way, she hurried back to the lake and aimed a rock at the light on her neighbor's boathouse. It took her four tries to hit the light bulb. Then she slid into the water so they wouldn't see her if they happened to look her way.

They groaned and snapped at each other as they came into view, hauling the TV. And then they stopped. Dana sucked in a deep breath, ready to vanish underwater if necessary. She could still see the boat, but the current had carried it farther into the lake. They might try to escape in her car, but she hoped the police would arrive before they left.

A squabble arose between Gabe and his friend. They cursed and blamed each other for their predicament. In the end, they picked up the TV and struggled to carry it back up the hill. Precious minutes ticked by. Dana swam closer to her own dock.

Headlights streamed through the darkness and the two men stopped. Dana squinted. Why hadn't the cops used the siren or flashing lights? A car door closed. Leaving the TV leaning precariously on the hill, the two men ran to the cabin. Dana did the breast stroke to her dock. Gabe and his friend would be caught red-handed, if not for attempted murder, then at least for burglary.

A gunshot rang out, echoing over the water. She gasped and clutched the edge of the dock, ready to disappear underneath. As she watched the house, a car engine started. The driver didn't turn on the headlights, and the sound died away as the car drove off.

Wary and alert to every sound, Dana forced herself to wait. She counted one-Mississippi, two-Mississippi until at least five minutes had passed. She eased herself out of the water. There was no sign of Gabe or his friend. Keeping to the trees, she ran up the hill in spurts. When she reached the side of the cabin, she looked through the window. A body sprawled on the floor. She tiptoed around to the driveway and her heart sank. The police car remained, but her hybrid was gone.

She quietly opened the front door and crept up behind the prone person. Her heart pounded when she saw a young woman wearing a police uniform on the floor. She slipped closer and a cloyingly sweet smell hit her. The same cheap perfume she'd smelled in the bedroom. Gabe or his friend had shot the wrong woman—they'd shot Dana's replacement. She felt for a pulse. The officer was still alive. Dana retrieved her cell phone.

A car raced up the driveway. Gabe and his buddy were back. She ran for the window, raised it, and slid out. She stood with her back flat against the wall. The sliding glass door on the lake side of the cabin creaked open. She peeked in. A man stood in the open doorway, his dark shape outlined by the lighter darkness of the night.

There was another shot and the man collapsed. The policewoman's hand fell to the floor, still grasping her gun. An owl hooted ominously and the world fell silent.

Dana's pulse hammered in her head. Where was the other guy? She called 911 again and asked for an ambulance, covering her mouth and speaking softly, in case both Gabe and his buddy had returned. She told the police an officer was down. When she hung up, she hesitated. She wanted to help the people who'd been shot, but the policewoman might shoot her by mistake. Her back mashed against the cabin, she strained to see in the dark and feared the sound of a twig snapping underfoot.

It seemed an eternity passed before she heard the faint peal of a siren. The light atop a vehicle strobed, eerily flashing through the branches as it approached. Would the second man run away?

She edged along the wall, and peered around the corner of the house toward the driveway, relieved to see emergency technicians, as well as a cop. She glanced around and darted to the front door to warn them that one killer might be hiding in the woods. After she explained the situation, they allowed her to enter the house for her own safety, but asked that she remain by the front door.

Flashlights blazing, cops strode through her beloved cabin, assessing the situation. The policewoman was still alive, but she had killed the man in the doorway. As the emergency technicians stabilized the woman, the cop called out, "Ma'am, can you identify this guy as one of the hired killers?"

Still shaking, Dana crept toward the officer. Even though she knew he couldn't harm her now, she stepped gingerly, as though he might suddenly revive to finish his mission. She hoped it would be Gabe, since she didn't know if she could identify the second man, whom she'd only seen from a distance.

She focused on his feet as she neared. Gabe and his friend had worn boots, but the dead man wore elegant loafers and chinos. Her throat constricted the way her son's did when he inhaled peanuts, and she knew the truth even before the orb of the flashlight reached the victim's face. It was Jeff.

Nationally bestselling author Krista Davis *writes the Domestic Diva Mystery series. Her first book,* The Diva Runs Out of Thyme, *was nominated for an Agatha Award for Best First Novel. Krista lives on a lake and ducked under the dock many times as a child. Visit Krista at divamysteries.com.*

THE PROFESSOR'S BOOKS

BY GLORIA ALDEN

William Faulkner gave Tilly the idea. Well, not the author himself, but a book of his. Not that Tilly had read the book. She didn't read much more than the obituaries or the advice columns in the newspaper. Sometimes she read Dr. Donohue's column if it wasn't about men's problems like prostate cancer. No, Tilly got the idea when she was dusting the Professor's books, something she spent a part of every day doing after she'd finished her other chores.

The book was *As I Lay Dying*, but because the capital "I" was so close to the capital "L," she thought it was *As He Lay Dying*, and that got Tilly to thinking about the Professor dying. Of course, ever since he'd casually mentioned to her that she would be remembered in his will since she'd been such a faithful housekeeper for so many years, she had started picturing the little house she would buy. She'd live there quietly with a cat and a canary. The Professor didn't care much for animals so she couldn't have any here. Those thoughts had just been daydreams of sometime in the future, but when he'd had his heart attack six months ago, Tilly thought maybe that time had come so she started reading the real estate ads in the newspaper, too. But in spite of his advanced age, he had rallied, and although he wasn't as spry as he once was, he didn't seem ready for death any time soon.

And so life went along in its usual rhythm with Tilly cooking for the Professor, doing household chores, and dusting the thousands of books the Professor had not only in his library, but also the piles of books found in every nook and cranny throughout his house. It wasn't a difficult life. The Professor was agreeable enough, and her work wasn't hard, so Tilly was reasonably content until the day before, when the Professor had announced that a book appraiser would be coming to catalogue his collection of special editions and re-evaluate their worth. He had given her a key to the locked bookcase and asked her to make sure the books were well dusted.

But Tilly had a problem. A year ago she had found a spare key in the Professor's desk to that bookcase. Curious, she had unlocked and opened the glass doors and took a few out to look at them. The first one was a volume of *Bleak House* by Charles Dickens. This surprised her. Why would this be so special when she remembered dusting one very similar to it on the Professor's book shelves? Just to be sure, she went to the shelf holding all of Charles Dickens's books. She pulled it out and compared the two. She couldn't see much difference. Someone had scribbled the name Charles Dickens on the inside flyleaf of the book from the locked bookcase, but it seemed to her that the one without any writing in it should be worth more.

Several days later an idea came to her. She was squishing along in the rain with one wet foot because her right boot had a leak. She was on her way to a shoe store to get a new pair when she passed The Emporium, a used book store. A sign in the window attracted her attention, "We Buy Used Books."

So over the months that followed, Tilly would take a book from the locked bookcase, replace it with another book like it, and take it to the Emporium to sell. At first the owner had looked at her with some suspicion, but he said she reminded him of a favorite aunt, and when she told him she was a widow and was trying to get a little extra money by selling her husband's books, he had accepted her story and offered her twenty dollars for the book. She accepted the amount gratefully. It seemed a lot for an old scribbled in book.

With each book she took, she was careful to skip around amongst the authors to make it less obvious, and she now looked at each one with new interest. She couldn't imagine a book by anyone with a name like Charles Lamb to be worth very much, especially such an old one, but the bookstore owner had given her twenty dollars for that one, too.

When Tilly was no longer able to find books with the same author and title, she substituted books that were similar in size and binding. The Professor never seemed to notice the missing books. It could be because his eyesight was failing. For a while he would have Tilly read to him, but that didn't last long. He got restless and annoyed with Tilly's slow reading. She used one stubby forefinger to follow the words, words she mispronounced no matter how many times he corrected her, so he had resorted to ordering books on tape from the library, which Tilly willingly picked up for him.

What should she do? None of the original books were left in the glass-fronted bookcase, and Tilly would be the only suspect when it was discovered they were gone. She would have to replace the money, but most of the almost two thousand dollars she had received was gone, most of it on lottery tickets. Would she go to jail? She'd lose her comfortable job with the Professor. The only way she could save herself was if the Professor died.

Now Tilly may not have been much of a reader, but she did watch TV, including crime shows, and she knew that killing someone and making it look like a natural death was not an easy thing to do. Even suffocating someone with a pillow could be proved to be murder.

Maybe it look like a burglary? But there were no guns in the house, and she'd never shot one in her life. Besides, she'd learned that gun sellers kept records so any gun she bought could be traced to her. Knives? She'd need an alibi. Where could she go to establish one? Most burglars came at night, and she had no family and very few acquaintances where she could just show up some night. It would look strange. She never went anywhere after dark.

Poison was out, too. She was the only one who fixed his meals, and he rarely had visitors anymore so she couldn't count on anyone coming before the appraiser showed up. Besides, who would want to kill the Professor? He didn't have any enemies, and the only family he had were a great-niece and a great-nephew, and they didn't live anywhere near. It had been several years since either one of them had visited.

Some medicines could kill. But the Professor took nothing but a heart medicine, and she doubted if that would work. If it didn't, either he or the doctor would wonder what had happened to the pills if he had to reorder early. As for Tilly herself, she had always been strong and robust. In fact, after the Professor's heart attack, she had often helped him get out of bed and into the bathroom. Tilly's medicine chest held only some vitamins and a small bottle of aspirin. Tilly knew an overdose of aspirin could kill, but she didn't see how she could administer that or even if she had enough to do the job.

Poor Tilly.

The following morning when the Professor came down, she had it. Drowning. Every morning before breakfast, the Professor went out for a walk around the pond behind the house. Sometimes he even did two laps. Before his heart attack he had done even more.

It wasn't a large pond. She had always thought it foolish since she wasn't much for exercising, but now she was glad that he did. After his walk, he'd stop to feed his koi. She couldn't understand why he liked his fish so much, either. It wasn't as if they were furry or affectionate in any way. Not like a cat or a bird.

This morning she watched from the kitchen door until he'd finished his second lap, and then she joined him on the small dock. He glanced up at her in surprise. She hadn't been out here since the first time he had shown her the fish years ago.

"I've come to look at the fish," she said as she walked up behind him.

He grunted in answer, and then let out a yelp when she pushed him in.

He struggled and managed to swim the few strokes back to the edge of the dock. He grabbed hold of the edge, sputtering and gasping. She knelt down as if to give him a hand, but instead grabbed his wispy hair, and pushed his head under. It was easier than she thought. He fought for a short while. Finally, he went limp. She waited a few more minutes before letting go and watched as he floated face down in the water while a few curious koi nibbled at him.

Then she went back to the house and started his breakfast. Today instead of his usual oatmeal, she fixed him bacon, eggs and toast. She fixed herself the same breakfast, too. When she had eaten and put her dishes to soak, she went out and pulled his lifeless body from the pond. Then she went in and called 911.

On the day of the funeral, the Professor's great-niece and her husband picked Tilly up to take her to the funeral home. They had chosen to stay at a nearby hotel rather than the Professor's house. Tilly settled in the backseat of their car, a little uneasy by its size and its soft leather seats. She had never ridden in such a car.

As the car moved smoothly away from the curb, the Professor's great-niece turned around. She asked Tilly about the Professor and his death and what Tilly would be doing now. Tilly's answers were stilted and brief. The great-niece turned around and talked to her husband.

Tilly felt shy. She was intimidated by their obvious wealth. Was she dressed all wrong, too? Maybe she shouldn't have worn the little black hat with a half veil. The great-niece wasn't wearing anything on her styled blond head, and she wore a stylish light blue dress. The last time Tilly had worn her black dress was at her mother's funeral twenty years before. Actually, it was the last funeral she had attended. Maybe people dressed different at funerals now.

Tilly hung back so the others could go in ahead of her. She carefully signed her name in the guest book in the hall and took one of the little religious cards for the mourners. It had a picture of Jesus on the front. She didn't know the Professor was a Christian. She had never heard him mention anything in the way of religion. She turned the card over and looked at his date of birth and date of death. He was eighty-nine. In two months he would have been ninety. If he were still alive, maybe she would have made a birthday cake for him. She could have put nine candles on, one for each decade. Of course, that would only have been if someone had called with birthday greetings or sent a card since she had never written his birthday down anywhere, and the Professor had never mentioned it. She couldn't remember any cards or calls for several years now. Maybe those who remembered his birthday were dead now, too. She slowly read the prayer on the back of the card. She didn't want to go in and bid a final good-bye to the Professor.

The church was empty except for a balding man standing at the head of the casket. The great-nephew. He'd lost a lot more hair since his last visit. She took a deep breath and walked up to the casket. The Professor looked so still, his skin so gray. She was glad his eyes were closed. Sometimes he had slept with his eyes slightly open. She turned away.

The Professor's great-nephew took her hand and smiled at her. He thanked her for all the good care she had given his uncle over the years.

Tilly nodded and took a chair near the back where she could see and yet not be noticed. The flowers were bright spots of color in a room with gray walls, gray carpeting and soft lighting. There weren't very many flower arrangements. The Professor's great-niece and great-nephew greeted the few callers who came. The great-niece's husband had taken up residence in another room with his Blackberry, so Tilly sat alone.

The Professor was to be cremated, so there was no procession to the cemetery. The funeral director had brought in a minister to say a few words. Since he had never met the Professor, the eulogy was brief. Tilly could have told him about the Professor if she'd been asked. She knew the Professor better than anyone else. Sadness seeped into her bones. What about her own funeral? Who would come? What would be said about her?

Later, back at the Professor's house, the lawyer met with the few beneficiaries of the Professor's will. The house went to the great-nephew along with a sum of money, and the furniture went to a great-niece with another generous amount.

"And to my faithful housekeeper, Tilly Swindler, I leave my collection of first edition and signed rare books that can be found in the locked bookcase. Enclosed is the list. This should allow her to live comfortably for the rest of her life," the lawyer read.

Tilly sat frozen. The lawyer pulled out the list. "Here's *A Dissertation Upon a Roast Pig* by Charles Lamb. What a strange title to be worth so much, six hundred seventy-five dollars. Hmmm. Here's another one by him, *Tales from Shakespeare: Designed for the Use of Young Persons.* It's worth five thousand dollars." His eyes skimmed down the list as he shook his head. "Wow! *As I Lay Dying* by William Faulkner is worth over thirteen thousand dollars. Professor Higgins must have thought a lot of you."

Tilly's vision blurred before she passed out.

Gloria Alden *lives on a small farm in Northeast Ohio with her collie and other assorted animals. Like the Professor, her library shelves are overflowing with books. She belongs to Sisters in Crime, Guppies, two writer's groups, and two book clubs. She's a retired teacher with a Masters in English and has had a short story and numerous poems win awards.*

KOI PALACE

BY HEIDI SAUNDERS

As it turned out, it was Maya's looks, not her brain, which snagged her the job at the Koi Palace. She came by her almond eyes and black hair via her Korean ancestors, but the owner, Mr. Chen, seemed confident he could pass her off as Chinese to restaurant patrons.

Maya smoothed her work uniform—a frilly apron over a faux-silk sheath that narrowed precariously at the ankles—and glanced at the wall clock. Feeding time again. She didn't have anything against fish per se, but hungry koi were another matter. The constant pulsing of their round gaping mouths, as if gasping for air, repelled her. Her hostess position at Louisville's newest Chinese restaurant required her to serve the clammy moochers twice a day.

Not that she had any right to complain. At least she had a job, unlike her indolent ex-boyfriend, Rob. A stagnant economy and military hiring freeze had forced Maya to accept an unpaid position at nearby Fort Knox. At least the internship with the Information Decoder department utilized her computer science degree. To cover her bills, nights and weekends found her at the Koi Palace.

When she'd been hired last week, Mr. Chen had explained her duties: greet and seat the customers, feed the fish, and let him know when any guests arrived asking for him by name. Those guests were to be seated in booth six near the front door. After their meal, Chen would personally serve them fortune cookies from a special trove he kept in his office. A treat for his favorite friends, he said.

Maya headed for the kitchen to retrieve desiccated fish food sticks. As she returned with the tray for the koi, children left their parents to follow her to the sunken pond in the center of the restaurant. A wrought iron fence surrounded the pond and kept children from falling in. An aroma of mildew and fish excrement hung in the humid air. Maya passed food sticks to the kids to throw into the water, which churned with writhing bodies lunging for the treats. The platter finally empty, Maya handed out plastic-wrapped fortune cookies from her apron pocket.

The noon feeding done, she headed for the hostess station and saw someone leaning against the podium watching her. The welcoming smile forming on her lips faded at sight of the dented motorcycle helmet dangling from the man's fingers. Rob stood there, thick hair pulled back in a ponytail, leather-clad arms crossed.

Maya walked toward him. His dark eyes never left her. She bent to slip the tray onto a shelf under the podium then stood to face him.

"Maya." Rob's voice, deep and seductive.

Her voice came out higher than usual. "What are you doing here?"

"Relax, I'm just here for lunch." He scanned the curves accentuated by her outfit. "You're looking well. I had no idea you worked here, or believe me, I'd have been in sooner."

An unbidden flutter twisted inside her. There had definitely been a strong attraction between them during their six weeks of dating. Then, after graduation last month, he'd joined a local biker gang and spent all his time with them instead of looking for a job. It was so out of character that she'd hoped he'd snap out of it. He hadn't, and a week ago she'd broken up with him.

She squared her shoulders. Their relationship was over. He'd chosen a lifestyle she couldn't accept. "Please leave."

His grin only widened. Aware that her boss's office door was ajar, Maya steeled herself to remain professional. Teeth clenched, she forced a fake smile. "Welcome to the Koi Palace. Just one today?"

"I'd like a seat near the front door, please."

Of course he would. So he could stare at her as she worked, no doubt. She grabbed a menu and led him to a front table.

She barely had time to return to her post before two stocky Asian men in black trench coats entered. Like Mafia thugs in a Hollywood film, Maya thought. The shorter one had a chunk of front tooth missing. In heavily accented English, he asked for Mr. Chen. Maya showed them to booth six then hurried down the short hallway to her boss's office.

Maya knocked gently on the doorjamb. Mr. Chen, his thin frame seated behind his desk, shot her an impatient look. "What?"

His reedy voice held an undercurrent of repressed rage, as if he had better things to do than manage a restaurant. Maya wanted to have as little to do with him as possible. She spoke calmly. "Two men asking for you, sir."

For a moment Chen tensed, then nodded and waved her away.

These were the first special guests since Maya had started her hostess job. Curious, she surreptitiously watched them in between seating other clientele. Both were Chinese, she was pretty sure. Despite the seafood the Koi Palace was famous for, they ordered only one bowl of soup each.

She begrudged a glance at Rob, seated across from booth six. He leered back. Although his waitress had already placed his check and fortune cookie on the table, he nursed a cup of hot tea, showing no inclination to leave.

Maya let out a frustrated breath and placed an X on the chart. She'd seated two men in the back room. Though in civilian clothes, their short hair and muscled physique suggested soldiers on weekend furlough from Fort Knox.

A commotion started behind her at the cashier's counter. An angry client lodging a complaint, something about dirty silverware and threats to call the health inspector. Not her responsibility. Mr. Chen emerged from his office to deal with the gesticulating man.

One of the special guests in booth six waved at her. No, he was looking past her, trying to capture Chen's attention. The guest jabbed a thick finger at his watch. They were ready to leave and wanted their fortune cookies. Those things tasted like sandpaper to Maya, but the customer always knew best. She turned and gestured to Chen.

Her boss excused himself and ducked into his office. He returned with a small tray with two cellophane-wrapped fortune cookies on it. The complaining customer's voice rose to a shout. Trapped, Chen held the tray out to Maya and pointed with his chin at the two men in booth six, then turned his attention back to the yelling patron.

She took the tray and headed around the koi pond, wobbling in the high heels Chen made her wear. For a brief moment she was out of sight of her boss and the impatient special guests. What was different about the fortune cookies from Chen's office, anyway? They appeared to have similar red lettering on the cellophane wrapping. As she raised the tray to examine the packets, her foot slipped on a dropped fish food stick. Before she could regain her balance, the tray tipped and one of the cookies fell into the koi pond. A foot long orange and white koi grabbed it and nosed it under a rock.

Maya froze. Mr. Chen was still arguing with the customer behind her. Her boss had been emphatic that his special guests receive the fortune cookies from his office. She could lose her job over this, and in this economy it might take her months to find another. She'd fall behind on her college loans, be unable to pay rent on her apartment. With a twinge of guilt, Maya drew a fortune cookie from her apron pocket and placed it next to the other on the tray. With luck, no one would notice the switch.

When Maya reached their booth, Chipped Tooth grabbed the packets, stuffed them into his pocket, and they left.

"Are those two here often?" Rob asked.

Maya jumped at the sound of his voice. She'd forgotten he was sitting across the aisle. "I've never seen them before." She hurried back to her station to seat a waiting family.

Chen finally appeased the irate patron with a free meal, and came over to Maya. Stepping close, he clutched her arm. "Did my guests receive their fortune cookies?"

Maya nodded.

His fingernails left red welts on her arm. Maya rubbed them as Chen returned to his office. Moments later, the front doors flew open and the two black-garbed special guests reappeared. They pushed past her and entered Chen's office, slamming the door behind them. Maya heard the scrape of a chair, a volley of angry shouts, then a loud smack and thud. Before Maya could react, the two men burst from the office and came up behind her.

They sandwiched her between them, and the taller thug hissed in her ear, "You've got something of ours, *bangzi*."

Maya flinched at the derogatory Chinese word for a Korean. The men grabbed her upper arms and dragged her toward the entrance. Maya cast a desperate glance at Rob and saw him moving toward them, talking into a cell phone.

From the other side of the seating area, the customer who'd complained to Chen stepped forward. "I'm dialing 911," he shouted. Chipped Tooth shoved past him and the two men quickened their pace toward the entrance.

"May I help you gentlemen?" Rob blocked the way, chin lowered, hands flexing. His voice held a sharp edge of command Maya had never heard before.

"Get outta the way," barked the taller man. They moved forward and Rob raised his fists. Chipped Tooth sniggered and flipped open a switchblade. The naked steel looked sharp enough to gut a fish in one swipe.

Maya snapped out of her shock. She raised one knee, ripping the shiny fabric of her narrow skirt, and slammed her stiletto heel into Chipped Tooth's instep. Rob lashed out with a booted foot and caught the taller one in the groin and, a split second later, pounded his fist into the other man's throat. The men released Maya and collapsed to their knees.

Adrenaline feeding her anger, Maya smacked the heads of both men together. They crumpled in a black heap on the floor. Customers and staff erupted into cheers and applause.

Rob relieved Chipped Tooth of his knife and searched both men. He found two pulverized fortune cookies. Pulling a pair of handcuffs from under his leather jacket, Rob secured the men to a pillar supporting the koi pond enclosure. Rob waved over the two soldiers she'd seated and asked them to keep on eye on the thugs. They nodded and stood over the prisoners.

Maya's heart thudded painfully. Had she really knocked two people unconscious? Rob had used moves out of a kung fu movie. And why in the world did he have handcuffs on him?

Rob wrapped an arm around her. "Slick moves there, champ. Surprised me and them."

"Who . . . who are they?"

"You tell me. What'd they want with you?"

"No idea. I didn't know you could fight."

"There's a lot you don't know about me."

Maya started. "Oh, no—Mr. Chen!"

They ran to Chen's office. Inside, the restaurant owner lay face up on the floor, mouth sagging open, lids closed. Was he dead? She staggered.

Rob placed his fingers against the man's throat. "Steady pulse."

Maya exhaled. She hadn't liked Chen, but didn't wish him dead.

Chen stirred, then sat up and massaged his head. "What happened?"

"Your so-called special guests beat you up and tried to kidnap me," Maya said.

Chen's face flushed dark red. "Where are the men who attacked me?"

"Handcuffed to the koi pond railing," Rob said.

Chen moaned. Maya grabbed a pillow off the sofa and eased him back down to the floor.

Rob stepped toward the office door. "I'd better go meet the authorities I called. They should be here soon."

Maya didn't want to be left alone with her boss. "I'll send Mei Mei to look after you, Mr. Chen," she said.

"I'll be fine." He groaned and shut his eyes. "I'm too groggy to move."

Restaurant employees congregated outside Chen's office. Rob asked them not to let anyone leave until the police had a chance to talk to everyone. Mei Mei went into Chen's office, and the rest of the staff went to calm the customers.

Maya leaned against Rob and shut her eyes. The image of Chen belly up, gaping like a fish, sent shivers down her back.

"I need you to stay alert," he said. "Tell me what happened."

"They went into Chen's office, then came for me."

"Why?"

"They said I had something of theirs. Must be the fortune cookie I dropped. A special one from Mr. Chen's office."

"Show me where it is."

They went to the pond, side-stepping the cuffed men who were just coming to. Rob and Maya peered into the koi pool. Maya pointed. "One of the fish shoved it under that rock."

Rob tested the strength of the wrought iron fence edging the pond. "This won't support my weight. You'll have to retrieve the cookie."

"I'm not sticking my arm in that water."

"Koi aren't carnivorous. They don't even bite."

"You're sure?" Maya found the food stick she'd tripped over and flung it into the far end of the pond, drawing the koi away. With Rob's hands gripping her waist, she leaned down until she could reach under the rock.

"Got it." She straightened, the dripping cellophane in her hand. The cookie appeared dry inside. Maya ripped it open and cracked the cookie. A narrow metallic rectangle a half-inch long dropped into her hand.

"What's that?" Rob asked. "A thumb drive?"

"Yes. This type holds huge amounts of data." She shuddered. "They thought I had this. That's why they came for me."

"Looks like your boss was passing information of some kind via the fortune cookies. I'd better go secure him." They hurried to Chen's office. Mei Mei lay unconscious on the floor. Chen was gone. Maya rushed to help the prostrate woman.

Rob swore under his breath. "I thought he was too incapacitated to run."

A man appeared in the doorway. Maya started as she recognized him from the security office at Fort Knox.

"Lieutenant Henchley?" she said.

He looked surprised to see her there, her Asian garb clearly confusing him. "I came to find Rob. He called me about those two thugs."

Maya glanced at Rob. Why'd he call Fort Knox security instead of the local police?

"You subdue them yourself?" Lieutenant Henchley asked Rob.

Rob smiled and shook his head. "I had help. Maya knocked them out."

Maya explained about the fortune cookie and the special guests, and showed Lt. Henchley the thumb drive. Before he could take it, the local police and ambulance arrived. As emergency personnel went to check on Mei Mei, Lt. Henchley explained to the cops that this was a military matter.

Rob touched the device in Maya's hand. "What do you think is on that thing?"

"One way to find out. My laptop's in my locker."

Her computer had protective spyware and had been scanned and declared clean by Ft. Knox, so Lt. Henchley agreed to let her try to read the device. Rob and Lt. Henchley followed her to the employee rest area where she retrieved her computer, set it on a table and inserted the memory stick.

Her fingers flew across the keyboard. "Encrypted, natch."

"We're sunk," Rob said.

"Have a little faith," Maya said. "The decoding software I developed for my senior thesis should crack it. Hold on."

A minute later, the computer dinged. "We're in." She let out a long whistle. Rob leaned over, his breath warm on her ear. Maya forced herself to concentrate on the screen.

Lt. Henchley read as she scrolled through the contents. "Military maneuver schematics, top-level strategy briefing documents, new tank specifications. You guys hooked a big one."

"How'd Chen get his hands on this?" Rob asked.

"I intend to find out," Lt. Henchley said. Maya removed the drive and surrendered it to Lt. Henchley.

Maya looked at Rob. "How come you had handcuffs on you?"

Rob glanced at Lt. Henchley, eyebrows raised.

"Go ahead," Lt. Henchley said. "She has security clearance."

"I'm working undercover for the military."

"So why did you let me think you're an unemployed loser who rides around on a big noisy machine with a bunch of hairy men?"

"Because of this." Rob extracted a billfold from his back pocket and flipped it open.

Maya sucked in her breath. "That's a Fort Knox identity badge."

"My first assignment was to go undercover in a motorcycle club that hangs out in a bar by the river."

"Why would the military be interested in a local biker gang?"

"One member was flagged as a possible terrorist threat. Turns out the rest are just a bunch of middle-aged thrill seekers who ride around on Hogs and collect toys for sick kids. I'm disappointed you were so ready to believe I'd thrown away my education and embraced unemployment."

"Next time I'll be sure to check if there's another explanation for your idiotic behavior." She paused. "Why didn't you tell me you had a job?"

Rob flushed. "I'm still on probation. Eighty percent of probies don't make it. I wanted to be sure I was in before telling you."

He met her gaze, and her stomach did another flip. She wanted to believe him, believe he was one of the good guys.

"I was reassigned today to come watch Chen's place," Rob continued. "He's been under suspicion since he opened."

"Those two guys you asked to watch the attackers?" Maya asked.

"My backup from the Army base."

Relief flooded through Maya. It was true—he wasn't a biker bum. Rob took her hand and pressed it gently. She squeezed back.

* * * *

By the time they gave their statements to the police and military, it was early evening.

Rob faced Maya and placed his hands on her shoulders. "I'm not letting you out of my sight."

"Oh?" Maya felt a surge of pleasure.

"You're a key witness," Rob said, his voice grave. "We only captured the couriers. Chen and whomever he's working for might try to silence you before the trial."

Her chest tightened. She was in danger.

"Lt. Henchley assigned me to protect you," Rob said. "I'm taking you to my apartment. You'll have to ride on the back of what you call my big noisy machine. And unless you're willing to ride with that torn skirt hiked up to your, um, thighs, you'll need to change out of that dress."

A few minutes later, dressed in blue jeans, her long hair stuffed inside a helmet, Maya clutched Rob's leather jacket and closed her eyes as he started the bike. Mercifully, he drove at a leisurely pace, following a meandering two-lane road along the Ohio River, almost empty on this Saturday evening.

The rumble of a powerful vehicle approaching fast made Maya turn. A truck bore down on them two car lengths away, accelerating as it came.

"Behind you!" Maya screamed in Rob's ear. He glanced back, and then gunned it, the cycle responding instantly. They sped down the road, outrunning their pursuer. Rob ran a stop sign, continued another half mile, then careened into the motorcycle-jammed parking lot of a ramshackle beer joint. He drove right through the bar's propped-open front door and rolled up to a table of leather-vested bikers.

"Who wants to catch a bad guy?" Rob yelled.

A dozen kerchief-headed men leaped to their feet and followed Rob as he backed out the door.

"Who are they?" Maya asked.

"The biker club I told you about. I'm an honorary member now."

"Terrific."

Just as they got outside, the truck barreled into view. The driver slammed on his brakes.

"Bring me the driver of that truck," Rob said.

The bikers raced to the truck and one yanked the driver from the cab. They brought him, struggling and swearing, to Rob.

Maya couldn't believe it. "Mr. Chen?"

Rob parked his bike and led the club members, dragging Chen, back inside. They tied Chen to a chair. Faced by a dozen tattooed bikers, even if they were more beer belly than muscle, Chen's bravado evaporated. He admitted he'd tried to run the motorcycle off the road to kill Rob and Maya.

Her thoughts whirling, Maya went outside to a deck overlooking the river. She gripped the handrail. She had misjudged everything—Rob's lifestyle, the Koi Palace. Nothing was as it appeared. Maybe if she'd tried harder to talk with Rob about the biker gang, she could have gotten him to admit what he was doing. Maybe she should have trusted him.

Rob appeared beside her and draped an arm across her shoulders. "I'm glad that's over. The authorities are on the way to pick up Chen. They'll get him to talk and capture his co-conspirators. You'll stay at my apartment until everyone connected with the plot is in custody."

Maya opened her mouth to protest, and Rob hastily added, "I'll sleep on the couch, if I have to." He nuzzled her cheek. "You'll get a citizen's award, you know."

"For dropping a fortune cookie into a koi pond?"

"For foiling a spy ring stealing military secrets and cracking the encryption on that device."

They stood silently for a minute, staring at the rippling water. A fish broke the surface, and then splashed under again.

Rob pulled her closer. "I'm really glad you were at the restaurant."

"We nearly got killed."

"But we didn't."

"I don't want to work there anymore. I quit. I'm not even giving two weeks notice."

"With Chen in police custody, the Koi Palace will probably be permanently shut down."

Was there a koi rescue league that would take care of the fish? They might be slimy beggars but she didn't want them to starve. "I'm sorry I doubted you. I've been wrong about a lot of things lately."

"I should have told you about my job. Trusted you." Rob gently kissed her. "We work well together."

"I wouldn't mind hearing how you managed to land a paying job with the military."

"How about over dinner?"

Maya grinned. "As long as it isn't Chinese."

Heidi Saunders lives on a Kentucky farm with a pond harboring one orange and white monster koi. Prior to writing mysteries, she worked as a wedding musician, canoe explorer, census worker, business consultant, and city planner. Vice President of her local Sisters in Crime chapter, she is polishing a political thriller.

SOMETHING FISHY THIS WAY COMES

BY DEBORAH J. BENOIT

Elizabeth found them down by the edge of the water, the old woman and the girl. Girl. She would probably always think of Sophie that way. She had to be in her twenties now. Elizabeth had known Sophie a long time, since Elizabeth herself was a young woman. Sophie had been a child from an inner city grammar school escaping to the country for a few weeks each summer. Part of some do-good program Aunt Josie and Uncle Pete had supported.

Uncle Pete was gone now. He'd been dead for nearly five years, a massive stroke. But Aunt Josie still clung to the life and the land. Growing frailty and the gout had failed to move her from the family homestead. Neither had a minor heart attack and all the persuasion her remaining family could muster. And now it was down to the two of them. And the girl.

There was no way a kid from the city was going to come to live in a cottage on the outskirts of a small, do-nothing New England town just to keep an old lady company. Especially not this kid. Elizabeth had listened to her blather endlessly on about childish schemes. People didn't change. Likely her reason for making nice was a nice cut of Josie's estate when the time came.

Elizabeth stood at the top of the path, watching. The old woman waved to a man in a row boat out on the lake. He waved back and turned the boat toward a spot further down the shoreline.

"Bye, Henry," the girl called. The two women turned and began to walk back. Sophie spotted Elizabeth first and nudged her companion. Josie smiled, hurrying up the path.

"Lizzy," Josie gasped when she grew nearer, pulling her niece into a hug. Elizabeth stifled her response. No one else called her Lizzy and she never hesitated to correct anyone who made the mistake. But this wasn't the time. Instead, she yielded to Josie's embrace, patting her back in response.

"I'm so glad you could come." The old woman wrapped her arm through Elizabeth's as they followed Sophie along the path to the house. "Sophie got here on the interstate bus last night."

Sophie laughed. "My old clunker would never make it this far. Busses are my friend."

At least she hadn't convinced the old woman to turn over the keys to Uncle Pete's Caddy. Josie kept it in prime running condition, taking it into town each spring for a bit of exercise and a tune up. The rest of the time it sat in the garage, waiting for its day on the auction block as some collector's fancy.

"We've been having a wonderful time catching up."

"Yeah," Sophie said over her shoulder. "You can help us celebrate. Auntie has asked me to stay for a while. Isn't that great?"

Not so much, Elizabeth thought. "Really?" she said. "How interesting. When did all this come about?"

"Just this morning," Josie said. "We got to talking over breakfast and it just makes so much sense. Why don't I make a nice pot of tea and we can tell you all about it?"

"That would be wonderful," Elizabeth said. What she meant was, tell me what that girl has convinced you to do and we'll put a stop to it here and now.

Today was well worth the change of plans. Even if this did make her second trip to the country this month. A week ago she'd talked herself blue in the face trying to convince the old woman to sign a power of attorney and move into a safe little retirement condo closer to civilization. But Josie remained adamant. She would not give up her home. Or her garden. Or the ladies' reading group at the church. Elizabeth couldn't help but smile picturing the girl accompanying Josie to the ladies' church group. Of course, it was never going to happen, but the image amused her.

Elizabeth had come with a purpose in mind. She'd been patient long enough, maybe too long. Now the girl was here and looking very much at home at Josie's side. If Elizabeth hesitated, she knew the girl would slide right in, snatch the old woman's attention away from the only family she had left. The conniver would wheedle her way in and send the old woman back into lost days where memories could be manipulated in her favor.

Not if Elizabeth had anything to say or do about it. And she did. She'd seen to that.

Josie turned watery blue eyes to her. "I am so glad to see you again so soon. You missed some wonderful fried catfish for dinner last night. Henry promised another treat tonight, but his luck ran out. No fish for dinner for any of us, not for a while. Henry and his wife are going to visit their grandkids for a few days. But I've made some shortbread cookies for our afternoon tea. You used to enjoy them as I recall."

"That I did. And you shouldn't be surprised to see me. You know how worried I am about you staying out here in that drafty old house, your nearest neighbor across the lake. That's why I'm trying to find something you'll like in town. Much better for all of us."

They moved up the wooden steps, through the front door and into the parlor where Josie settled onto the overstuffed chintz sofa.

"No need to worry, Lizzy, dear. I've told you a thousand times." She raised a finger to silence Elizabeth's protest. "And I have Sophie here now. She'll keep me company, for a while at least. I haven't quite convinced her of the joy of wintering in the Berkshires, but I'm working on it. She's trying to convince me to take a trip to Florida before we get snowed in." She grinned in the girl's direction, winking as she did so. The girl laughed a little too enthusiastically, Elizabeth decided. Who was she trying to impress—Elizabeth or her aunt?

It looked as if she'd already made progress in whatever her plans were for the old woman. Florida, indeed. Elizabeth was certain of one thing: Sophie was up to no good. She hadn't trusted the girl since the day she'd stepped off the bus nearly twenty years ago looking like a fish out of water.

It hadn't taken the girl long to figure out there was profit in cozying up to the childless couple. Summers in the Berkshires, gifts for birthdays and holidays once she was back in the city. Extras in between. Lots of extras as the years passed. Time and such things that should have been reserved for family. As Josie's last living relative, Elizabeth had no intention of allowing Sophie to horn in on what was rightfully hers. Now it seemed the time for patience had passed.

"What shall we do about dinner since Henry left us high and dry?" Sophie asked from her perch on the sofa's arm. "Do you think there's enough of that beef stew left in the freezer?"

"Not enough for a meal for three, I'm afraid. Perhaps I could stretch it with some vegetables. I have a good supply down in the cellar," Josie said.

"Let me get them for you," Sophie offered. "It'll save you going down those rickety cellar stairs."

"Oh, I don't use those any more, dear. I use the outside stairway. Fewer steps and not quite so steep," Josie said with a grin.

"Either way," Sophie began.

"Either way," Elizabeth cut in, "I think I'd prefer a nice steak. Sophie, I have an idea. Would you mind driving down to that store on Route 116—what's it called, Mason's? —and picking up what we'll need? When I stopped for coffee on my way home last week, I noticed they stocked organic beef from a local farm. You could take my car."

Sophie glanced in Josie's direction.

Josie nodded. "Even at my age, I appreciate a good steak, some nice baked potatoes. They should have some fresh from the Browns'. Yes, do go, dear. It will give Lizzy and me a chance to catch up."

"Sounds like we've got a plan." Elizabeth smiled. The country store was a good twenty minutes away. With a big "closed" sign hanging on the front door.

Elizabeth handed her keys and some cash to the girl, gave her a few instructions on driving a quality vehicle and watched as Sophie drove off in her car. The idea of that girl behind the wheel of her pride and joy didn't sit easy with Elizabeth but it was a small price to pay to get her out of the way. With any luck, she'd drive on to the next town and the market there. It should be open and have what they needed. Besides, the trip presented Sophie with an opportunity to drive a car she could never hope to afford herself. Why should she resist? And she was trying to curry favor. Do good and she'd expect Elizabeth to buy into her act. As if she'd fall for that routine. She was no foolish old woman vulnerable to the attention of a wily con artist.

"I put the kettle on," Josie said. "We could have a chat while we wait for Sophie to get back."

"Why don't you make yourself comfortable and let me get the tea? I think I remember where everything is." Elizabeth didn't wait for a reply. Before she'd finished speaking, she was half way across the room. Once inside the small kitchen, she rinsed the teapot in hot water from the kettle just as Josie had taught her to do as a child. She topped off the kettle and returned it to the stovetop.

From the cupboard she selected Josie's spicy herbal blend. The pungent flavor was far from her favorite, but it ought to hide any bitterness from the heart medication she'd appropriated from Josie's medicine cabinet during her last visit.

Just an accidental overdose by a forgetful old woman. What could be simpler? And if anyone suspected? Well, the girl's un-expected appearance could work in Elizabeth's favor. Who had better access to Josie's medication than her houseguest? And if a couple of the pills happened to be found in the girl's room along with a valuable broach or ring from Josie's jewelry case, so much the better.

Elizabeth carefully emptied the capsules into the tea infuser along with the tea leaves. Finally she emptied the pot, added the tea infuser and poured in hot water from the kettle. While the tea steeped, she gathered the pot, cups, saucers, honey, and a plate of shortbread cookies. That should do it.

"Here we are." Elizabeth settled into one of the overstuffed chairs by the sofa. "A lovely pot of tea for us and some time to talk."

"What did you want to talk about?" Josie asked as she took a bite from one of the cookies.

Elizabeth poured a cup of tea and placed it in front of Josie. She poured another for herself, holding it in her lap. "Don't let it get cold."

Josie picked up her cup and took a long sniff. "It smells won-derful." She thought for a moment then put down the cup. "Do you know what we need? We need some apricot preserves to go with these cookies. It'll be just the thing." She began to get up but Elizabeth waved her to stay.

"Let me get it." She headed back toward the kitchen. "Which cupboard is it in?"

Josie got to her feet and followed. "Oh, it's not up here. I need to go down to the cellar. Oh, I do wish I'd asked Henry to fix those cellar steps this summer. I kept putting it off. He always looked as if he was having such a pleasant time out on the lake. Then his wife had him painting their house and, well, I just put it off so long. Maybe it's not too late. The snow hasn't started to fly yet, though heaven knows the nights are cold enough. Soon, though, and I don't want to be using the outside hatch to get to my stores this winter."

"The cellar? Really, Aunt Josie. I'll never understand how you can store food in a place with a dirt floor and rock walls."

Josie smiled. "It's the best place, really. Even temperature most year round in the root cellar in back. Pretty much the same in the front section if the hatchway is kept closed. 'Course, summer heat and winter cold seep in if it's left open. And despite what your Uncle Pete said, I don't think his putting in a concrete floor in front by the hatchway stairs made one bit of difference."

This was far more information than Elizabeth cared to know about cellar storage. What she did want was for Josie to sit down and have some tea.

"We really don't need any jam with the cookies. Why don't we just enjoy our tea?"

"Nonsense, Lizzy." Josie grabbed a sweater from the hook by the back door and headed outside.

When she reached the hatchway, Elizabeth stood watching as the old woman heaved the heavy upper door aside.

"I won't be a minute." Josie stepped gingerly down the stone stairs. She paused at the bottom to flick on the light.

Elizabeth watched from above as Josie disappeared into the shadows, chattering away about the quality of last summer's harvest. She soon returned, smiling triumphantly, a jar of something or other in hand. She stopped abruptly at the foot of the stairs. A moment later, she recovered.

"Oh, my, I seem to have lost my breath. Perhaps you were right, Lizzy, dear, I have been over doing it." She reached out her hand. "Can you help me?"

Elizabeth glanced down at the uneven stone steps. Carefully, she stepped over the threshold, one toe into the dimness. Josie took a hesitant step up. Elizabeth took a step down, one hand gripping the edge of the opening. She reached down to Josie.

"That's it. You're doing fine," she said. "Just another couple of steps. Take my hand and we'll get you out of there and you can have your tea."

Instead of continuing up the stairs, Josie stepped back. Before Elizabeth could react, something pushed at the small of her back. Her fingers slipped from the casing and she lurched forward, landing hard. The air was driven from her lungs and her mouth filled with the taste of dirt and blood. Her cheek was raw against the concrete flooring at the base of the stairs.

"What—" The word caught in her throat. She tried to pull herself upright. Agony ripped through her. She tried to move her left arm. She couldn't feel it, yet she could see it twisted at an odd angle. She tried to move again and cried out in pain.

She focused on the old woman's shoes as they moved into view.

"She's awake," Josie said, her voice strong and clear. "But it looks like she's hurt bad. I don't think we should move her."

"Definitely not." Sophie's voice came from up above. "Did you think I wouldn't see through your game, Elizabeth? That Josie wouldn't notice the missing pills? She thought she might have miscounted, but I thought differently."

Elizabeth tried to speak, failed.

"I bet she's got those missing pills of yours just waiting for the chance to use them. Maybe right there in her pocket."

The old woman's feet moved back a step.

"Or in the tea," Josie whispered. "Is that why you've been so accommodating today, Elizabeth?" Her voice cracked. "She kept telling me to have some tea."

Elizabeth's arms and legs grew numb.

"Let me get you out of here," Sophie said. "It's starting to rain and the temperature's dropping fast. We can leave the hatch open. If her injuries don't kill her outright, exposure will. Eventually."

"It seems a cruel thing to do." Doubt tinged the old woman's voice.

Help me, Elizabeth wanted to plead, but she could only moan.

"What do you think she would do if it was you lying on the cellar floor?"

Josie let out a long sigh. "I suppose you're right. I just don't like to cause any creature pain."

"I know how you feel, but think about Henry's fish. You sure enjoyed the catfish last night and the fish chowder you made for lunch today. Sometimes someone else does what's necessary. Sometimes we have to do it for ourselves. This time I'm here to help you. Can you make it up the stairs okay?"

"I don't think I can get around her. I'll use the stairs to the kitchen. I should be fine as long as I watch where I'm going."

"Be careful."

"I will, dear." The old woman took in a deep breath, let it out slowly. "Lizzy, would you have pushed me down these stairs when I thought you held out your hand to help? You know there's more than enough to share when I'm gone. Not that you need any of it. But you wanted it all. You turned against me."

Elizabeth tried to focus on the old woman's words. This was wrong. They should be having tea, the old woman growing sleepy, her breathing labored. Soon Elizabeth would be calling 911 to report . . .

"Josie? We should get going," Sophie said.

"Yes, dear, I know. Lizzy, you wanted my house. Enjoy it while you can. Sophie and I will be heading south a little earlier than we planned. Your Uncle Pete always did enjoy a visit to the Magic Kingdom. I think that will be a fine place for us to begin our winter holiday. Goodbye, Elizabeth."

The old woman moved a step closer to the hatchway. "I'll be just a moment, Sophie. I need to rinse the teapot and get a few things together. Will you put my bag in the car? The keys are on the hook just inside the garage door."

The soft padding of the old woman's footsteps echoed across the dirt floor and up the wooden steps. With the click of a switch, the light blinked out and plunged the cellar into murky gray, the only light seeping in from the hatchway. The sound of footsteps crossed the floor above.

Elizabeth heard the sound of running water through the pipes followed by the creaking of the back door and a soft thump as it closed overhead. For a time, there was nothing but the beating of her own heart.

Voices melted down from somewhere beyond the opening at the top of the stairs, moving away from the hatchway toward the garage.

"It will look like an accident. She came out, expecting to find you, went looking in the cellar and fell."

"In a few days I can call Henry and ask him to check on the place while we're gone. I'll tell him we forgot to close the hatchway before we left, thinking about the trip and all."

Elizabeth heard the Caddy's engine roar to life and listened as the crunch of its tires on the gravel driveway faded into the silence of the coming night.

Deborah J. Benoit *is a Master Gardener living in western Massachusetts. When she's not plotting mysteries, she can be found digging up plots in her garden. Deborah is a member of Sisters in Crime, Mystery Writers of America and the Short Mystery Fiction Society.*

PALACE ON THE LAKE

BY DARYL WOOD GERBER

I sat in the passenger seat of Lucy's black Honda Civic, binoculars pressed so tightly against my face that I would look like a raccoon in the morning, but I didn't care. My heart thudded as I peered across the lake and searched for signs of my errant husband at the Polka Palace. I would've driven myself, but my prosthetic leg was in the shop for repairs, and hopping along the icy lakefront on one leg would have been a little precarious.

"Are you sure Edward's here?" Lucy whispered.

Did she honestly think anyone other than the two of us could hear? We had the windows rolled up and the lake was empty of swimmers and boaters due to the fact that it was colder outside than a Popsicle in an igloo.

"He's here, all right. That's his Buick in the parking lot."

"That low-life." Lucy's mouth drew down in a frown.

My husband, a high school math teacher, had recently taken up ballroom dancing, but not to bone up on counting to three. He was more interested in learning how to two-time.

"What made you suspicious?" Lucy continued to whisper.

"I found the dance studio's business card, a condom, and a little blue pill in his pocket."

"A little blue pill?" Lucy sputtered the words.

"Viagra, darlin'. My silly husband thinks he needs it to be potent. He doesn't, but he won't listen to me."

"So you still have—" She nodded her head in a leading manner.

"Of course, we still have s-e-x."

"Then why would he be having an affair?"

"Because he wants more s-e-x."

Lucy could be a little prim at times. I never asked, but I was pretty sure she hadn't dabbled in sex before taking her vows. She adjusted the white bib of her habit.

"Pull to the side, would you?" I said. The front window, clouding with fog from our conversation, was becoming difficult to see through.

"You're not getting out, are you, Eileen?"

"And risk falling into the lake?" I sniggered. "Nah, I don't think so. I'd either rust or freeze."

"Not funny."

A year ago, I had lost my leg, not my sense of humor. In a hit and run at midnight. By a white car that could have been driven by anybody, just not my husband. His Buick LeSabre was cherry red, the only flashy thing about him, and he had been out of town at a math competition. I rolled down my window. "Aha, there he is, doing the mambo with Hot-to-Trot Paula."

"Paula Peabody?" Lucy sounded more distressed than me, probably because ours was a small town. We knew everybody in it. Back when Lucy and I were in high school, Paula was the most popular girl with the guys. We knew why. Everybody did.

"She's not Edward's type," Lucy said.

"And what type is that, Lucy? Huh? If you were having an affair, wouldn't you choose the easiest—"

"Hide!" Lucy slumped in her seat. "Edward's coming out."

I scooched down, the upper rim of the binoculars barely peeking over the door's rim. My husband stood on the pier, alone, a cigarette glowing in his hand. The Polka Palace owners had taken over the long-abandoned Lake Lodge Inn and reformed it into a wonderland of twinkling lights and music and oom-pah-pah. The twelve cabins went unused. Perhaps the owners intended to utilize them come the summer. Maybe they would consider having a *Dirty Dancing* retro weekend.

Edward took a long drag and breathed the smoke out in circles. More than once I joked that he would die from so much smoke ring practice. Nowadays, whenever I said that, he sneered at me. I wasn't sure why. I had the feeling he couldn't stand the sight of me anymore because of the one leg thing.

Don't get me wrong. I don't walk around sighing *Oh, poor me.* I couldn't tolerate myself if I did. Jokes and humor are what keep me going. I post a slew of legless jokes on my blog. For example, what do you call a guy with no arms and no legs in a lake? Bob. What do you call that same guy a week later? Fish food. Ha-ha, right? Edward doesn't laugh at my lame humor. Get it? Lame? My name is Eileen. Do you want to know how many times I've heard the joke about the girl who has one leg shorter than the other? Humor is good for the soul. I need all the help I can get.

"Eileen, I don't think he's seeing anyone," Lucy said. "He's alone."

"Just because no one's standing in the friggin' cold with him doesn't mean he's celibate." My throat tightened. What did I do to deserve this . . . this pain? I've never wronged anyone. I obey the rules. Other than the bum leg, I keep myself in shape, drink lots of water, pet stray dogs. So why doesn't my husband love me anymore? I sucked in a long breath and told myself to snap out of it. Self-pity doesn't heal wounds or broken hearts.

"He's going back inside," I whispered.

"Roll up the window, would you? It's freezing in here."

"I can't. I'll lose visibility."

"Fine." Lucy shoved her hands beneath the folds of her habit as I shimmied up to a full sitting position.

"I thought he was seeing Paula," I said.

"Why?"

"I found orange lipstick on his collar. She's always wearing orange."

"Not everyone matches their lipstick to their outfit. If I did, I'd be wearing black."

I chuckled. Lucy's only foray into fashion was swishing on gloss for Easter and Christmas dinners. I said, "Okay, Miss Marple, who would be your guess?"

Lucy cut me a harsh look, harder than I thought she was capable of. What was she so uptight about? This wasn't our first caper. Back in high school, I was Ethel to her Lucy. We short-sheeted the camp counselor's bed, purloined chemistry exams, and toilet papered Edward's house. Crazy stuff. She changed after sophomore year. Grew quiet. I'd asked what was wrong, but she wouldn't bare her soul. I hadn't pressed. We'd grown apart until two years ago, a chance meeting at the local diner.

"C'mon, who?" I said.

"I have no idea." With the energy of a riveter, Lucy tapped her foot on the floor of the car. "How long are we staying here?"

Through the binoculars, I could see my husband back on the dance floor, cozying up to a woman of Amazonian proportions. He shot his arms out rigidly, like he did when he practiced air-dancing around the kitchen. The Amazon stepped toward him, grabbed his hand, and off they whirled, his nose nestled in her massive cleavage. I hated to admit that Edward looked more than capable as a dancer. Maybe that was why he wasn't in love with me anymore. I couldn't dance. Sure, I had seen *Dancing with the Stars,* and I had been told I could do what Paul McCartney's ex-wife did, but that wasn't me. I couldn't dance before the accident. I sure as hell couldn't learn now, could I? As a high school gymnast, my floor exercise routines always stunk. I was an uneven parallel bars girl. To this day, I could probably fly around the bars with ease. The dismount, however, would be a bitch.

"What else tipped you off?" Lucy whispered.

"Tipped me off about what?"

"About the affair?"

Duh! Our mission. To spy on my husband at the Polka Palace. As I refocused on the task, the sights and sounds of night swelled around me. Waves lapped the shore. An owl hooted then soared silently across the water, its yellow eyes eerie. Someone once told me that seeing an owl was a harbinger of bad news. I shuddered.

"Eileen!" Lucy flicked my shoulder with her finger. "How did you know about the affair?"

"Edward has been losing weight." He had tried this diet and that, and then, pow, he started a serious regimen. Daily he did two hundred crunches. Twice daily he walked on the treadmill. And then he took up ballroom dancing. In just a few months, he had lost over eighty pounds and looked sharp. Better than sharp. He looked as handsome as the day I met him in English class. I will never forget the way he recited Shakespeare's eighteenth sonnet. *Shall I compare thee to a summer's day?* He had looked straight at me, the right side of his face quirked up in a smile.

"That's pretty flimsy," Lucy said. "Do you have any other proof?"

"He's humming all the time."

"Humming?"

"Some song. I can't place it, but it's very familiar." I tried a few notes but sounded like a screechy violin in desperate need of tuning. I can't dance and I can't carry a tune. Broadway is not in my future.

"I'll pray for you," Lucy said, a much-missed hint of humor dancing in her eyes.

Suddenly I felt as if an army of creepy-crawlies had invaded my veins. "I'm going up there." I reached for the glove compartment handle.

Lucy snapped her hand over mine to prevent me from opening the compartment.

"I need your flashlight," I pleaded.

"To do what?" She reverted to that no-nonsense nun tone that I loathed. "What are you going to do, Eileen? Make a fool of yourself? Accuse him? Men don't appreciate women who make a scene."

I snorted. Like she would know. "I want to see the women, up close. That way I'll be able to tell which one he's been screwing."

"Will you?" She seared me with a look. "What makes you so sure?"

"I . . ." I licked my lips, more chapped than ever. I had been biting them for months in an effort to hold back my screams.

I released the latch of the glove compartment and batted away the tears slipping down my cheeks. Flashes of the accident that changed my life whirled in my head. I had rounded the corner at Main and State, grocery bags in both arms blocking my sight like blinders on a horse. A white blur of metal smashed into me.

"Eileen, are you okay? Your eyes—"

"I'm fine! Please, Lucy, I've got to go inside."

"No! You might slip and fall into the lake. We never found that ice fisherman last year, remember?"

"I've got my crutches." I slung my arm over the car seat and groped for my sticks, but I couldn't reach them.

"You're insane," Lucy said.

"Insanity isn't a sin." I winked brazenly and reached again for the glove compartment. "I need that damned flashlight."

"He's not right for you." On more than one occasion, Lucy told me that I should have moved to California after college and become an Olympic coach. She said I squelched my dreams when I married Edward and settled down as a gym teacher. Maybe I had. So what?

"So who is right for me, huh?" My nerves felt like they were firing up for a rocket launch. "I've got one friggin' leg, Lucy. I'm a gimp. I sit in a chair all day and do research on the Internet for peanuts. I can't teach gym any more. I can't support myself. My insurance ran out." No matter what anybody says, get more insurance coverage than you think you need. You never know when you'll be hit by a rotten driver who won't fess up. I slapped my hand on the console and screamed.

"Stop it! You're freaking me out." Lucy gripped my wrist. Her nails dug into my skin.

"Let go of me. I need to find out who Edward's seeing."

"And what if he won't stop? What if he's in love with her?"

"With one of those clowns in there?"

"Maybe she's not a clown. Maybe you know her. Maybe you like her."

"So I'm supposed to wish them well? Hey, you lovebirds, have a happy life. Don't worry about me. I'll just hobble alone into the sunset. Ta-ta! Not on a bet." I wrenched free of her grasp, then opened the glove compartment and dug beneath a wad of papers crammed into the slot. A few of them flew out as I removed the flashlight. "For a nun, you're sure a slob."

She grunted.

"What are all these? Parking tickets? Don't nuns have an agreement with the traffic cops?" I switched on the light and flared it at her. She looked as white as the bib of her habit. "You okay?"

"It's cold."

"Good deduction, Sherlock." I started to shove the papers back into the glove compartment when one sheet, yellow and flimsy, caught my attention. From the Goose Creek Body Shop. "What's this?"

"A receipt. Nothing."

"Why'd you need your car repainted?"

"A dent."

"What did you hit?" My heart hammered at another memory. A blur of white metal. I fell to the ground. The car tore away. As I lay on the pavement, head twisted, breasts pressing against a loaf of white bread, cans of Campbell soup clattering toward the gutter, I thought about the dinner I was planning to make Edward. His favorite. Grilled cheese sandwiches and tomato soup. I tried to move, but my leg wouldn't budge. "What did you hit?" I rasped.

"Nothing. Give it to me."

While I was in the hospital, Lucy had her car repainted. Black to match her habit, she said.

"Lucy?"

The blare of horns and shrieks of horror had been deafening. I'd passed out. Edward showed up at the hospital around midnight. He held my hand and cooed encouraging words, but something changed in him the next day when the doctor whispered that I would lose my leg. Edward didn't cry, but he turned rigid, as if the thought of me without a limb was repugnant. And then he grew distant. A frosty smile, a withered kiss. We made love, but every time we did, it seemed perfunctory, like he felt it was his duty. Time drifted, he started humming, and then I found orange lipstick on his collar.

"It's the theme from *I Love Lucy*," I blurted.

"What is?"

"The song that Edward hums." I made another poor attempt at the tune. "It's you. He's having an affair with you."

Panting, Lucy pulled a gun from beneath her habit and aimed it at me. "He's mine. He's always been mine."

I whipped the flashlight across my chest as if it would stop a bullet. "But you don't wear orange lipstick."

"That's the real question, isn't it?" she hissed. "Who's been kissing my Edward?"

"Your—"

"You stole him from me."

"Stole him?"

"He loved me, but then he met you."

I gaped. Was that what had changed the dynamic between Lucy and me in our sophomore year? I'd met Edward on a warm day in September. The classroom windows were propped open to let in a breeze. I was wearing a floral sun dress. Edward sat to my right, Lucy to my left. He stood to quote Shakespeare and looked directly at me. I had flirted outrageously, even twirled a strand of my hair. He had winked at me.

"I never knew you were a couple," I said in my own defense.

"He and I were best friends."

"Best friends aren't necessarily—"

"Zip it!" She waggled the gun.

I pressed my lips together.

"You were so pretty, so talented," she said. "How could he resist?"

What was she talking about? I was a geek back then. I had zits and no tits. Edward threw me a bone, and I gobbled it up.

"All he could ever talk about was you," she went on. "I never had a chance until . . ."

"Until you hit me with your car."

Lucy barked out a hyena-shrill laugh. The gun shook in her hand.

My stomach wrenched. "Did you try to poison me, too?" Last Christmas, I had gone to the hospital with severe vomiting. Lucy had brought my favorite yam casserole. Edward hated yams.

Lucy huffed. "The labels never tell you how much to put in."

"And the mugging?" I had suffered a bout of bad luck since reconnecting with Lucy. None of the incidents had seemed related until now. How could I have been so stupid?

"You're such an easy target," she snarled.

I'm trusting. Is that a bad thing?

"I was supposed to die in the hit and run, wasn't I?"

"You were supposed to die every time." Lucy frowned, like she couldn't wrap her mind around the idea that she had failed not once but three times. "Finally, Edward came to church to talk to the priest. He wanted to come to grips with your . . . your stump. He was making progress, but then one day, the priest was making a house call and Edward talked to me-e-e-e." She dragged the word out, as if caressing it. "I told him you cheated on him."

"You lied? How could . . . You're a nun, for heaven's sake."

"Not out of choice."

"By default?" I swallowed hard. I believed in God. I had chosen my faith. It had wavered after the accident, but in the end, I held strong. "Don't your vows mean anything to you?"

"Not since Edward gave in to me."

"Gave in?"

"I seduced him." She cackled. "Yes, me, the high school prude. Lucy Wouldn't, they called me. Well, I would. Again and again. And I did. And Edward liked it. A lot." There was a crazy rapture in her eyes. Had something about being a nun made her loco? Or was she loco before, and I had missed the signs? Did that say something about me? I've heard you can tell the merit of a woman by the friends she keeps.

"Get out of the car."

"Lucy—"

"Out. Time for a swim."

"Is that why you agreed to come with me?" When I'd first asked her to help me spy on Edward, she had resisted. "Were you hoping I'd slip into the lake like the fishermen?"

She growled.

"Does Edward know you tried to kill me?" Even in the dim moonlight, I could see Lucy blanch. "No, of course, he doesn't. You seduced him when he was vulnerable, when he was steeped in doubt." If only I could get hold of my crutches. I shored myself up, grunting to cover my clumsy attempt to reach along the side of the seat. My fingers grazed the seat adjuster lever. "What do you think Edward will do when he finds out?"

"Love me for putting you out of your misery."

"I'm not in misery."

"Sure you are. You want him, but you can't have him."

"And neither will you."

I jerked the seat lever. The seat back lurched. As I tumbled with it, I hurled the flashlight at Lucy. It struck her gun with a clank. A shot fired and hit the dashboard. Lucy dropped the gun, then pitched forward, searching for the gun on the floor. At the same time, I groped for my crutches lying on the backseat of the Honda. I caught hold of one and lifted it, but I couldn't get it to arc over the headrest. It wedged against the roof.

Lucy lifted the gun. "Say bye-bye, Eileen."

"Help!"

The sound of lapping water and the hoot of an owl was all I heard. And then footsteps. Smacking the icy path. A skid. A shout. The driver's door whipped open. A hand reached in, grabbed Lucy by the shoulder, and wrenched her out of the vehicle. She shrieked. The gun fell onto the floormat. I lunged for it. Grasped it. Lying half on my belly, I swung it up and aimed.

"Don't, Eileen, stop! I'm here."

Edward peered over Lucy's shoulder, and I caved in to tears and cascades of hiccupping coughs.

"You . . . you love her," I said. "You're having an affair with her."

"No, I'm not. Did she tell you that? She's been stalking me. She's delusional. I've informed the priest."

Lucy struggled in his grip. "Liar!" She tried to pry off his fingers, but he held her tightly.

"I'm not lying."

I scooted into the driver's seat, slung my legs out of the car, and clambered to a one-legged stand. "Why didn't you tell me she was harassing you?"

"Because she was your friend. I didn't want to make you anxious. I wanted the church to handle it." With one hand, he whipped off his necktie and looped it around Lucy's wrists. She moaned as he pulled tight, and then she grinned, open-mouthed, like a monkey at the zoo who knew it was getting away with some lewd gesture.

I shivered and yanked my gaze back to Edward. He wasn't entirely off the hook yet. "I found things in your pocket."

"What things?"

I told him.

Edward shook his head. "Oh, babe, there's a simple explanation. Remember when I had to supervise that group of sophomores?"

I did. He hadn't wanted to, but the principal had forced him.

"On the trip, the kids were making orange Jell-O shots. I confiscated everything, including the condom and Viagra one boy filched from his father's stash. I'd forgotten I put them in my pocket. The kid wrestled me for the junk and smeared wet orange Jell-o on the collar of my shirt. I meant to tell you about it."

He looked like he was telling the truth. His eye contact was unwavering, and he hadn't looked at Lucy once since he had arrived at the car. I said, "What about the Polka Palace business card?"

He smiled. "I found the card on the bulletin board at the grocery store. I thought dancing would shake up the workout routine, you know? I was getting tired of the treadmill. You were the one who said there was a spring back in my step."

"And the humming?

"What are you talking about?"

"You're always humming the theme from *I Love Lucy.*"

His forehead creased. "No, I'm not."

"You are." I made another futile attempt at carrying a tune.

Edward burst into laughter. "Sweetheart, that's *The Theme from the Godfather.* All men hum that."

A red-hot flush swept up my neck and into my cheeks. What a fool I'd been!

He stroked my hair. "I love you. I'll never stop loving you."

"What about . . . my leg?"

"You're my little leaning tower of Pisa."

"Oh, Edward, you made a joke!"

He chucked my chin with his knuckles. "If you can, I can."

I threw my arms around his neck and kissed him with abandon.

The next week, Lucy was put in a cell. Not a nun's cell, a padded one. It turned out I wasn't the only woman that she had tried to intimidate. Three girls from college and one other parishioner pressed charges.

As the memory of her attacks faded, I secretly took up ballroom dancing. A challenge at first. I hobbled for the good part of two weeks, certain the prosthetic would give out and I'd fall flat on my face, but after I blabbed my secret over a candlelit dinner, Edward set down his knife and fork and guided me onto the kitchen floor for a dance. Oddly enough, I didn't care any longer how stiff and stupid I looked.

Getting the Polka Palace to host a *Dirty Dancing* retro weekend is my latest project. After that, who knows? Maybe I'll work up the courage to return to teaching.

Daryl Wood Gerber *writes thrillers and amateur sleuth mysteries. For the latter, she writes under the pseudonym "Avery Aames." Avery is the nationally bestselling author of the "A Cheese Shop Mystery" series. The first in the series,* The Long Quiche Goodbye, *was nominated for an Agatha Award for Best First Novel. Find Daryl online at darylwoodgerber.com — and find Avery online at averyaames.com and mysteryloverskitchen.com*

FATAL FISH FLOP

BY BETH GROUNDWATER

"The guppies killed him." The middle aged woman with teary red eyes stood in the open door.

Detective Nora Stewart stiffened in surprise. She'd heard all sorts of accusations in her twelve years on the homicide force, even "The butler did it" by those making a lame attempt at gallows humor. But she'd never heard fish blamed.

"Pardon me?"

The woman tucked a lock of gray-streaked hair behind her ear, sniffled and wiped her nose with a balled up tissue.

"See for yourself." She stepped aside.

Nora entered and waved for her crime tech to follow.

A short entryway led into a living/dining room with green and brown overstuffed furniture and a hardwood floor. The body of a middle-aged man lay on the floor, blood congealing on a gash in his forehead. An EMT looked up and solemnly shook his head.

The dead man lay next to a shattered glass-topped coffee table. The nearest corner of the table had blood on it. A grocery bag, leaking milk and broken eggs, lay on the glass fragments.

A few steps from the front door was a large pool of water, a split plastic bag, and the smear of smashed guppy bodies leading from the spill to the bottom of the man's left shoe. Other dead guppies lay with glassy eyes in the entryway, and one lying in a large puddle gave a weak flop before expiring with a last flap of its gills. The smell that overlaid the familiar coppery scent of blood was fish. Dead fish.

"I see," Nora said.

The crime tech nodded his sage agreement.

"He must have dropped the bag of guppies when he came in the door," the woman said. "He's always bringing home either guppies or goldfish to feed to his precious Oscars. They're carnivorous, you know."

She waved at the large tank resting on a metal stand. Large red-marbled fish looped lazily through the water while an air hose burbled from behind a multi-pronged piece of bleached coral.

Nora's eyes narrowed. That word "precious" caught her attention.

"Are you Mrs. Hammond?"

"Yes."

"Can you tell me what happened?"

"After we watched the football game, I went to the neighbor's to have a cup of tea and some gossip while Herb went out. When I came home, I saw this." Mrs. Hammond's voice hoarsened and she took a moment to compose herself before continuing. "I checked for a pulse, but his hands felt cool and his face was gray. I knew he was dead. That's when I called."

Mrs. Hammond seemed awfully coherent for someone who had just lost a loved one, so maybe no love was lost. And maybe this "accident" had been staged. It was hard to believe the man couldn't have checked his fall to avoid the coffee table—unless he was drunk or drugged.

"Have you touched anything besides his hands?"

Mrs. Hammond shook her head. "I watch CSI. I knew I shouldn't disturb the scene until you came."

The crime tech, who had moved into the room and opened his case, rolled his eyes.

"Was anyone else here?"

"Yes," the woman said with a sigh. "My son. He lives with us. He left college, and he's delivering pizzas now while he figures out what to do with his life."

"Where was he this afternoon?"

"He watched the game with us then went to his friend Tom's house. I haven't called him yet to tell him his father—" With a moan, she put a fist to her mouth, obviously dreading the task.

"I'll need the name and address of both your neighbor and this friend Tom." With a gentle hand on Mrs. Hammond's elbow, Nora steered her toward the kitchen. "And I need to ask you a few more questions for my report. How about sitting down over a spot of tea before you tackle calling your son?"

* * * *

After taking Mrs. Hammond's statement, and providing a steadying presence while the woman called her son, Nora popped in on the neighbor. She confirmed Mrs. Hammond had indeed been there for about an hour, that a Sunday afternoon chat was regular thing for them. While there, Nora asked the neighbor if she knew if the Hammonds had any marital problems, but as far as the neighbor could tell, they were a happily married couple.

Tuesday afternoon, Nora received a call from the coroner.

"Got a bit of news on that fish flop case of yours," the coroner said without preamble.

"Spill it." Nora couldn't help herself.

The coroner chuckled. "Good one. We did the toxicology test, as you requested, to look for alcohol and drugs, and discovered an overdose of eszopiclone. Mixed with the alcohol he consumed, it would prove fatal. So, the guppies didn't kill him."

"Interesting." Nora made a note to find the pills. "Don't people usually upchuck when they OD on sleeping pills?"

"Not with eszopiclone."

"When did he die and how long before his death did he take the pills?"

"I figure he died about a half hour before you arrived. The drug entered his system probably a couple of hours before that. It usually takes about an hour for the drug to take effect, but he'd consumed a large, fatty meal with them. That slowed the absorption."

"So he could have made it to a neighborhood store and back home again?"

"If the errand took less than an hour. His central nervous system would have been depressed, though, causing lack of coordination toward the end."

"Okay, then." Nora made another note. Canvas neighbors to see if anyone saw the man walking—or stumbling—home from the neighborhood strip mall, with its pet and convenience stores.

"Think he staged the accident?"

"To cover up a suicide? Maybe."

But why go out for guppies, then? Nora tapped her pen on her desk. Maybe Mr. Hammond was so fond of his precious fish that he wanted to make sure they were well-fed before he died. His widow would have so much to deal with after his death that she might forget to feed them. Did the man actually care more for his fish than his wife? Nora made another note to look into Mr. Hammond's mental state and finances.

Over the next couple of days, Nora visited Mr. Hammond's place of work, a seafood import business. His boss and co-workers could throw no light on his mental state or his marriage. He'd been a quiet man, not inclined to socialize much or to get too personal in his water cooler chit-chat.

The pet store owner said that Mr. Hammond fumbled for change and his speech was a little slurred on the day of his death, but he chalked it up to mid-afternoon drinking, since the football game had been on earlier.

"Has he come in inebriated before?" Nora asked.

"No, but Sunday's game was special, our first chance to get into the finals in years."

"How did you know he was watching the game?"

"Oh, I'm a big fan." The rotund man waved his hand at the triangular banners hanging above the shelves lined with bags of dog food and birdseed. "After I discovered Mr. Hammond followed the team, too, that became a topic of conversation when he stopped in twice a week to buy feeder fish."

Mr. Hammond's finances told an intriguing story. A second mortgage had been placed on the house, and his and his wife's joint credit card account was maxed out. He also had taken out a sizeable life insurance policy a year ago, more than enough to pay off his debts and leave his widow and son, joint beneficiaries, financially secure.

When Nora got a copy of the Hammonds' credit statement, she saw numerous cash advances drawn at the Howling Wind Native American casino an hour's drive away. The pattern was weekly, and a quick check of the calendar showed her they were always on a Tuesday evening. A gambling addict? Maybe. Time for another visit with the widow.

The second time Nora knocked on the Hammonds' door, a skinny young man with long dark hair, a soul patch, and an eyebrow stud opened the door.

"Yeah?"

"I'm Nora Stewart," Nora said. "I have an appointment to talk to Mrs. Hammond."

"Mom," the kid yelled over his shoulder. "Lady here to see you." He stepped aside to let Nora enter.

Mrs. Hammond led Nora into the living room. While Nora settled herself in the side chair and Mrs. Hammond took the sofa, the young man leaned over his mother. "I need some smokes. Can I borrow a twenty?"

Mrs. Hammond sighed and waved a hand at her purse sitting on the dining room table. "Go ahead, Billy, but don't be long. After I finish talking to the police detective, I need you to go with me to the funeral home."

Billy's head snapped up, and a look of fear briefly passed over his features. He quickly extracted not one, but two, twenties from his mother's purse, stuffed them in his jeans pocket and walked out.

Nora suspected that this was one of many "loans" that never got repaid. And that look of fear could either mean Billy hated the thought of seeing his father's dead body or he was doing something he didn't want the police finding out about. Smoking more than cigarettes, probably.

"How's your son doing, dealing with his father's death?"

"Poor boy was pretty broken up when I told him." Mrs. Hammond swallowed a few times. "He's been a great help to me since then, though. I don't know what I would have done without him."

She turned back to Nora. "What was it you needed to talk to me about?"

"I'm sorry to bother you again so soon, but we need some additional information. Was Mr. Hammond taking any medication?"

"Blood pressure medication, that's all." Mrs. Hammond looked puzzled.

"Did he ever take sleeping pills?"

"Oh, I do. I have a prescription for them. Very rarely, Herb might take one if he had trouble sleeping."

"Do you know if he took any Saturday evening or Sunday?"

"I don't think so."

"May I see them?"

Nora followed Mrs. Hammond upstairs to the master bathroom, but when the woman went to open the medicine cabinet, Nora stopped her and opened the mirrored door herself. She put her hand inside a baggie, picked up the bottle with it, slipped the bottle into another baggie, and sealed it.

"Sorry, I'm going to have to take these." She labeled the bag and wrote down the prescription label information to give to the coroner, noting that the primary ingredient was eszopiclone.

"Why are you taking my sleeping pills?"

"The toxicology report found a sedative in your husband's bloodstream."

Mrs. Hammond gasped. "But if he took one Saturday night," Mrs. Hammond said, "it would have worn off by Sunday, right?"

"He may have taken more than one," Nora replied. "Maybe they made him unsteady on his feet, especially in combination with the beer he drank during the game. How many beers did he have?"

"Just two." The same answer every drunk driver gave to Nora whenever she pulled one over while she was on patrol.

"Herb didn't drink to get drunk," Mrs. Hammond continued. "He savored the taste of microbrews. Ales, porters, stouts. And he never took more than one sleeping pill. I don't understand."

"Do you still have the beer bottles from Sunday?"

"They're in the recycling bin."

"I'll need to take those, too." Nora steered Mrs. Hammond to a chair and took her own seat on the side of the bed. "Now, I need to ask some more questions that may be difficult for you to answer. What was the state of your marriage?"

Mrs. Hammond stiffened. "We had a solid, steady marriage, just what you'd expect for a middle-aged couple. No fireworks, but no problems either."

No mention of the word love. "What about his mood lately?"

"He was working hard the last couple of weeks, trying to find a new salmon supplier and replace a driver who quit. But he's gone through busy times like this at work before."

"We also found quite a few debts," Nora said, "such as a second mortgage on the house."

"We had to take that out to cover Billy's college expenses." Mrs. Hammond's hands were tightly clasped in her lap now.

"And your joint credit card account is maxed out. Many cash advances were drawn at the Howling Wind casino nearby. Can you shed some light on these?"

Mrs. Hammond looked shocked. "I didn't know about the credit card. Herb paid the bills. Are you sure those charges are correct? Herb never said anything about going to the casino."

"They all occurred on Tuesday evenings. Did he go out Tuesday nights?"

Mrs. Hammond's eyes widened. "Tuesday's my Bunko night. I'm gone every Tuesday, and whenever I hosted, Herb went to a movie . . . or so he said." She unclasped her hands and flexed her fingers. "Why are you asking about all this? What does it have to do with his death? That was an accident."

"Maybe," Nora said softly.

"You're not saying he committed suicide?" When Nora didn't answer, Mrs. Hammond's chin quivered before she clamped her teeth and took a deep breath. Anger flashed in her eyes. "Herb would never do that. Never!"

Was Mrs. Hammond angry that people thought her husband killed himself? Or because if his death was ruled a suicide, the life insurance company wouldn't pay on the policy, since the two-year timeframe in the suicide clause hadn't expired yet?

"I need to check out every possibility." Nora saw a family portrait on the dresser. "Do you mind if I borrow that photo for a few days?"

* * * *

After obtaining the photograph and box of beer bottles from Mrs. Hammond, Nora returned to her office. She left the evidence with the fingerprint technician, with directions to pass the beer bottles on to the crime lab for content analysis. Then she called the coroner and gave him the prescription information.

"Could Mr. Hammond have been given the pills without his knowledge?"

"They could be dissolved in a beverage, but they'd give it a bitter taste."

"What about beer, say a strong tasting one, like a porter or stout?"

"Maybe. If I was to do it, I'd add some sugar to mask the extra bitterness. Do you think this guy was knocked off?"

Given Mrs. Hammond's remark about the precious fish, her coherent responses on Sunday, the impersonal replies today, she could be angry that the police would find out she killed her husband. Her grief about her husband and her surprise about their credit card debt could have been acting.

"It's a possibility I'll have to rule out. Maybe Mrs. Hammond found out about her husband's gambling addiction, decided to put a stop to it—permanently. Or maybe she was the gambler, and Mr. Hammond found out she really wasn't playing Bunko all those Tuesdays."

"The case smells fishy, huh?"

Nora smiled. "Touché."

Nora hung up. The accident scene had been a little too pat, too perfect. As if it had been set up to hide the poisoning. Well, this open-and-shut case had become very interesting.

* * * *

Late Friday afternoon, Nora drove out to the casino. When she entered, her eyes and ears were assaulted by neon lights in bright colors, the hypnotic, musical pingings of electronic slot and poker machines, and the clinking of coins dropping into payout trays. The next assault—to her nose—was the stench of cigarette smoke from the garish carpets, the gamblers' clothing, and the cigarettes clasped in their fingers.

Nora asked for the floor manager and gratefully followed him into a clean, quiet office in the back.

"Thank you for agreeing to see me," Nora said after taking a seat. "I'm investigating the death of a person who seemed to be a regular customer at your casino. I'd like to see if you or any of your workers recognize this person."

"Glad to be of help," the manager answered. But, after looking at the Hammond family portrait, he shook his head. "I don't recognize any of these people, but if your deceased was a drinker, our bartender or cocktail waitresses might. If not, we can check with the blackjack dealers and cashiers."

He escorted Nora back out onto the noisy floor and led her first to the bartender, then to the cocktail waitresses serving customers. Nora hit pay dirt with the third waitress.

The young redhead tapped the photo. "I recognize that one. Been coming in every Tuesday night for the past few months. Poor thing never seemed to leave happy."

"Thank you very much," Nora said. "You've been very helpful."

* * * *

The next day, when Nora visited the Hammond home, she took a patrolman with her. After Mrs. Hammond opened the door, Nora asked if her son was home.

The woman gestured to the stairs. "He's in his room."

"I think it would be best for him to join us."

Mrs. Hammond put a hand to her face. "Oh no, you've got bad news."

Nora remained silent, and Mrs. Hammond called her son. When he entered the living room, Nora nodded to the patrolman. He positioned himself in the kitchen doorway.

Nora asked Mrs. Hammond and Billy to sit on the sofa. She took out two pieces of paper and two pens and laid them on the new oak coffee table. "I'd like each of you to sign your name on the paper, as if you were writing a check."

With quizzical expressions on their faces, Mrs. Hammond and her son signed their papers then looked up at Nora.

Nora clasped her hands behind her back. "And now sign Mr. Hammond's full name."

Two pairs of startled eyes stared at her. Then Mrs. Hammond bent her head to sign her paper, while Billy said, "What? Why do—"

"Just do it, Billy," Mrs. Hammond said with a tense jaw.

Billy glanced from her to Nora and back again, and then with an air of resignation, he scrawled his father's name on the paper and threw down the pen.

Nora picked up the pens and papers and stowed them in a large office envelope. She placed another piece of paper on the coffee table and pointed at it. "That's a copy of some cash advance slips from the Howling Wind casino, Mrs. Hammond, and signatures of your husband's name."

Mrs. Hammond looked at the signatures. A look of horror dawned on her face. She faced her son. "Billy, it was you!"

Scowling, Billy glared at Nora.

"And we have a witness," Nora said. "A cocktail waitress has identified Billy as a regular Tuesday night customer."

Mrs. Hammond shook Billy's arm until she caught his gaze. "How could you? And how did you get the credit card?"

Billy clamped his lips tight.

"He took it out of your purse, Mrs. Hammond," Nora said. "The same way he gets cash from you."

She turned to Billy. "And I suspect your father kept quiet about the charges for awhile, thinking your mother was gambling and wondering how to confront her. Until he followed her one Tuesday night and confirmed that she was playing Bunko. When did he figure out it was you, Billy? When did he confront you?"

Looking at his mother's incredulous face, Billy seemed to shrink. "Three weeks ago. Told me I had to stop and pay the money back."

Nora tapped the copy of the cash advance slips. "This one is for last Tuesday. You couldn't stop, could you?"

Grinding his teeth, Billy stared at the floor. "No. That's when he yelled at me, called me a loser, and said he'd turn me in for stealing."

Mrs. Hammond stifled a sob and addressed Nora. "Herb would have felt awful about turning Billy into the police. So awful that he, he might commit suicide, so the bills would be paid from his insurance settlement. Is that what you think happened?"

"No," Nora said. "While you watched the football game, Billy thought he would neatly solve his problem and slipped a fatal dose of your sleeping pills into his father's beer."

Mrs. Hammond gasped.

Billy crossed his arms. "No way."

Nora slid another two pieces of paper onto the table. "The first is a copy of your fingerprint record from a juvenile shoplifting arrest years ago. The second is a copy of the fingerprints taken from an empty beer bottle I removed from this house. Along with your father's fingerprints, Billy, two of the prints match yours."

"So? He asked me to fetch him a beer." Billy's feigned nonchalance was belied by the sweat beading on his brow.

"That bottle had residue of your mother's sleeping pills in it." Nora added a copy of another fingerprint document to the pile. "And we found your fingerprints on your mother's prescription bottle."

A tear ran down Mrs. Hammond's cheek. "No, no, no . . . ." The words came out in a strained whisper.

Billy's eyes took on the wild look of a trapped animal. The case was solid, but she wanted a confession from Billy.

Time to fish or cut bait. "Are those the shoes you were wearing Sunday?"

"Yeah, why?"

"May I have them, please?"

"No."

"Billy," Mrs. Hammond said, "give Detective Stewart your shoes."

Nora held her breath.

When Billy didn't move, his mother reached down and jerked a sneaker off his nearest foot. She handed it to Nora.

Nora fished a magnifying glass out of her pocket. "Tom, Billy's friend and alibi for Sunday afternoon, told me something interesting."

She studied the waffle sole of the shoe. "He said you took a long break, supposedly to use the bathroom, while you two were playing video games. I think you returned to your house, to see if the sleeping pills had killed your father or not. When you discovered that he'd gone out, you waited for him to return home."

She lowered the magnifying glass and stared at the young man. "You knew he'd be unsteady on his feet and carrying packages, so you hid behind the door and tripped him when he entered, hoping to set up what looked like an accident scene. After he conveniently hit his own head, you waited, didn't you? Watching until he drew his last breath. Then you ran back to your friend's house."

Mrs. Hammond burst into tears.

Pointing at the sneaker, Nora said, "I'm sure the lab will verify that these two bits stuck between the treads of your shoe are guppy remains."

Billy's mouth gaped open like a fish out of water. He collapsed back on the sofa. "I'm screwed."

His mother clutched his arm with fingers curled like talons. "Why would you kill your father, Billy? Why?"

"For the effing insurance money, why else?"

Nora breathed a sigh of relief. Thank you, Mrs. Hammond.

Billy moved toward the kitchen, where the patrolman stood, slapping his nightstick against his palm. When Billy turned his wild gaze to Nora, she shook her head.

"You're under arrest for murder, young man. You've got nowhere to go. Nowhere at all."

Beth Groundwater *writes the Claire Hanover gift basket designer mystery series and the RM Outdoor Adventures mystery series. She enjoys exploring her native Colorado outdoor settings and sports for both series. Beth's a proud Guppy and grateful she's been allowed to stay in the pond. Find out more at www. bethgroundwater.com.*

THE FRAIN LEGACY

BY DARLENE RYAN

Reid Frain pulled his Lexus into the driveway and shut off the engine. He peered at the old house through the rain spattered windshield. Lord, it was ugly. Those old windows with the thick glass made everything outside seem slightly out of focus, and the worn wooden shingles needed scraping and painting every second year. And stuck on the end, that stupid round room, the Frain library, that looked like it should have been part of a castle with some blonde babe up in the turret hanging her long hair out the window. Two floors of musty, moldy books that should have been hauled away in a Dumpster years ago.

He glanced at his watch. Good. He was three minutes early. The last thing he wanted was a lecture from Aunt Grace about punctuality. Frain men were always punctual. And according to Aunt Grace, Frain men were also well-mannered, impeccably groomed, restrained in their behavior and opinions, and maintained good posture. Frain men didn't have much fun, either. As the last of the line, Reid figured he had an obligation to all his polite, well-dressed, standing-up-straight-and-had-to-be-miserable male ancestors to enjoy life any chance he got.

He pulled up the collar of his coat and ran for the house, stopping in the back porch to shake off the rain. How many times had he told her to keep the doors locked? Stuck out here by herself, who knew who could come walking in, hit the old girl over the head and . . . what? Reid shook his head. What was there to steal? Old books? Old wood furniture? Old velvet curtains and lace tablecloths? Who'd want the stuff?

"Reid, is that you?" a distant voice called.

"It's me, Aunt Grace," he replied, stepping into the kitchen. "Where are you?" He heard the sound of creaking wood and slow footsteps coming up from the cellar. The basement door opened and Grace Frain appeared.

She crossed to the sink, set a large flashlight on the counter, and began to wash her hands. She was, as always, dressed in a blouse, dark skirt and matching cardigan, with her gray hair twisted in a bun at the back of her head. She looked like the librarian she'd been. Reid tried to picture her dressed like the old doll in the condo next to his. Mrs. Minton wore sweatpants and sneakers all the time and had an outlandish collection of tee shirts. That morning in the elevator she'd been wearing one that said, *I'm Old But I Have Money.* Reid couldn't help smiling. He couldn't imagine Aunt Grace in sweatpants. Her only vanity was shoes—high heeled ones. Except when she was working in the yard, heels were what she wore from morning to night. In his opinion she was way too old for that kind of shoe. One misstep could end in a broken hip. He'd even tried to talk to her about it. She'd dismissed him with a wave of her hand.

"I put on my first pair of heels when I was twelve years old," she'd said. "I didn't fall then and I'm not going to fall now."

Reid rubbed his hands together. "It's cold in here," he said.

Grace finished drying her hands on a small white towel. She hung it on a hook by the sink, and turned to face her great-nephew. "I've told you before, Reid, a good quality thermal undershirt and a sweater vest and you wouldn't notice the cold nearly as much. Your grandfather added a sweater vest to his suit on the first day of October every year and wore one every day until the fifteenth of April."

His grandfather. The sainted stick-up-his-butt Eben Alexander Frain. In the almost twenty years since he'd died he'd gotten more perfect. The great Eben Frain went to the office until the day he died. That was *where* he'd died. The great Eben Frain didn't smoke, didn't drink, didn't swear. The great Eben Frain was in the second pew on the right every Sunday morning. It sometimes amazed Reid that he had the great Eben Frain to thank for his existence. It was hard to believe the old guy had ever done the deed that resulted in Reid's father.

He took a breath and let it out. "Aunt Grace, it would take more than a vest to be warm in this house today."

"I'm aware of that," she said. "That's why I was in the cellar. I was putting wood in the furnace. It seems ridiculously early to have to do so, but that's what happens when as a society we allow development to go on unchecked. The ground and air become contaminated and we have December weather the last week of September."

He'd heard Aunt Grace's speech about development dozens of times. Frain land went back for acres and acres behind the house. Across the road, just beyond the trees, was a small pond where Reid had gone skating as a kid and where he'd stuck his tongue in the warm and willing mouth of thirteen year-old Lacy Dennis. All of that was Frain land, too. One developer or another had been trying to buy some part of their property for as long as he could remember. And Aunt Grace had been saying no. Reid had tried a couple of times to convince her to sell. One small section could easily bring in a million dollars.

"That land is part of the Frain legacy," she'd say, squaring her shoulders. "Your legacy."

The freaking Frain legacy. The land, the old house and Lord knew how much money, his legacy, all in the hands of his Aunt Grace. Reid's grandfather had died at ninety. Eben's other sisters had made it to ninety-six and ninety-nine, respectively. Grace was only eighty-four and the healthiest of the lot. Reid's father was the only Frain to die young and that had nothing to do with his genes and everything to do with a drunk behind the wheel of an SUV. By the time he got his hands on the Frain legacy, Reid was going to be too old to enjoy it.

The furnace came on then with a groan and a whoosh. Reid put his hand over the grate in the floor. The air was barely warm. "It's not very hot," he said. "I'll go down and take a look at it."

"Here, you better take the light." Grace handed him the flashlight. "Though I don't know what you think you can do."

Reid felt his way down the steps. The light wasn't much help. The basement air was stale and cold. The stone foundation may have been old, but it was solid.

The furnace sat in the middle of the cellar like a giant gray octopus, ductwork snaking out from it like tentacles. It was noisy, inefficient and older than he was. It was like everything in the house—past its time. Of course Aunt Grace wouldn't have it replaced—it still worked. She used the oil as little as possible. Instead she hired someone to cut, split and stack wood from Frain land to heat the house, just the way it had always been done.

Reid looked the furnace over—not that he knew anything about how it worked. He tried moving some of the leads. Maybe they were clogged and he could shake something loose. Everything seemed solid until he got to the flue, snaking into the stone chimney. It would come out in his hands if he pulled. He sighed. That meant a trip to the hardware store for some duct tape to seal it in place until he could get a technician out to check the furnace and be sure the house wasn't going to fill up with carbon monoxide.

He trudged up the stairs. Aunt Grace was waiting in the kitchen. Behind her the cold water tap dripped steadily in the sink. The faucet was so old they didn't make washers for it anymore, but she refused to have a new one put in. "That would be money down the drain," she'd said. He didn't think she'd intended the pun. So instead she shut the water off under the sink when she wasn't using it.

Reid opened his mouth to tell her he was going to the hardware store but she spoke first.

"You bought a new car," she said.

"I did," he said. "Do you like it?"

"Since it's not my car it hardly matters whether I do or I don't like it." Her hands were clasped in front of her, her stance as perfect as if she were balancing a book on the top of her head. "What does matter to me is the amount of debt you're carrying. That condominium, the furniture you bought for it, that was all completely unnecessary. You could be living here with me. There's plenty of room for the two of us."

Right. Move in to the mausoleum with her and never have a bottle of wine, a cigar or a woman ever again.

"Now you've added to that debt with a new car."

Reid ran a hand through his hair. It was the only part of the Frain legacy he'd gotten so far. Thick, blond and it didn't go gray until way after everyone else. Of course, as far as Aunt Grace was concerned, it was always a bit too long to be respectable.

"I can handle the payments," he said. And he could. He'd done well for himself in the almost ten years since he'd graduated from college. Frains had a knack for making money. His grandfather had been a successful stockbroker. So had his father. So was Reid. He didn't know if it was talent and their la-di-da private school educations or more the Frain looks, charm and a healthy dose of good luck.

"That is not in dispute," she said, primly. "What concerns me is the way you're managing your money and your life."

"I'm taking care of everything, Aunt Grace," he said evenly, forcing a smile he didn't feel. "You don't need to worry."

Anger gathered into a tight, hot knot in his stomach. He wouldn't have had to take on any debt if she'd given him some of the Frain legacy she was always going on about. He wouldn't have had to spend his days sucking up to people who didn't have one tenth his skill at making money. He should have been the one managing the Frain legacy and turning it into a Frain fortune.

She looked at him for a long time and when she spoke it seemed more to herself than to Reid. "I guess there isn't anything else to say." She brushed some invisible lint from her skirt. "Reid, would you bring in some wood from the pile by the back door, please?" she asked. "I have a phone call to make." She turned on those ridiculous high heels and left the room.

He just stood there for a moment. Then he remembered that he hadn't told her he needed to get to the hardware store before it closed. His hand was on the handle of the French doors into the living room when he heard her on the phone. He squinted through the wavy glass.

"Timothy Hawthorne, please," she said. "It's Grace Frain calling."

Timothy Hawthorne, of Harris, Hawthorne & Townsend, the Frain lawyer. He reminded Reid of a lizard with his thin lips and knobby head. Reid could picture the man, sitting behind the massive desk in his stuffy office, his tongue darting out to lick his lizard lips

He took a step back from the door. What was she doing?

"Timothy, I need to see you tomorrow," Grace said. "No, it can't wait. I need to make some changes to the family trust. I'm sorry it's come to this, but it has, and I have to do the right thing."

The right thing. The old bat was going to cut him—him, the last Frain—out of the Frain legacy. Reid turned and walked carefully, quietly, all the way out to the porch. His heart was pounding. He clenched and unclenched his hands trying to somehow get hold of his anger.

The cold seeped through his trench coat and suit, but it didn't cool his temper. How many holidays had he spent sitting in that gloomy dining room eating freaking roast beef and Yorkshire pudding—the Frain tradition for all holiday meals—when he could have been skiing with his friends, or lying on a white sand beach with a blonde in a bikini? How many Saturdays had he given up to clean half-rotted leaves out of the gutters, or pick sour, spot-pocked apples? How many armloads of wood had he lugged down those creaky old basement stairs?

He glanced over at the cellar door. The furnace was still laboring to warm up the old house. The furnace, with that loose, leaky flue that needed fixing. The flue that could be leaking carbon monoxide into the house.

Then again, what did he know about furnaces? As Aunt Grace was always pointing out, he hadn't inherited his grandfather's mechanical abilities. He could be wrong.

He stepped out the back door and quickly gathered an armload of wood. Downstairs he dumped it in the wood box. There was a blue silk handkerchief in the breast pocket of his suit. (Frain men always wore a matching tie and handkerchief.) Reid used it to cover his hand before he took hold of the pipe leading into the chimney. He pulled it from side to side. Bits of some kind of seam sealer, dried-out and gray with age, fell onto the floor. He bent down and scooped them into his handkerchief, stuffing the whole thing in his pocket. Yes, that pipe definitely was loose.

Upstairs Grace was waiting in the kitchen. It was surprisingly easy to smile at her. "I just took some wood down," he said. "I'm going back for another load."

He made three more trips down to the cellar. "The wood box is full and I've stoked the furnace as well," he told her after the last trip. "Is there anything else you need?"

"No, thank you, Reid," she said. "But I do need you to come back tomorrow. There are some things I need to talk to you about."

"I could come out about six," he said. He was confident nothing in his face was giving him away. There was a reason he was such a good financial advisor. Not to mention a damn good poker player.

"That will be fine."

"I'll see you tomorrow then," he said.

Reid glanced back at the house in his rear-view mirror as he wound his way down the driveway. That musty, dreary old place would be the first thing to go, he promised himself. And old lizard lips would be the second.

* * * *

Timothy Hawthorne called Reid's office right after lunch the next afternoon. "There's been an accident," the lawyer said.

Reid's hands were shaking. "I'm on my way," he said, and hung up. He tried to swallow and couldn't. *Oh, God,* he thought. *What did I do? What did I do?*

He drove out to the house, pushing the car way beyond the posted speed limit.

Hawthorne's dark sedan was parked by the back door, along with a couple of police cars, an ambulance with its back doors open, and the rescue squad truck.

The lawyer was pacing in the kitchen. "Ah, Reid, you're here," he said, offering his hand. He was wearing fine grey leather driving gloves.

"Where is she?" Reid asked. His heart was pounding so loudly in his ears he wondered if the other man could somehow hear it too.

"They're still down there, trying to get her stabilized before they move her."

"Stabilized? You mean she's alive?"

Hawthorne gave him a look Reid couldn't quite make sense of. "Yes, she's alive."

Reid put a hand on the counter to steady himself. She was alive. He hadn't . . . She was alive. Then the rest of the sentence sank in. "Wait a minute, you said, 'down there.' What do you mean? What happened? Where is she?"

"Apparently the furnace stopped working sometime during the night. This morning she must have gone down to the basement to see if she could get it going again. It looks as though she caught her heel a couple of steps from the bottom. I heard them say her hip is broken."

"You found her?"

Hawthorne nodded. Pacing back and forth in front of the sink he explained that when Grace hadn't shown up for her appointment he'd telephoned the house. When she didn't answer his repeated calls he'd driven out to see if everything was all right. That was more an indication of just how much the Frains were worth than because of any great concern for Aunt Grace, Reid thought. Still, he was glad the lawyer had come out.

"She was unconscious when I found her. The mailman arrived just as I did. It seems he's been bringing her mail to the door instead of leaving it in the community box out on the road—even though it violates the delivery policy the post office put in place last year." There was a slight tone of disapproval in the lawyer's voice.

"She wasn't breathing, but he knew CPR. I called 911, and then I called you. If it hadn't been for him coming with the mail your aunt would be . . . gone." He kept running his thumb over the edge of his gloved fingers.

Reid let out a breath he hadn't realized he was holding. "Thank you, Timothy," he said. "You saved her life. That, man . . . the mail carrier. I'll have to get his name. I . . . I want to thank him."

He heard the sound of voices then and footsteps coming up the cellar stairs. "Easy, easy now, one more step." The door swung open. A muscular young man lifted his end of stretcher over the top step and into the kitchen.

Grace Frain's eyes were closed. Her skin was the color of newsprint. She looked small and old. Reid reached for her hand and gave it a gentle squeeze. "I'm here, Aunt Grace," he whispered. He felt a faint squeeze back. *Lord, what had ever made him think he wanted her gone?*

The paramedics loaded the stretcher into the back of the open ambulance. "I'll be right behind you," Reid said to the two men.

"I'll go." Hawthorne was behind him in the doorway. He pulled a white handkerchief out of an inside pocket and wiped the sweat off his forehead. "The police are going to want to talk to you," the lawyer continued. "I'll be with her. You come as soon as you can."

"All right," Reid said. "I won't be long." He went back into the kitchen and down the cellar stairs.

The officer in charge was a woman. He introduced himself.

"Your aunt seems to have caught her heel on the step, fell and broke her hip," she said. "She did hit her head on something when she went down. We're not sure what, yet. Go to the hospital. I'll talk to you there."

Reid started back upstairs. Halfway up he paused and turned. "I'm not so sure that furnace is safe," he said. "Even if you could get it to come on."

"That's not a problem," the officer said. "I used to work in Goose Bay. This isn't even chilly."

* * * *

Timothy Hawthorne was waiting by the triage desk when Reid arrived at the emergency room. The lawyer's navy wool coat was folded neatly over his arm. His color was back.

"They've taken her for a CAT scan," he said.

Reid sank into a chair and ran his hand across his neck. "I'm going to have to get some help in for her," he said. "At least in the daytime."

The lawyer nodded. "That's going to be expensive."

Of course cost would be the first thing he'd think of. Timothy Hawthorne was the third generation of Hawthornes to handle the Frain legal affairs. He couldn't have been much more than his mid-forties, but he dressed and acted like a man twenty years older. Reid had a feeling Timothy Hawthorne had been born old.

"And that furnace will have to be replaced," Reid said.

"Are you sure you can afford everything?"

Reid looked up at the other man. "What do you mean? There's all kinds of money."

"In the Frain trust, yes. But your Aunt Grace depended on her pension for all of her own expenses. It's really unfortunate that she fell before our scheduled meeting today."

Reid could hear his heart begin to thud again in his ears. "I don't understand," he said, slowly.

"I guess there's no harm in telling you. Your Aunt Grace was planning on changing the structure of the family trust, having you take over management. As she explained it to me, despite your personal spending habits, she had come to the conclusion that blood is thicker than water. But since she didn't make our appointment, none of the changes will take effect."

She was going to give him a chance and he'd almost . . . Reid swallowed. "But what does that have to do with the money, with paying for her care?"

Hawthorne looked almost . . . smug? "All the Frain assets are held in trust. You can't touch any of that money. My firm manages everything on a day to day basis. When Grace is gone it all goes to several charities. Didn't you know?"

All of the money? All of the land to charity? That was the Frain Legacy? Reid let out a breath. That didn't matter right now. All that mattered was making sure Aunt Grace was taken care of. "She can still make changes. As soon as she's settled in a room you can draw up the papers."

The lawyer shook his head. "I'm sorry. I should have told you right away."

"Told me what?"

"Grace had a stroke, in the ambulance on the way here." The lawyer's voice seemed to be coming from farther and farther away. "Her heart is strong, but there appears to be massive brain damage. There was bleeding under her skull. So unfortunate that she happened to hit her head on a piece of wood when she fell." He smiled down at Reid. "But at least she has you to take care of her."

His lizard lips were moving so Reid knew the lawyer was still talking, but Reid couldn't hear him anymore.

Darlene Ryan *is an award-winning young adult author and mixed-media artist who lives on Canada's east coast. Her teen novels include* Rules for Life, Saving Grace, Responsible, *and* Five Minutes More. *She is also the author of the memoir,* A Mother's Adoption Journey *and the children's picture book,* Kisses, kisses, kisses. *As Sofie Kelly she writes the Magical Cats of Mayville Heights mysteries. Visit her online at www.darleneryan.com*

THE CRITIQUE GROUP

BY PATRICIA GULLEY

Blood on the Manuscripts, Patti Priestly thought as she watched Lana Kimble open the next submission covered in red ink. This one wasn't hers, but her turn was coming. Everyone had a chapter in for critique this week, and already the fur was flying. Patti had no idea what had gotten into Lana these days. Well, she did, if she believed the rumors circulating around the moorage about Lana's husband seeing another woman.

Normally, Lana was the punctuation high priestess, while Betty Opals had a propensity to circle every -ly and -ing word and Joanne Jeffers disapproved of any form of the verb "to be." Winifred Whitmore worried about too much description and Patti had to admit, she always wanted to know where the story was heading.

Today's critique meeting started off with Lana calling Winifred's romantic suspense a virginal delusion, and Joanne's farmhand mystery clichéd cornball. Next up was Betty's erotic vampire slayer, and Patti's ghost story would be last.

The five members of the group had formed after a moorage meeting of their one-hundred-and fifty floating home community, when they discovered that they were all writers of mystery or romantic suspense. Patti and Joanne, who were long time friends, were happy to join the other three and form a critique group and rotate the every bi-weekly meetings between their five floating homes.

Lana added more red marks to Betty's manuscript before beginning the critique by telling Betty that her heroine sounded like a nymphomaniac on uppers, dressed like a hooker and needed to learn to curse.

"Okay, stop!" Patti shouted, and got approving nods from Winifred and Joanne. Betty stared daggers at Lana. They had gathered at Patti's house on I row today, and Joanne had brought the goodies. "Let's eat. Maybe some dessert will sweeten our attitudes a bit."

They were all in their sixties, with Betty the youngest at 64 and Winifred the oldest at 69. Dressed comfortably in Bermuda shorts and sandals or boat shoes, they trouped into Patti's kitchen to partake of Joanne's frosted pistachio orange cobbler. The coffee and tea for hot July were iced.

Winifred leaned her ample hip against a counter. "I think our critiques are getting a little too vicious. We're supposed to point out problems and give suggestions on how to fix them, not rip each other's works apart."

Lana tossed her head, though not a strand of her champagne blonde hair moved. She stabbed a fork into her cobbler and said, "If the work is lousy, it's lousy! Can't stand the heat, get out of the kitchen!" She put a piece of the cobbler in her mouth and chewed it like she had to kill it first.

Betty refused a piece of cobbler. She was always dieting and her thinness bordered on scrawny. Sleeveless blouses did not suit her boney shoulders. She put three packets of Splenda in her iced tea. "And who would know more about lousy writing than you, Lana?"

Winifred, Patti and Joanne completely forgot that frowning wasn't good for already lined faces as Lana hauled back and threw her fork at Betty. The foul language that followed between the two combatants could have made a hardened criminal blanch. They lunged at each other and only the fast action of the other three women kept them from tearing each other's hair out. Patti and Joanne pulled Lana into the living room, while Winifred held onto Betty in the kitchen.

"Okay! Let me go!" Lana demanded, then instantly broke into tears.

From the kitchen, Patti heard her screen door slam. Lana collapsed onto the sofa and cried into her hands. What a mess, Patti thought, as Winifred came into the living room to say that Betty left.

Lana looked up. "That scheming little witch! I'll kill her if she tries to take Stan away from me!" She looked as shocked at her words as the others did. Embarrassed, maybe, she wiped her face with the back of her hand, grabbed her stuff and stomped out of the house.

Patti, Winifred and Joanne stared at each other for several seconds.

"Let's get our drinks and the rest of that cobbler and go out on deck to relax, girls," Winifred said. "I think we deserve some comfort gorging after that scene."

"I guess!" said Joanne. "So, I'm assuming that means the rumors are true?"

"In spades," said Winifred, more calmly than the statement deserved. "I don't know who Lana was trying to fool with that comment about 'if she tries.' I heard Stan already moved out, though no one has seen him move in with Betty yet."

* * * *

Early the next morning Patti stumbled to her computer with her first cup of coffee. She liked to begin her day by reading one of her on-line writing lists. Suddenly, footsteps pounded down the ramp and sirens sounded in the distance. She couldn't look out to the main walkway anymore; a new two story house recently moved in and blocked her view. Moving to her front window, she saw a squad car most assuredly breaking the fifteen-mile-an-hour speed limit. It was followed by an ambulance.

Winifred rushed down the row heading for her house. Patti had the door open when Winifred stepped on to the deck.

Wheezing from the exertion, Winifred spoke in spurts. "Lana. Found her. Between the ramp and deck. Drowned."

She was stunned. Lana had looked distraught yesterday. Should they have talked to her more?

"Come in and rest a moment while I throw some clothes on," she said.

Ten minutes later, they turned off Patti's row at a slow trot onto the main walkway and met Joanne coming towards them.

"I was just coming to get you," Joanne said, and the three broke into a quick fast walk. Joanne looked and sounded shaken. "A neighbor found her this morning on his way to work. The cops have the row blocked off. I heard a guy who must be a detective—plain clothes—say to one of the uniforms that it looked suspicious."

"Geez, do you think it could be suicide?" Winifred turned pale and slowed.

"Lana?" Patti asked. Should they tell the detective about the events from the previous day?

"Never! Not Lana!" Joanne said. "I heard that detective say something about 'the head.'"

Sure enough, when they got there, yellow tape was strung across the entrance to Lana's row, and two uniformed cops stood guard.

"Any information yet, officer?" Winifred asked, in her best curious-little-old-lady voice, which generally got her what she wanted to know. "We're her friends."

"You are, are ya?" the cop answered. "Stay here and I'll tell the detective. He might want to talk to you." He turned and headed down the row to Lana's house.

The detective approached them with a frown.

No introduction. "You knew her? Lana Kimble?"

And in each their own way, they told the detective how they knew Lana, what everyone wrote, and a lot of innuendo concerning the current gossip going round about Lana, Stan, Lana and Stan, Betty, Lana and Betty and the possibility of Stan and Betty.

When he finished scribbling in his notebook, the detective looked up. "And where does this Betty Opals live?"

A brush off. In their best-ditzy-old lady personas, they vaguely waved towards the row Betty lived on. He thanked them courteously, took their addresses, and told them to go home.

Fat chance! They made a bee-line for Betty's house. When they got there, Joanne leaned on the doorbell and didn't let up until Betty answered, dressed in a flimsy nightgown.

"Knock it off!"

Before she could say more, the three women began telling her what happened. Betty's gaze moved from one to the other, then her eyes went wide. They turned. The detective, hands on hips, stared at them.

"I thought I told you to go home."

"We're not leaving." Patti said. "Betty needs us." And she and Joanne each took one of Betty's hands.

"Is Stan here?" Winifred whispered.

Joanne gasped.

"Yes, he is," said Betty.

They all moved into Betty's living room, the detective clearly displeased. When Betty tried to go upstairs to get Stan, the detective told her to just yell up. Stan came down, dressed in Bermuda shorts and a polo shirt, his full head of white hair still wet from a shower.

"Stan, they've found Lana in the river," Betty said. "It might be murder."

This was no way to tell a husband about his wife's death. The detective looked put out. Mildly surprised and upset, Stan asked what happened.

The detective asked if he'd like to sit down, and maybe they could go into another room for privacy.

"No, here will be fine." Stan hunted through a candy dish, unwrapped one and popped it in his mouth.

The detective's brows rose. "So, you were here all night. Didn't go home for any reason?"

"This is a temporary home for me now, Detective. I moved in two days ago. And no, I didn't go back yesterday. I took what I needed when I left."

"Did you leave this house at anytime yesterday evening or last night?"

"No, I did not."

"And you can vouch for this, Ms Opals?"

"Yes, sir, I can. We ate in last night, watched a movie in bed until almost midnight."

"And neither of you saw Mrs. Kimble last night nor heard anything this morning?"

"I sleep like the dead, Detective," Stan said. "A bomb could go off and I wouldn't hear it."

"Which means you can't really vouch for Ms. Opals being in bed all night." He looked at Betty. When Winifred lifted her finger and opened her mouth, the detective gave her such a sharp look, she closed her mouth.

"Well, I guess not."

"And Ms Opals, you saw Lana Kimble at your group meeting yesterday afternoon?" Betty nodded, her eyes going wide. "And you stormed out after throwing a fork at Mrs. Kimble when she accused you of having an affair with her husband?"

Betty glared at her friends, and the detective raised his voice. "Isn't that right, Ms Opals?"

"No! It was over her vile critique. It was vicious and useless!"

"But you did throw the fork?"

"Well, I guess—"

"You guess? You don't know?"

"Yes, I did, but it didn't hit her and she lunged—"

"She lunged? Didn't your friends have to hold you apart?"

At that moment Betty looked as if she could have committed three murders.

"Lana attacked me! I only attempted to defend myself, and they did pull her away into the other room. Then I left!"

A short silence followed

"I suggest you get dressed, Ms Opals. I'm going to need statements from both of you." The detective nodded at Stan. "And I may need you to come downtown to do so."

He turned to leave. At Betty's scowl, the other three members of the critique group followed close behind him.

"So much for standing by Betty," Joanne muttered when they reached the main walkway. The detective returned to the murder scene.

"Gosh, I never thought telling the detective what happened would have such dire consequences," Winifred said.

"You'd think we'd know better, since we write this stuff." Patti shrugged.

"Do you think this tells us something about why we're not published?" Joanne said.

They stared at each other.

"But since we do write this stuff, is there anything we can do to help prove Betty didn't do it?" Patti said. "We weren't as close to her or Lana, but they were our critique buddies and, well, I just feel so sad . . ."

"We can investigate!" Joanne bounced on her toes. However, five minutes of suggestions revealed nothing that the police wouldn't do themselves or let them get involved with. They eventually drifted home.

Later that evening, the phone calls started. According to the grapevine, Betty had been arrested. The police found something at Lana's house that proved she did it. A row-captain meeting, which included Patti and Winifred, was set for the next morning at the moorage office. This was a perfect opportunity to find out what the neighborhood knew. Gossip ran rampant amongst the inhabitants of the moorage.

* * * *

It didn't take long to get the row-captain business out of the way. "Okay, now we can talk about the murder!" said Cheri, the office manager.

"Let's hope we learn something useful," Patti whispered to Winifred.

Everyone had a tidbit. A neighbor said that Stan had been slowly moving stuff out of the house for over a week, so he hadn't just marched out with a suitcase two days ago. And he had gassed up his boat the day he left, but hadn't moved it over to Betty's house. According to another neighbor, Lana had been screaming at someone the night before they found her. However, no one screamed back. A friend of Stan's assumed she was on the phone, and it looked as if Stan wasn't at the house that night.

Winifred told everyone about Stan being a heavy sleeper and what he said that made Betty look guilty. Unfortunately, the others believed Betty was guilty as opposed to thinking Stan a real heel.

"Talk about different points of view," Patti said.

"Just remember, we don't know exact time of death yet. Stan could have killed her earlier," said Winifred.

"I don't think so." Cheri's remark caught everyone's attention. She sounded smug. "They found Betty's finger prints on the murder weapon. Her head was bashed before she was dumped in the river." Cheri's cousin worked in the morgue.

"Do they have the murder weapon?" Patti asked.

"Yes! It was Lana's laptop computer."

Lana had frequently brought her old, large and heavy laptop to their meetings. On their slow walk home, the three women agreed it could do a lot of damage to a human head. Cheri's cousin said that Lana had been hit several times.

* * * *

The next morning, Patti woke up to the doorbell ringing non-stop and sirens blaring in the parking lot. Joanne and Winifred stood on her doorstep.

"More murder!" Winifred wheezed.

"This time it's Betty!" Joanne wailed, tears flowing.

"I thought she was in custody?" Patti said, shocked.

Joanne shook her head. "Let her go. They found her in the river this morning."

"How?" Patti whispered.

"They think it's suicide."

"Do you think someone is out to murder the critique group?" Joanne said.

"Don't be silly." Patti invited them in. She made a fresh pot of coffee and cracked a package of cinnamon rolls. It seemed the perfect time for comfort food. She was frosting them when the doorbell rang again.

It was the detective. He helped Patti carry the coffee, cups and rolls out to the deck to join Winifred and Joanne.

After everyone had finished their first roll, the detective glanced at them. "Okay, which one of you killed your two friends?"

Joanne choked and Winifred looked appalled. "You mean we're suspects?" Patti said.

"Absolutely!" The detective took another roll. But he was openly surprised when Joanne sniffed dramatically and began rattling off possible motives.

"Maybe Stan really loved Patti and Lana found out. And Lana wrote a novella that Winifred stole. She killed Lana because of the manuscript and Betty found out. And I hated both of them because they ripped my manuscripts to pieces so often I now have writer's block and can't write anymore."

Winifred chimed in. "Maybe I made sure Betty touched the laptop before I deleted the story from it, then clobbered Lana with it. Betty remembered and confronted me. So I drowned her."

"And my love for Stan could not allow him to be tied to that woman," Patti added. "I had to get rid of her. When I found out he'd slept with Betty, I went ballistic."

The cop stared. "How did you know Lana was killed with her laptop?" he said.

So they explained about Cheri. He was on his feet in a flash and gone without so much as a "Just the facts, ma'am."

Patti's cell phone rang with news from a neighbor of Lana's. Stan was loading up his boat with stuff from Lana's house. Patti still had her phone to her ear as they ran down the walkway. The neighbor explained how she couldn't help overhearing when Lana's daughter showed up this morning and told Stan that Lana's new will didn't leave him a dime. When the daughter left, Stan started loading up his cabin cruiser, which was parked along side Lana's back deck.

They ran along the side decking and caught Stan coming out of the sliding glass doors of the house carrying Lana's jewelry box.

"Watcha doing, Stan?" Patti demanded.

"None of your business!" Stan practically growled.

"You have no right to take any of Lana's belongings," Patti said. They blocked his exit from the house. "You're not in her will, and this is still a crime scene." Stan pushed past them heading for his boat.

"You better stop, Stan," Winifred shouted. "Or we'll call the cops!"

His face red, he ignored them and climbed into his boat. He started up the ladder to the flying bridge, but they followed him, grabbed his legs and pulled. He fell backwards and all four landed in a heap. Still clutching the jewelry box, Stan scrambled into the cabin. The women followed, jumped on him and flattened him to the floor. Patti and Winifred sat on him while Joanne hauled back to punch him.

"That's enough! Get off him!"

Cheri, the moorage office manager, stood in the doorway holding a gun.

"Step in, honey, so no one will see you," Stan gasped. He shoved Winifred and Patti aside, raised himself and kissed Cheri's cheek.

"Cheri! You're with this goofball?" said Patti, still on her knees.

"We love each other!" Cheri said, her tone low and deadly. "What are we going to do with them?"

"Let me load a few things, and then we'll take off. We can dump them out where the slough meets the river. They won't be able to stay afloat for more than a few seconds there."

That area was the location of some of the roughest waters on the fast running Columbia River. Patti didn't want to die.

"So, Cheri," she said. "I guess you killed Lana while Stan alibied himself with Betty. You kill her too?"

"Stan put sleeping pills in her wine, and we both put her in the water."

Cheri glanced sideways at her lover. The women rushed her with enough momentum to carry them out on to the boat's deck where a free-for-all broke out as all four women fought for possession of the gun.

Suddenly Stan was in the fray too and with all the hysterical pushing and shoving the boat began rocking wildly. A final lunge carried all five combatants over the railing and into the river.

Patti surfaced quickly and scrabbled for a dock ladder. A police launch maneuvered to block Cheri and Stan's escape. Police helped Joanne and Winifred climb out of the water. Finally, Cheri and Stan were hauled out of the water and handcuffed.

The detective looked at the three women. "That was a pretty stupid thing to do. The hint about knowing the murder weapon was enough."

"What?"

"She doesn't have a cousin at the morgue. Several people knew Stan and your office manager were together, even though they thought they were being discreet. Only the murderer would know what the murder weapon was, and that she'd been hit several times."

"So, poor Betty was set up to be an alibi and a victim?" Joanne cried.

"'Fraid so!" The detective patted Joanne's shoulder.

It was a hot afternoon, and they'd dripped dry long before being allowed to go home. They thanked the neighbor who had called the police when they confronted Stan.

"Do you think we can get a book out of this?" Winifred said.

Joanne looked stunned, but Patti considered. "Each of us?"

"No," said Winifred. "We can collaborate and make up one name for all of us."

Patti chuckled. "Like Patti Jo Winifred? Maybe we can get a short story out of it."

"No, a book!" said Joanne. "With lots of really good motives for everyone in the critique group."

However, several minutes of brainstorming did not produce any more motives than the silly ones they'd offered the detective.

The detective walked up to them.

"So tell us, Detective," said Patti. "What motives for us did you come up with?"

Patricia Gulley is the Docket editor for the Sisters' newsletter, In SinC. *Her novel,* Downsized To Death, *was published in April 2010 by Wings E Press. A retired travel agent, she still travels frequently. She lives on a floating home in the Columbia River. Visit her at www.patgulley.com.*

ABOUT THE EDITOR

RAMONA DeFELICE LONG is an author, independent editor and writing instructor. She has co-edited a collection of stories by Delaware authors as well as FISH TALES, and her clients include published as well as new writers. As an author, her fiction and non-fiction have appeared in literary, regional and juvenile publications. She's received grants and fellowships from the Delaware Division of the Arts, the Pennsylvania State Arts Council and the Society of Children's Book Writers and Illustrators. A native of Louisiana now living in Delaware, Ramona was recognized by the DDOA in 2009 as an Established Artist in Fiction. She is active in the Delaware Valley arts scene, and her literary blog may be found at ramonadef.wordpress.com.